CRITIC
STEVE
MATADOR SERIES

**Including *The Man Who Never Missed*, *Matadora*,
The Machiavelli Interface,
and *The 97th Step***

"A crackling good story. I enjoyed it immensely!"
—Chris Claremont, author of *FirstFlight* and *Grounded!*

"Great fun, a rousing *Planet Stories*—style adventure with a
touch of *The Shadow* thrown in . . . Enjoyable."
—*Science Fiction Review*

"Heroic . . . Perry builds his protagonist into a mythical
figure without losing his human dimension. It's refreshing."
—*Newsday*

"Noteworthy!"
—*Fantasy and Science Fiction*

"Another Sci-Fi winner . . . cleanly written . . . the story
accelerates smoothly at an adventurous clip, bristling with
martial arts feats and as many pop-out weapons as a Swiss
army knife!"
—*The Oregonian*

"I look forward to Perry's next!"
—*Amazing*

"Plenty of blood, guts, and wild fight scenes!"
—*VOYA*

THE ALBINO KNIFE

STEVE PERRY

ACE BOOKS, NEW YORK

This book is an Ace
original edition, and
has never been previously
published.

THE ALBINO KNIFE

An Ace Book / published by arrangement with
the author

PRINTING HISTORY
Ace edition / July 1991

ISBN: 0-441-01391-0

PRINTED IN THE UNITED STATES OF AMERICA

10 9 8 7 6 5 4 3 2 1

*In case any of my usual fans haven't figured
it out by now, this book is for Dianne;
And also for Mike Byers and Kiel Stuart.*

ACKNOWLEDGMENTS

There are always people who help whenever I'm working on a book. For supporting me technically, morally, financially or otherwise, my thanks go to: Dianne, Dal and Stephani Perry; for assorted other reasons best not mentioned, I'd like to thank Conan the Barbarian, the kids at PULPHOUSE, Frank Aquino, LeAnne Killian and Ashley Wallingford, and especially Pamela Mohan, who knows why. Oh, and Ginjer Buchanan, long as I'm at it. Thanks, folks.

"In all forms of strategy, it is necessary to maintain the combat stance in everyday life and to make your everyday stance your combat stance."

—*Miyamoto Musashi*

"Only those defenses are good, certain and durable, which depend on yourself alone and your own ability."

—*Machiavelli*

PROLOGUE _____

1.

DEATH CAME FOR them on electronic wings.

It came silently. No whisper betrayed its presence, no
false move disturbed the intricate viral/molecular twined
and interlocked essences of the ship's computer. The bioelectric brain continued to hold the Republic ship *Khadaji* in
tight orbit around Earth, performing ten thousand functions
with ease, never a pause, never an error, cupping the lives
of the Republic President Rajeem Carlos, his wife and
companions and operators within the shell of spun carbonex
fibers and denscris, proof against the hard and cold vacuum
of space.

The ship was armed as well as any Republic destroyer,
crewed by the best troops available from any of the fifty-six
planets or eighty-nine wheelworlds. Named for the hero of
the revolution, the *Khadaji* was the acme of galactic
technology, virtually impervious to intentional harm from
without when lit, top of the line, triple backups for every
system onboard right down to the toilets. But there was no

1

obvious enemy for the doppler guns to track, no visible incoming attacker to outrun or destroy. Death came wrapped in grinning stealth and waited for its proper moment.

President Carlos walked with his wife Beel toward the dinner at which he was hosting the new governors for the five planets of the Shin System. Just ahead of them, dressed in his characteristic dark orthoskins and spetsdöds, was Jarl, one of the family's four matador guards.

Carlos had been President for nearly five years, the term was almost over, and he was looking forward to stepping down. They had come a long way since the Confederation had been toppled. Time for somebody else to continue the work. He had done his part and he was ready to rest and let history judge his actions. From Prebendary to President, it had been a far road and a perilous one.

As they entered the corridor between the dining room and the commons, the thin-sheet carbonex safety door above the hatch ahead of them snapped down from its slim tube and shot into place, forming an airtight seal over the portal.

Jarl spun away from the door, his right hand extended, the barrel of his back-of-the-hand weapon seeking any attacker from their rear.

There was no one behind the trio. Almost in the same instant, however, the safety door at the opposite end of the corridor popped into place.

Jarl came up from his crouch. Beel looked at Carlos, puzzled. The President watched the matador's jaw muscles flex as he bit down too hard on his dentcom and subvocalized a question.

"A breach in the hull—?" Carlos began.

"No, sir. The comp says the hull is patent—"

The lights went out.

A heartbeat later the wall batteries lit the thin line of emergency beamers along the floor and ceiling. The corri-

dor was darker, but the beamers gave enough illumination
so they could see to move. If there had been any place to
which they could move. They were bottled up.

Where were the warning sirens and emergency instruc-
tions?

"Rajeem—?"

The President turned to his wife. "I don't know."

It was quiet in the hallway, and it took Carlos a few
seconds to figure out why that was wrong.

The air blowers were off.

Impossible. Every enclosed space on the ship had its own
backup air supply, compressed tanks that were supposed to
go online instantly if the main pipes were shut off for any
reason. Where were they?

Jarl had already noticed it. The matador moved with easy
grace to the manual hatch crank. The safety door could be
opened with that, in the unlikely event of a total power
failure. Not that Carlos thought there was any real danger.
There was probably enough residual air in the corridor for
the three of them to breathe comfortably for several hours,
even without the backup tanks; somebody would come for
them long before it ran out. Meanwhile, he could hurry
things along by calling them.

"Intercom," Carlos said.

The ship's integrated com was silent. Very strange, that
the com should go out, too—

"Damn!"

Carlos looked at his bodyguard. Jarl, like most of the
matadors he had known, was usually calm and unflappable.
"What is it?"

"The crank cover is jammed shut."

Carlos felt a coil of coldness grip his belly. "Somebody
will miss us."

Jarl shook his head. "Maybe not. The comlink is down.

Now I can't get through to the computer on my set, either."

The matador walked to the rear door and tried the manual control cover. It wouldn't open.

Carlos moved closer to his bodyguard and dropped his voice so that Beel couldn't hear. "What else?"

"My personal channel to Shum and Lil is being flossed."

That was bad, Carlos knew. The matadors had their own comlink, independent of the ship's computer, a short-range radio connection run off the dentcom's bioelectric batteries. If that was blocked, somebody was doing it on purpose.

They were trapped like bugs in amber, communications cut off.

Carlos stated the obvious. "This isn't an accident."

"No, sir. I had Lil online for a few seconds and she said the airdoors are down in the crew's quarters and in engineering. Lifesupport is turned off there, too. Only the comp can shut that down, and then supposedly only during a coded maintenance interlock with the chief engineer and a repair dock chief working together. Can't be done in Deep with people onboard. And the comp is supposedly rascal-proof, too."

"It would seem that such things are not absolute," Carlos said. His voice was dry, but there was a trace of humor in it. They were trapped, but nobody was shooting at them. Not yet, anyhow.

Jarl nodded. If he were afraid, it didn't show. "So it would seem."

"Rajeem? What is it?"

"We are under attack, somehow," Carlos said. "They've gotten control of the computer and cut lifesupport and dropped the airdoors. We're stuck here—unless Jarl can get us out."

The matador grinned. He reached into a pouch on his belt and pulled out an oval pellet about the size of the tip of his little finger. He moved along the corridor toward the door behind them. He pressed the pellet against the base of the carbonex where the lock mechanism joined the vacuum-proof barrier to the floor, then turned and walked back to where the President and his wife stood. "It's newton-bleak, but you might want to cover your ears. About five seconds from now."

Carlos and Beel put their hands over their ears, as did Jarl.

Five seconds later the carbonex shattered under the force of the stikcap. It was only a handsized piece—carbonex was stronger than denscris or squashed steel—but it was enough to destroy the imbedded lock. Jarl moved to the door again, and used his dotic boot to pull the door upward high enough so he could grab it away from the hot spot and lever it completely open.

"I hope the pilot can hold orbit on manual," Jarl said.

"What does that mean?" Beel asked.

"It means we are going to have to shut the computer down," Carlos said.

Carlos stood in the computer hutch next to Jarl.

"Shum has got the radio working. There's a boxcar and a tug on the way, and the guard ship is synchronizing. The comp never altered the security pulse the whole time."

Beel said, "What about our children?"

"Lil put in a *betydelse* com to Drean. No problems on Earth."

Carlos nodded. Drean was the matador in charge of the detail watching the children. Normally Lil would be with him. "Any idea as to how they did it?"

Jarl shrugged. "It's not my field. I dropped a white cell program into the system but it came up blank. Maybe a compdoc can find out."

"It could have killed us. Everybody on the ship."

"Not if that was the best it could do. Airdoors won't stop a prepared matador. If we hadn't gotten here first, Shum or Lil would have, soon as they'd figured it out. But that's not what worries me."

Carlos nodded again. He understood what Jarl meant. Whoever had gotten to the computer could have put a nuke under a chair somewhere instead and blown the ship into radioactive slag. Their defenses had been breached, and if whoever it was hadn't been intent on making it look like some kind of computer malfunction, an accident, they could have easily wiped out a lot of important people.

Carlos was used to enemies—the old regime had not left willingly—but this would-be assassin was very clever.

And clever enemies were dangerous.

2.

Juete left her station at the casino and strolled through the contiguous corridors toward her quarters. She didn't have to work, not with Emile's annual stipend still coming after all the years, but she had to be with people, and she enjoyed doing it in a setting she could control. As an Albino Exotic, she always carried her pheromones with her, and time had been very gentle with her. Even among her kind, Juete was still considered more attractive than average, and there were few normal humans or compatible mues who could look at any albino without feeling desire. Albinos had been bred for beauty, originally as sexual playthings, and the genes had been hardy ones. Where they were unprotected, the Darkworld albino population tended to be raped or murdered more frequently than any other ethnic group in the galaxy. Governments changed but human nature did not. Beauty carried its price, sometimes a fatal one.

The corridor wound through the upper reaches of the

casino, away from where Juete greeted the wealthy patrons who came as special guests of the management. Since the Confed's destruction five years earlier, things had loosened up considerably, travel restrictions were gone, and those who had been nervous about star hopping before now came in droves to the pleasure world of Vishnu to spend their standards.

Through the denscris half of the tube, Juete watched the people on the multiple levels of the main casino. There were dozens of ways to win or lose money operating on the floors, and the house percentage was high enough so that it never lost.

Vishnu sold pleasure in most of its acceptable forms and once, Juete would have been a more direct seller. In theory she couldn't work or even live full-time on the world, one of three large moons orbiting Shiva in the Tau System. Residency and employment privileges on Vishnu were reserved for natives. People often made exceptions for Exotics, however, and Juete was comfortable with exceptions in her favor. She didn't work hard, got to meet rich and interesting people, and lived in a safe environment. The security in the casinos was necessarily strict; access to the corridors through which the staff traveled to their cubicles was guarded by EEG recognition electronics and full-scan electropophy gear, backed by zap-field wards. Nobody would wander in by accident and so far, nobody had been able to get inside intentionally.

Juete's cubicle was just ahead. The tell-tale and recording din built into the door showed three green diodes and one red—nobody had called, nobody had opened the door or left messages, and the alarm was armed.

Juete wore skintights, colored jet to contrast with her skin, and her pale hand flashed white against the black of her sleeve and half-gloves under the portal light as she handprinted the lock.

"Shooo-et-tay?" the din's slow and gravelly chipvoice asked.

"Yes, of course."

The viral/molecular electronic brain thought its security thoughts, scanned her for the proper EEG pattern and the truth of her reply, then opened the sliding panel door.

Juete stepped inside and the door slid soundlessly shut on its cushion of magnetic flux behind her.

"Don't make any sudden moves," came a deep male voice.

She was startled but she tried not to show it. The Exotic woman turned slowly. Two men. One stood in the doorway of her fresher, the other sat on the leather and spidersilk form-chair, enjoying the massage machinery built into the unit.

The one standing was tall, but not overly so, average-looking, medium skin color, pale brown buzzed-and-dubbed hair, the kind of face you'd forget a minute after you saw it, a zero.

The one in the chair was darker, almost swarthy, black hair spun into a conservative halo cut, harder features, with a long nose, big chin, and large muscles, to judge from the thickness of his neck and forearms where they protruded from his three-quarter sleeve, loose-weave tunic. Genuine cotton, if she was any judge of these things, stained with organic dyes in bright blue and green. A man of taste and money—or one who could fake it.

Muscles produced a small blue plastic airpistol from under his tunic, held it up so Juete could see it, raised his thick eyebrows for emphasis, then tucked the gun back out of sight. A threat, but more subtle than many she'd received. I have a gun, he said. See? No need to point it at you, is there?

How was it possible they had gotten in here? What did they want? What were they going to do to her?

The man in the chair interrupted her thoughts, as if he could read them, answering broadly the first of her unspoken questions. "The galaxy is full of miracles, isn't it?"

She blinked but did not speak.

"Shall we go?"

"Go? Go where?"

He smiled, a lazy, genuinely happy expression. "I could hardly say that in front of the room's recorder, now could I?"

"If you know that, you know I'll be missed."

"To be sure. Eventually." It didn't seem to worry him. He stood, moving smoothly, effortlessly, and nodded toward the door.

Juete sighed. These two were expert and dangerous and if they wanted to kill her, likely she would already be dead. To resist would be foolish. She had not lived as long as she had by being foolish.

Juete turned and walked to the door.

3.

In the small museum that served the Siblings of the Shroud in the main compound on Manus Island, Earth, the two most respected teachers of the order were being given a tour of the new exhibits. Pen and Moon were being led by Spiral, himself nearly as venerated as they. The trio were in their early eighties, late middle-age for a healthy terran. All three wore full shrouds, covering them everywhere save for their eyes and hands in the nearly-living one-way osmotic cloth called *kawa*. The material was produced in only one place, this compound, and used exclusively for the shrouds.

At one time, each of the three senior siblings had been the Elder Brother or Sister in charge of the order.

"There's the mock-up of Wall's private quarters," Spiral said.

It was a big room, even at quarter scale, with an indigo and scarlet rug covering the floor, waxed wooden walls, and a sheet of mother-of-pearl spider silk tenting down from the ceiling. A trio of custom orthopedia backed by a give-all drug and liquor dispenser and a computer console completed the main furnishings.

"Denying himself luxury wasn't one of his handicaps, I see," Moon said.

Spiral's eyes crinkled in a smile. "The late Factor did indulge himself at times."

"What is that carpet? Yinguala?" Pen asked.

"Bioengineered *tuch* wool, from Rangi ya majani Mwezi."

"Green Moon fiber. I hear it's as comfortable as *kawa*," Pen said, "and costs ten times as much to make."

"I'm only a poor sibling," Spiral said. "I wouldn't know."

The three laughed.

Moon said, "How about the projections? Anything new we should know about?"

"That glitch is still there. The comp gives us a spike in the near future."

"How near?"

"What time is it now?"

"That soon?" Pen turned away from the exhibit and looked at his friend. They had been half-naked students together and he could hear the concern in Spiral's voice. Spiral had felt the Cosmic Lightning, the *Relampago*, more than a quarter century past, and few things had seriously disturbed his *wa* since. That this did bothered Pen.

"That soon. And close to home, too. We are fine-tuning the expectations."

"Take away the Confed and still there are problems," Moon said.

"The nature of life," Spiral countered. His voice was full of mock gravity.

They laughed again.

The three of them strolled away from Factor Wall's exhibit and down the hallway through the rows of holo-projic dioramas. Many of the displays had been here for fifty years before Pen had first come to the compound as a new student, and he was as familiar with them as he was the bonsai and gardens outside in the tropical air.

"Here, have you seen this one?"

Spiral nodded at a full-scale display of a pair of spetsdöds mounted inside a block of clear plastic. The weapons were small parallelograms, nearly diamond-shaped, each with a thin spun-fiber barrel. The magazine ejection button was the only visible control, since a spetsdöd was fired by touching the barrel with the tip of the index finger. This rather tricky operation was made possible by the position of the weapon where it rode securely on the back of the operator's hand, held there by a thin slab of artificial flesh. A spetsdöd operator learned care quickly.

Moon stepped close to the exhibit. "Khadaji's?"

"Yes. That's his signature, authenticating them as one of the sets he used. The Smith has another set, and there's a pair in the Provincial Museum on Greaves. As far as we know, those are the only ones on public display."

"Nice of Emile to give them to us," Pen said.

The three started to move on.

Behind them, there was an explosion. The force of the blast knocked all three siblings sprawling. Debris sleeted past, spattering the walls and exhibits.

Pen raised from his face-down position and shook his head, trying to clear the ringing in his ears. An alarm began to hoot, over and over, and he rolled onto his side from his belly, afraid, but not for himself.

"Moon—!?"

"Chang and Buddha on a goddamn stick!" she said.

Thank all the gods. They had been living together for so long that the idea of being without her was inconceivable. Ever since he had left Rim. Twenty years.

"Spiral."

"I'm okay."

"Pen. Your arm!"

As Moon sat up and pointed at him, Pen became aware of the pain in his left shoulder. He looked at it.

A shard of thincris had buried itself in his deltoid. The force of the explosion was such that the handsized sliver had pierced the rip-stop weave of the *kawa* shroud. He touched the clear crystal section with his right hand. It didn't move. Must be all the way to the bone, as solid as it felt. And now it really began to hurt. Blood oozed out through the torn cloth and dripped from the thincris onto the floor. Still, it was a small price.

He took a deep breath and tripped a mental kuji-kiri to stop the pain. The shoulder continued to throb and he was aware that it was injured, but the hurt diminished greatly.

Four siblings came running into the museum, all trying to talk at the same time.

Spiral looked at Pen and Moon. "I don't remember getting an exhibit that blows up," he said.

4.

On Thompson's Gazelle, first planet of the three-planet Delta System, the Civil and Criminal Complex in Evets

City came to its last proceeding before the midday meal recess.

In Sentence Room A, the judge sat at his podium facing a single prisoner flanked by four planetary cools. The room was old; the air conditioning unit whistled somewhere in the low ceiling, sounding like some trapped beast unhappy at its fate. The room was empty, save for the six people who had to be there.

"Criminal Sleel—" began the sentence judge.

"I'm Sleel," Sleel said, interrupting. "Stuff the criminal part." He was a fair-sized man, well built but not extremely so, dressed in a prisoner-white coverall and neoprene slippers. He was held in place by a pressor field mounted beneath the floor. The field was keyed to movements involving more than a few kilos' effort. He could breathe or blink, but any real effort to move would activate the pressor and it would clamp him like a vise. The field was rated at a thousand kilos and there was no way a man or mue, no matter how string, could break its grip. But because he was Sleel, he kept trying.

"Can't" was not a word Sleel used very often.

The judge ignored the interruption. "You have been found guilty of tampering with protected artifacts—"

"This is all lizard shit and you know it."

"—and in addition, you have also been convicted of resisting arrest, assaulting planetary officers, third-degree mayhem, damaging property in excess of five thousand standards, and attempted escape. I am required to ask you if you have any final statement, which must be limited to one minute or less, before I pass the sentence."

"Yeah, I got a statement. You and everybody connected with this dick-twisting extrusion are gonna be sorry you were ever fucking born."

"Is that your statement?"

"You heard it."

"Then by the authority of the Galactic Republic and in accordance with the law of Thompson's Gazelle and the state of Bingington's Peninsula, I hereby order that you shall be removed to the General Power Complex on Bantu Island where you shall repay your debt to society by fifteen years at hard labor."

Sleel stared at the judge as if his eyes were charged particle spitters and he could cut the man to shreds with his gaze.

"That's it. Take him out."

Sleel gathered himself for the moment that the pressor field would let go. Hell, there were just four of them, and armed with only hand wands. Any matador worth a damn ought to be able to take these balloos without working up a good sweat. He grinned at the thought.

"Should I shut the field off?" one of the guards asked.

The head guard, one who had been knocked silly by Sleel during an earlier escape attempt, smiled to match the trapped matador's expression. "Just a second," he said. He pulled his hand wand, a standard issue straight tube, but one that had been customized with pearl inlays and a Pachmayr one-piece stikgrip. He pointed the weapon at Sleel. "Have a nice nap, elbowsucker," the guard said.

Sleel had time to realize what was happening before the guard flashed him. Dammit, they were gonna blast him *before* they let the pressor down.

Shit—

5.

Saval Bork was of homomue stock, born of a heavy gravity world, and big by any man or mue standard. On a one-gee planet like Fox, he weighed nearly a hundred and twenty-five kilos, and he stood not quite two meters tall. Between the high-gravity upbringing and his subsequent work with lifting weights, Bork had built his body to impressive proportions, with power to match his looks. He knew his own strength, after a fashion, but he sometimes did things without thinking that other men could not do with all-out effort. What he considered hard made most strong men quail.

As he walked along the quiet street in Zor, the main city on the Little Island, Bork was once again lost in memory. It had been five years and more since Mayli had died, cut down by the guns of the Confederation. The wound to Bork's heart seemed as fresh as if it had happened yesterday. He had loved only one woman in his life, a woman who had been many things, doctor, whore, teacher, matadora. She had called from his depths an emotion he had not known he'd had, and his life had truly begun on that day; now, she was dead, and not a waking hour passed without Bork's regret.

This town, this planet, this system, they were backrocket places where even a man who had been one of the heroes of the revolution could mostly stay lost. Not unnoticed, because someone who looked like Bork always drew stares, but at least he wasn't bothered very often. Last year, when one of the entcom channels ran a lurid vid about the last days of the Confed, they'd gotten some giant actor to play his part. A few people had asked him about it then, but Bork had simply stared at them until they shut up and went away. He rarely lost his temper and, looking as he did, most people didn't want that to happen. He'd shucked his spetsdöds and orthoskins for anonymous gray coveralls and he'd gone back to his old line of work, security in a local pub. After he warned a couple of overchemmed and drunk patrons to quiet down, once by lifting a big man clear of the floor by his shirt front, word got around the neighborhood that it was probably better not to get in Bork's way.

He was on his way to his cube from work, the corpse-stealer's shift, and Fox's sun had yet to come up, though it was trying. The narrow street was quiet, only a few electric carts humming along, no other pedestrians up at this hour.

Ahead four men came out of a pub, laughing too loudly and making broad gestures in the dimness of false dawn. They looked like an all-night party winding down, but as Bork walked toward them, he saw that they were watching him and pretending otherwise.

He was used to being the object of awed stares, but this was different. Alarms tripped in his head.

He no longer wore the uniform, nor did he mount the standard weaponry, but the training he'd gotten as a matador did not disappear so easily. A man could not graduate from the elite bodyguard school without learning how to recognize a potentially dangerous situation. After all the years of instruction and practice, it was nearly a reflex.

Bork altered his path and started to cross the street. He had no client to protect and the simplest way of avoiding trouble was to be elsewhere when it came down. After Mayli and Red died, Bork decided he did not want to be involved with death again. He carried no weapons, save his own skills and strength, and he would avoid using these if possible.

The four men pretended to ignore him as two of them stumbled out into the street and began a showy, fake argument. The other two played at encouraging the first pair to fight.

None of the four were drunk or stoned, Bork realized. They all moved too well. You could hide a lot, you were a good actor, but body control and balance were hard to disguise. Little moves gave it away; a stumble uncontrolled made the hands and arms go out reflexively, and the motion was different if you faked it. Bork had been taught by the best. These four were fairly big, if not as big as he was, and they moved like men who knew how to fight.

Worse, this wasn't some random act. These four were set to attack him, and he was the target they'd been awaiting.

He didn't see any weapons, but that didn't mean anything. He was too close to turn back without exposing himself to a hidden gun.

Bork took a couple of deep breaths and moved to meet the four. That was a bad number; fewer could be danced around, and more only got in each other's way. The why of it could wait until later; now, it was time to deal with how.

Despite his size Bork was as much a matador as any. He would never be as graceful as Dirisha or as fast as Geneva or as cocky as Sleel, but he'd learned to walk the Ninety-seven Steps of sumito from start to finish without missing one or stumbling or losing his balance, and that made him one of only a few in the galaxy who could do so. Any man or woman who could dance the sumito pattern could also rank in the top players of the Musashi Flex, did he or she choose that path. None had, but the flexers were professional fighters who could hand-kill most men without much effort, and even the hardest of them respected the priests who had created sumito.

Bork smiled broadly and shook his head as he neared the four men. They turned to watch him openly now, and maybe the smile gave them a false sense of confidence.

The big man caught the first of the ersatz drunks unprepared. Bork snatched him up as a boy might pick up a pet cat. He twisted through the Magician's Hands, spun through Helicopter, threw the startled man into the face of an equally startled second would-be attacker, and danced into Laughing Stone at the third man.

The third man was good, he was fast, and he was ready. He ducked and sprang away to Bork's left, but made the mistake of going for a weapon instead of following up with a kick or punch. Bork altered his dance and skipped to the Braided Laser.

The assassin managed to clear his shotpistol from his hidden holster and had it halfway up when Bork's fist hammered down in the form of the Sword of the Sun.

Too hard, Bork realized, as the man's skull cracked under his blow. Well. That's why they had medics.

The fourth man was blinking away his surprise when Bork twirled toward him. Steel Circle and—

The man lifted his hand to the back of his neck and snapped his elbow and wrist down in a blur. The throwing steel spun toward the charging man. Bork tried to shift, but his forward momentum only allowed him a quarter step to one side. It was enough so that the point of the steel hit him just above the belt, but outside the rectus abs proper, on the hard knot of lateral muscle. Another three centimeters and it would have missed entirely. The steel sank half its length and stopped, not doing any real damage.

Bork hoped the blade wasn't poisoned.

It worked out that when he reached the wide-eyed knifeman, who was going for a second steel, the best of the nineteen dances to use was the last one. Bork shifted his feet and slid the final half meter and brought the heels of his hands together in front of his chest in the first part of Mimosa Sleeps Softly.

Unfortunately for the knifeman, his temples were in the way of Bork's hands.

Too hard again, Bork. Emile would give you static for that.

Bork pulled the knife from his side and looked at it. Didn't look like it was coated with chem. That was good.

Now. He needed to find out who these people were and why they had come for him.

6.

When the motor of the aircar exploded, both Dirisha and Geneva bailed out. Fortunately the car was moving slowly and only a few centimeters above the road. It wasn't a big blast, just enough to wreck the repellors and coil, but Dirisha knew it wasn't an accident. She hit the road rolling, tore the shoulder of her orthoskins, and came up with spetsdöds extended.

There were six, no, seven of them, coming out of the brush on both sides of the outback road, and it couldn't be anything but a set-up.

"Geneva! Four on your side!"

The aircar was still skidding to a stop on the hard surface, shredding the plastic skirt before the safety wheels had a chance to kick out fully, when the first spring gun twanged and sent a needle her way. Dirisha pointed her finger at the shooter and the spetsdöd coughed twice. The two shocktox darts hit the woman in the face and she started to fall.

Dirisha rolled again, felt more spring needles thwip past her, and came up with her left spetsdöd on full auto and her right tracking the sound of the spring gun.

She had only three on her side. The second caught the hail of full auto darts across the hands, twelve shots, and screamed before he fell. The third man ate a single dart from the right spetsdöd; his mouth was open and dark against his white face, and that was where Dirisha aimed.

The black woman twisted toward her friend and lover, hearing Geneva's spetsdöd fire. But only a single weapon.

Dirisha saw that three of the four attackers on Geneva's side were already down. The fourth fired a shotgun at the blonde, who was sprawled on her side on the road.

Dirisha screamed "No!" as Geneva's body rocked under the force of the hit. Dirisha leaped up, right hand pointed at the shotgunner. Her weapon rasped. Three small spots appeared in a short line on his neck. He fell.

She ran to Geneva.

"W-w-we get th-them all?"

"Yeah, hon. Hold still, let me see."

"I h-hit a bump on the r-road," Geneva said, the pain heavy in her voice. "Sn-snapped the b-barrel on the left clean off."

Blood welled from the wound on the blonde's chest. The shotgun blast had hit her high and to the right. Missed the heart, Dirisha hoped, but the splash of red bubbled. Got the lung for sure.

"I b-broke my left wrist, Dirisha. And t-took the shot in the—" She winced and ground her teeth as a spasm of pain hit her. Her pale skin seemed waxy and lighter than normal.

Dirisha slid her arms under the wounded woman. "Hang on, brat, they'll have transportation close. We'll go let you dance with the medics."

"You th-think?"

"Yeah. No problem. Looks like you might have to take it easy for a few days, though." Dirisha tried to sound offhand, as if she weren't worried in the least. It was a lie.

Green eyes narrowed in concern, the black woman stood and started for the place where she would have hidden her transport if she'd been mounting the assassination attempt. Halfway to the thick brush, she spotted the flitter. Good.

She put Geneva into the flitter, and sprinted back to their ruined aircar for the medkit she always carried. The coags would slow or stop the bleeding, the stupecomp would pump whatever it thought the patient needed into her, and then it would be up to the medics to repair the damage.

The matadora hurried back as fast as she could move to

Geneva, put the medkit over the chest wound and triggered the machine to life. It hummed and clicked, and Dirisha had already gotten the flitter online and into the air before the medkit finished its diagnosis and emergency treatment. The flitter's engine screamed as Dirisha jammed the forward speed control to maximum and headed back toward Flat Town. Five minutes, she figured. Geneva had wanted to see where Dirisha grew up, and so they had come to the planet for which the black matadora had been named.

As she drove, fear making her mouth dry, Dirisha added things up. A bomb in the aircar's engine, set off where seven attackers lay waiting. Probably a radio pulse rather than a timer. Somebody wanted the two of them dead? Who? Why?

Later. First thing was to get Geneva somewhere they could take care of her. After that, Dirisha would figure out the rest of it. And when that happened, somebody was going to be in a pile of shit a klick deep and as big around as Mount Ziwi.

Tape it, deuce. Somebody was going to pay big for this. You could spit on that and make it *shine*.

Part One
The Albino
Knife

ONE _____

THINGS WERE QUIET in the Red Sister, which was not unusual. Winter had laid its cold hands across Muto Kato's single continent and a meter of fresh powder lay piled upon twice that much older packed snow. Those families who usually favored the pub with their patronage were slow in coming on this frigid evening. Half a dozen regulars sat drinking or smoking and the muted hum of conversation was mostly about the weather. Somewhere in the distance a snowmachine whined as it carried its passengers through the world made white.

Emile Antoon Khadaji, hero of the revolution, *instigator* of the war that brought low the repressive Confed, wiped the already-clean bar top with a rag. He was medium tall, still in good shape under his thermoskin coverall, though not muscular enough to draw stares. His dark hair had gray in it, mostly along the sides, and his face bore smile wrinkles and character lines. A first look might make him about forty T.S., a more careful examination could up that closer to fifty. The blue eyes were still clear and alert. Here, the patrons and workers he employed knew him under a

pseudonym. It had been five years since anybody had called
him by his true name, and none of the locals knew who he
had been before. He was a man who had gone to ground,
hiding who and what he had been.

The outer door slid open and then closed, the hard plastic
squeaking a little as it moved along its track. Have to get
that fixed, Khadaji thought.

He turned to adjust the nozzle on the liquor dispenser as
the inner door opened, so that he caught only a peripheral
flash as the single customer entered the pub. He noticed
nothing unusual about the figure from his quick glimpse.
He—she?—wore a heavy, gloved and hooded parka over
thermoskins and extrusion boots. The whine of the snow-
shoes as they retracted over the second dump grate just
inside the door was a sound he heard frequently. There was
nothing to set the customer apart from any other, and yet—

Khadaji turned and looked at the woman. He was sure it
was a woman, and something about her movement as she
reached up to untab her parka and face shield seemed
familiar, even though he felt certain he had never seen her
before. What would bring a stranger here? The last person
he hadn't known personally who'd come to the Red Sister
had been a miner from Delton City, and he'd stopped in
only because his flitter had broken down on the way home.

When the woman removed the parka, Khadaji thought his
heart was going to stop.

Juete!

It couldn't be, and yet, there she was.

Khadaji stared, unable to get his mind working. It had
been more than twenty years since he had seen her, and she
looked exactly the same. There was the white skin, the
white hair, the pink eyes—she wasn't wearing colored
droptacs—and the beauty that hit you like a fist to the solar
plexus, stealing your breath and your soul at the same time.

Even as he saw her, he knew it could not be. Juete had never told him how old she was, but surely twenty years had to show somehow? If anything, she looked younger than she had when he'd seen her last.

She walked toward the bar. Every customer in the place stopped and turned to watch, caught by the genetic magic that was the Albino Exotic's birthright. Those closest to her would have felt the call most, for her ancestors' pheromones had been tailored to attract virtually any man or woman of human or human mue stock.

As she drew closer, Khadaji saw that he had been mistaken. This was not Juete. There were small differences in her face, the shape of her nose, her lips, her jaw. She was close, very close, but not Juete. A relative.

The woman reached the bar and looked at Khadaji with a gaze that seemed to penetrate to his essence.

"Hello, Emile," she finally said. Her voice was honey on denscris, smooth and clear. "My name is Veate."

That she used his name, one he hadn't heard directed at him for five years, was not lost on him. And in that instant, he knew who she was.

"You're Juete's daughter," he said, his voice full of wonder and a certain kind of joy. Juete had a daughter. Amazing.

She gave him a brief nod. "And yours," she said.

Veate had played this scene a hundred times in the theater of her mind and in none of those rehearsals had he reacted quite the way it turned out now, finally, on opening night. She was watching carefully, very carefully when she announced her news, and save for a slight tightening around the eyes, he had shown no reaction. He hadn't suspected, she was pretty sure of that; it was a true surprise, but he'd

handled it well, better than she'd expected. She wasn't sure
exactly *what* she thought he might do: he could have denied
it, maybe; or maybe his mouth might have gaped in shock;
yes, and maybe he could have fallen down and frothed at
the nose, too. But she could see that he didn't doubt it for
a second, that he knew the truth when he heard it.

There was a way in which she hated him, but she was
also curious. One did not meet one's father every day, and
she had been nervous about it, frightened in some nonspe-
cific way. Not every young woman was the daughter of a
certified hero, a man who'd taken his lever and found a
place to stand and then moved the whole damned galaxy.

Not that he looked it. He was ordinary enough, handsome
in a rough way, but nobody she'd cross the street to view
better. She had seen the holoprojic representations her
mother had, some of them full size, and even so, she'd
expected him to be taller, to be larger than life, to be
arrogant.

He turned to a young man stacking bottles near the
opposite end of the bar. "Shel, watch things here for me,
would you?" Then he turned back toward her. "I have an
office in the back; we can talk there."

Damn. He sounded so fucking calm! She'd wanted to
rattle him, offbalance him, at least a little, and he was
taking this in stride as if she'd offered him nothing more
than the weather.

He grinned, and Veate tried to read it. Was he laughing at
her? Could he somehow tell she'd wanted to rock him? Or
was he smirking for some other reason?

Maybe he's glad to see you, hey?

No. Discount that. She didn't want him to be glad to see
her. She didn't want him to have any redeeming virtues,
save his much-vaunted abilities with guns and intrigue. She

needed his help; that was the only reason she'd come to
him. The only reason.

Yeah, said her little inner voice, *right*.

The small room Khadaji used for an office was not much.
It had enough space for a desk and a couple of chairs, with
an old couch against one wall that sometimes served as a
bed for customers too stoned or drunk to try to make it
home. Over the couch there was a painting of a figure
wrapped in dark robes against a background of a starry
night. The figure was of one of the Siblings of the Shroud
and it was the only reminder of his past life that Khadaji
kept in his office. Except for the pair of loaded spetsdöds
locked in the center drawer of the desk.

Khadaji stood next to the desk, looking at the young
woman who claimed to be his daughter. To say it had
come as a shock was a massive understatement. He had a
daughter, by Juete? She had never even hinted at it. She
must have been pregnant before he had left her on the Darkworld, and for some reason, had decided to keep the child.

That she was Juete's child he did not doubt; he could see
her mother shining through her face. But that she was also
his offspring still vibrated through him like a sudden
thunderstorm. He had a child. It was not something he had
ever seriously considered. His path had been in a different
direction from home or family, and while he had sometimes
wondered at that which he had turned away from, he had
never regretted his choice.

He believed her when she'd said it. He was not naive, but
the truth had rung for him like a crystal bell in a quiet
mountain zendo. He looked for some sign of himself in her
features, but could not see it.

The truth did not preclude the questions that arose in him,
the thousand things he wanted to know all of an instant.

"Your mother never told me," he said.

"I know."

It was said coolly, matter-of-factly, and it brought up in him another raft of emotion bouncing in the rapids of his amazement. "Do you know why?"

"You left and went to save the galaxy. You were busy."

Again, the comment was spoken evenly, without apparent anger or censure.

"Even so, I loved her."

"She has always spoken well of you," Veate said. "That I am alive indicates something."

Khadaji nodded. Juete couldn't have known that he would become rich a few years after they parted and that he would arrange for her to be supported by part of his wealth for the rest of her life. Bringing another Exotic into the universe was risky, especially during the days of the Confederation.

"And I've read all about you," she said. "The Man Who Never Missed, the father of the revolution that cleared away galactic injustice, the living legend who vanished after he had done his job. Some people think you're right up there with Chang or Buddha or Christo."

There was the barest hint of sarcasm in her voice this time. He did not know her, had not known that she even existed before a few moments ago, and certainly he did not need to justify his actions to a stranger, albeit that this stranger was like no other to him. But it bothered him that she seemed to dislike him somehow.

"But you don't approve," he said.

"It's not my place to say."

He let it pass. "How did you find me?" He already knew, but he wanted to hear how she would play it.

"Pen told me."

He nodded again. Pen was the only person who knew

where Emile Khadaji had gone. And he would never send on anybody who didn't have good reason to see Khadaji. Surely this was as good a reason as he was likely to come across. Must have surprised the old man. Or, given Pen's integratic philosophy, maybe not.

"Why now?"

A fugue player would find worlds to think about in those two words, but it was not his intent to play fugue with his daughter. The simple answer to the basic question would do for a start.

"I need your help." The cool reserve in her voice was still there, but for a moment, he saw the girl underneath the composure. Albinos had to learn early how to deal with a galaxy that wanted them, wanted to own them, wanted something from them even if it had to take it by force. Exotics had to develop walls to protect themselves, hard shells to absorb the blows, and he could not imagine Juete failing to teach her child—*their* child—what she must know to survive. But for an instant, the walls cleared and her fear and vulnerability were there for him to see.

"Someone has kidnapped my mother," she said. "Will you help me find her?"

He had left it all behind when he'd come to retire on Muto Kato. The killing he had done while a soldier, the manipulations after that, the war against the Confed. Oh, he would sometimes take the spetsdöds out on a free day to plink at old drink containers, trying to keep skills that had once been razor-edged from rusting completely. He had put it all behind him, the danger and intrigue, and he had never regretted it. He'd done a lifetime's work in a decade and a half, and walked away without a backward look. He had done what he had been driven to do by a mystical battlefield revelation that he could not ignore, but he was long past that. It seemed sometimes when he thought about it as if it had all happened to another man, in another life, one he knew only slightly, if at all.

All these thoughts ran through his head in a jumble, and it was only a few seconds before they were done. This was a test; the gods were not done with him yet. Comfortable in your little pub, Khadaji? Really? Here. Chew on this.

"Yes, of course," he said. "I'll do whatever I can."

Veate smiled at him, the relief bright behind her expression, and he mirrored her smile with one of his own.

"Thank you," she said.

He stared, entranced by her. He had a daughter.

But the joy was mitigated by what she had said. The woman he had loved above all others, the mother of his child, had been kidnapped. He hoped he wasn't too late to do something about it.

Veate slept in the spare room of his cube. Khadaji sat at the keyboard of his computer and called up his communications program.

"Online," it said.

He gave the computer the com number of the Siblings of the Shroud's main compound on Earth. It was billions of klicks from here but White Radio had a hundred-LY armspan, if you could afford it. And at this distance, the time lag would be almost nil. Odd, that, since the farther away one got using White Radio, the less lag there was.

"Linked," the computer said.

The face that peered from the holoproj over Khadaji's computer was completely covered save for the eyes. The hood was part of the shroud all members of the order wore. Khadaji kept his own visual transmission blank.

"Yes?" A woman's voice.

"I would like to speak to Pen."

"He is unavailable at the moment."

"It's important."

"This makes him no more available." There was an edge to the woman's voice, something Khadaji could not quite identify. Anger? Worry?

"I see. I would like to leave a message, then. Tell him to call Emile when he can—"

"Emile? Will you give me visual?"

Khadaji hesitated. The Siblings were as trustworthy as they came, but the habits of the last few years were hard to break. What the hell, he thought. I'm leaving here anyway. Maybe I won't ever come back. He said, "Transmit visual."

The computer obeyed.

"It is you," the woman said. "This is Moon."

Moon. Pen's mate. Khadaji had met her before he'd left for his new life. He should have recognized her voice.

"Ah, Moon."

"Pen is having a cut on his shoulder bonded," she said. "I'll put you through."

"Nothing serious, I hope?"

"We had an explosion. He was hit by a shard of denscris."

"An explosion?"

"An attack, of sorts."

Something torpid stirred in Khadaji's mind. Juete kidnapped and Pen injured? It was possible that it was coincidence, of course, but his reptile brain knew otherwise. It sent a cold tendril to chill his scrotum, another to tighten his belly.

The reptile knew that something was very wrong here and that he should stay the hell out of it.

TWO _____

KHADAJI HADN'T BEEN offworld in five years, and when he booked passage for himself and Veate, he was mildly surprised. The old Confed-run system had been inefficient on its best days, with no apparent logical reason for various transit times. The Bender-driven ships often seemed to go out of their way to drag things along slowly, and when he'd come to Muto Kato from Earth, it had taken the better part of three weeks, with side jaunts to systems that made no sense whatsoever. Now, the trip to Earth could be done directly, with an elapsed time of just under four days. The deregulation of the star lanes and opening them to private companies had apparently done wonders for the industry.

Other things had changed, too. Where once there had been Confederation troopers and military flight controllers, they had been replaced by ship company employees and civilians. Bribes were not necessary, and any galactic citizen with a basic ID cube could travel virtually anywhere he or she wished, with few restrictions save those of common sense. And enough stads, of course. Access to classified military areas was forbidden, as was spacing to a planet where some new disease might be loose. Local restrictions had to be dealt with, naturally, now that the planets could set their own rules, but by and large, few worlds tried to keep strangers from visiting.

The ship, the *Pride of Bocca*, was an old deep spacer that had been extensively refurbished. The vessel was the size of a small ocean liner, and could carry five hundred passengers in comfort, with choices ranging from basic accommodations to luxury in the extreme. Years past, when he had waged war upon the Confed, Khadaji had put virtually all of his own money into that battle, keeping out only enough to buy the pub—and a certain reserve, just in case of emergency. The stash was of precious gems and rare metals, easy to convert to stads, and it was upon this fund that he drew to buy passage to Earth. If anything, the freebiz Republic prices were cheaper than the old government-run ships had been. Very interesting.

Veate spoke little as they took the boxcar into orbit and rendezvous with the *Pride*. She seemed lost in her own thoughts and Khadaji respected her privacy. Probably worried about her mother, he thought.

For himself, Khadaji had yet to get over the shock of the young woman's sudden appearance in his life. As they left the gravity well of Muto Kato, he turned the new sensation of being a father around in his mind and looked at it from various angles. He would have thought that at his age and after all his experiences, he would not have been rattled by anything. But he was wrong, for this was one hell of a surprise.

The deep space ship was shaped more or less like a brick, with odd protrusions jutting out along the sides here and there. He watched the holoproj unit built into the back of the seat in front of him as they approached. It would be a few minutes before the boxcar docked. Khadaji turned to Veate.

"Tell it to me again," he said. "I might have missed something the first time."

The young woman came back from her long stare. "I was skiing on Mount Rama," she said. "I was with four friends and we were in the lodge. I called Juete's cube and got the recorder. I asked that she be paged—she was considering coming out to join us—and the page went unanswered. It worried me."

"Any particular reason?"

"Only that my mother was a careful woman. When she wasn't in the casino, she usually was in her cube. If she went outside the safety of those places, she always did so with an armed casino guard."

He nodded. "Go on."

"I had the cubecomp page security. They didn't know where she was. I got nervous, and I had the cube's recorder give me a recent playback."

"You had the override code?"

"Yes. And you heard the recording."

Khadaji leaned back in the form-chair and sighed. Juete had been abducted from her electronically secured cube on Vishnu by two men. They had vocal and visual records of the kidnapping, and he had seen the holoproj three times. Neither of the kidnappers were familiar to him, but that in itself meant nothing. The men had managed to rascal their way in, but had made no attempt to stop the room's recorder from working, and they had known that somebody would collect the voices and images sooner or later. They could have been skinmasked and wearing voice distorters, of course, but even so, a computer aug could do wonders with somatic patterns and speech cadence based on the recordings. They had not seemed particularly worried. It was as if they wanted people to know what had happened.

Why had they taken her?

Khadaji stared, as if he could see across time and space to the event. If he knew the "why," he might be able to figure out the "who," and the "where."

He had certain resources upon which he could draw. He had never traded on his status as the man who focused the revolution that toppled the Confed. It had been five years, but there were those who owed him, and others who might not reject a call for help. He would go to see Pen first and then he would call in his favors. The mother of his child—he had a daughter!—was in danger, and he would do whatever it took to try to save her.

"How are you feeling, brat?"

Geneva was sealed into a Healy medicator, and her voice when it came through the speaker sounded hollow behind the thick, clear plastic of the lid. "I've felt better. I itch all over."

Dirisha smiled down at her lover, her teeth white against her dark sin. Geneva was naked, and the thin silk sheet put inside to cover her was bunched up under her feet. Even with the wound sealed under an ugly glob of mediflesh, she was still quite beautiful lying there. Dirisha put one hand onto the plastic, pressing down with her palm; inside the machine, Geneva matched her move so that their hands, the dark and the pale, were separated by no more than a half centimeter of the hard clearness. The danger had passed and Geneva would live. The medics had dug the metal shot from her, stapled and glued her punctured lung and torn blood vessels back together, and stuck her into the Healy. The machine's computer monitored every system and adjusted the flow of medicine and ultrasound and coherent healing light and magnetics as needed. Another week or ten days and the blonde could pick up her life where she'd left off, not much the worse for her experience.

"I thought you knew how to roll without breaking your damned spetsdöd barrel."

"I'll work on it."

Dirisha's smile beamed down brightly.

"Hey, Rissy? Thanks."

"No problem, brat. I didn't have anything better to do."

"I love you, too. You find out anything about the reason they hit us?"

"Not really. By the time the cools got there, a couple of them had come out of the shocktox and taken off. The cools got four of them in custody. They are contract workers, anything for money SOF's, and they got paid through a computer drop. Never saw the man or woman who hired them."

"Why would mercenaries set up a splash on us?"

"I dunno. Maybe somebody with an old grudge. They were definitely waiting for us—the aircar engine was rigged to blow from a coded pulse and one of them had the button. They knew which way we were heading and they were loaded for battle."

"I don't remember pissing anybody off that bad," Geneva said.

"Some people take things real personal."

Dirisha tried another smile to hide what she wasn't ready to say, but the woman inside the Healy had been with her too long to miss the undercurrent.

"What is it? There's something else, isn't there?"

Dirisha shifted her stance a little. Might as well tell her; she wouldn't rest until she knew. "Yeah. I got a call from Bork. He sends his best, by the way."

Geneva nodded, but didn't speak, waiting for Dirisha to finish.

"Bork got jumped around the same time we did."

"Is he okay?"

"Yeah, you know Bork. Drop him off a tall building and he'd just tighten up and bounce a few times. Four men, also meat for hire. Two of them survived."

"Odd coincidence," Geneva said.

"Yeah. And that isn't all of it. There was an explosion on Earth, in the Siblings compound. Nobody really hurt there. And Sleel has dropped from sight. I couldn't raise him."

Geneva considered it. "Not good. We got some kind of conspiracy here?"

"Looks like it. I've got some feelers out, but so far nothing is twitching."

"What are we going to do?"

"*We* aren't going to do anything. You are staying put until you get well. I'm going to poke around a little and see what I can find."

Geneva knew her well enough to know there was no point in trying to talk her out of it. So she said, "You be careful."

"I will. You remember Grandle Diggs?"

Geneva looked puzzled for a second. "Starboard?"

"The same. He happened to be in the neighborhood so he dropped by. He's gonna set up camp in here for a few days until I get back."

"You think I need a bodyguard?"

"Probably not, but what the hell, I'd feel better." With that, Dirisha reached down and activated the food tray slot. The small drawer extruded itself from the Healy, and the matadora removed a flat package from her jacket and dropped it into the drawer. As the drawer cycled shut, Dirisha said, "You know where the override in that thing is?"

"Of course," Geneva said. She gave her lover a disgusted look. Nobody with her training would get into a box like this without knowing how to get out of it in a hurry.

"Sorry. There's a pair of spetsdöds and ammo in that

pack. And a personal communicator you can bounce off the
comsats to get to me anywhere onplanet, if you need me. If
somebody gets past Starboard, you can pop the lid and
throw something at them other than your good looks."

Geneva smiled and peeled open the package. She removed the two back-of-the-hand weapons and, moving with
some care, managed to seat them in place. Another two
seconds and both spetsdöds were loaded. "Ah. Now I'm
dressed again."

"I ever tell you how beautiful you are?"

"Not nearly often enough. I could move over and maybe
make enough room to squeeze you in here."

Dirisha laughed. "You heal up, brat. I've got some
errands to run. I'll check back with you later."

"You be very careful, Dirisha."

"Always."

The General Power Complex on Bantu Island was not a
pleasure club. The men, women and mues sentenced there
were not in the same class of hardcore criminals shipped to
the Omega Cage for life, but neither could the GPC
prisoners be called upright cits. Many of them were violent,
most of them were going to spend an average of fifteen
years in custody, and all of them would have rather been
elsewhere.

When Sleel was mustered into the system, he was
unhappier than most of the population on the island. He
was set up, by whom and why he didn't know, but he was
damnsure gonna find out and when he did, there were folks
gonna be sorry they were ever born.

Sleel was stubborn, but he wasn't a fool. Until he could
find a chance to escape, there was no point in making too
much trouble for himself. So he went with the guards

quietly once the transport touched down. That all five of them held leveled hand wands helped his decision.

He was processed, shaved bald and put through chemsprays and scans, then given a floppy gray coverall, slippers, underwear and a packet of personal hygiene gear. A pair of guards took him to a single-occupant cube that was three meters square. A thin bedpad was drawered into the wall and a toilet and shower occupied one corner. There was a small cabinet to stow the packet they'd given him, and any personal belongings he might have or acquire.

He pulled the bed out and examined it, pushed it back, and looked around.

Welcome home, Sleel.

"Come with me," said a voice from behind him.

Sleel turned to see a man dressed in a coverall like his own.

"I'm Brunder," the man said. He was average height, fair-skinned, and had been here long enough for his hair to have grown out to shoulder length.

"I'm Sleel. Where are we going?"

"To the converter room. You'll be loading carts for your first rotation."

"Nice of you to give me time to settle in."

"'Idle hands are the devil's workshop,'" Brunder said.

Sleel followed the other prisoner down a series of interlocked corridors. If there were guards around, he didn't see them.

The converter room was a high-ceilinged rectangle maybe twenty meters by fifty meters, and a bank of humming rectification units lined one of the long walls. Maybe twenty prisoners, mostly men, worked in the room, moving around the machines, pushing carts full of electronic parts and coils of wire. As Sleel followed Brunder into the big room, he saw a bank of flashers along the doorway, indicating that the door was wired into some kind of scanner. Sleel figured that anybody who tried to take home a souvenir from work, a tool, some cable, whatever, would probably get nailed by the HO scan and no doubt be made to suffer for the effort.

Sleel turned to Brunder. "Who is the hardest man in the place?"

"You done time before?"

"Not your business. The guy who runs things?"

Brunder nodded. "Truck. Big man with the spacer's buzz, sitting at the desk next to the dollycrane." Brunder did not point and he kept his voice low.

"This place covered by video?"

"Sure."

"How long for a guard to get here?"

"Thirty-one seconds is the record. Forty-five is average."

"Okay."

Sleel walked over to where the man called Truck sat. He was big, not as big as Bork, maybe, but not much smaller, and he had a face that had taken a few shots. The nose was slightly bent, the eye sockets padded with some scar tissue, one ear thicker than the other. Sleel would have been a lot more impressed if the guy had been beautiful. A hard with a pretty face meant he didn't let it get hit and that was worse than somebody who looked like this guy. Still, you never knew what an opponent could do; looks could fool you sometimes. There seemed to be a fair amount of muscle under the tight coverall.

Truck looked up. "Yeah?"

"I'm Sleel. I mind my own business and I don't take any shit."

Truck grinned. "Yeah?"

"You heard it."

Truck stood, and Sleel saw his intent as he did. Might as

well have a big flashing sign over his head, the way his muscles tightened, the way his hands curled into fists and his breathing altered. Stupid.

Truck was still gathering himself when Sleel kicked him. The matador's foot snapped out precisely, smacked into Truck's testicles and flattened them briefly against the man's pubic bone.

Truck sucked in a quick breath, which was good, because it was the last one he was going to get for a few seconds. Sleel stepped in even as Truck reached for his injured scrotum and put everything he had into a flat punch into the man's solar plexus. The punch stole the man's ability to breathe and drove him back half a meter.

With Truck now having two things to worry about, Sleel gave Truck a third. He spun, his arms drawn in tight, and when he opened out, his right fist formed a hammer that connected with Truck's forehead.

Truck fell backward like a chainsawed tree and hit the floor.

The room got very quiet.

Sleel took a deep breath, let it out, and moved to sit in the unconscious man's chair. With any luck at all, he'd have almost another forty seconds before the guards came to get him. He smiled at the other prisoners and waved one hand jauntily at them. Good to get that out of the way.

Now he could concentrate on finding a way out of this pit.

THREE _____

BORK WAS NOT stupid. People sometimes had the idea that all big men with muscles had less on the ball mentally, and Bork had long ago realized that he could turn this into an advantage. A man who was busy patronizing you would often let something slip that he might not if he thought you could keep up with him. That was good, and Bork knew how to exaggerate his normally easygoing attitude to the point where he might seem less than bright. He was doing it now.

He stood at the front of a long line waiting to do business with the woman behind the counter of the computer message service. As backrocket as Fox was, most people didn't carry personal comps capable of linking into the larger com and info nets. Therefore, such places as this did a fair amount of work requiring personal contact.

It was nearly lunch time, and Bork was being deliberate in his speech and action. Very deliberate. The place had that stale office smell that came from recirculated air, along with a slightly acrid tang due to overused computer solidstates. The line of operators was busy, and looking forward to a break soon; that was fairly apparent. Nobody really wanted to be here, not those in line, not those servicing them. The woman behind the counter was already overworked and Bork was politely making things harder for her.

The four men who had attacked him had gotten their contract via this compservice; at least, that's what the two who'd survived had said. He hadn't hurt them, only lifted one of them up by his shirt front and held him dangling in a one-armed curl that frightened the other one so bad he was willing to talk. Nothing personal, the man allowed, and Bork had nodded and said fine; killing them wouldn't be personal either. The guy had gotten positively loquacious at that point. They were supposed to send a message when Bork was dead, and pick up a response thereafter. So Bork had the talker send the message; that could be done over any comcircuit, but the response had to be obtained in person, and the cools had arrived too soon for that to happen.

Talk to the cools about this, Bork had said, and I will be displeased with you. Neither of the survivors wanted that.

"What did you say the name was?" the woman behind the counter asked Bork. She was not far from the edge of her patience.

"Timmer su Lock," Bork said, allowing a big grin to spread over his face. That was the name of the man who'd been so eager to tell him anything he wanted to know.

The woman spoke to her computer, giving it the name. "You have identification?"

Bork nodded slowly. "Yes, I have identification."

"May I *see* it, please?"

He gave it another two seconds. "Huh? Oh, yeah. Sure." He reached into his jacket pocket and produced Timmer su Lock's credit and ID cube. This was a standard thumbtip-sized chunk of hard black memory plastic with information embedded in it. The would-be assassin hadn't been so unprofessional as to have it on him when he and his friends had tried to splash Bork, but he'd been almost eager to tell him where it was.

Bork watched as the woman inserted the cube into her computer's scanner slot. The UV lasers played their invisible questions upon it.

After a second, the air over the comp lit with the holoproj of the cube's contents. Bork could see the back of the image; the words and everything were reversed, but he could easily see that the cube had been damaged: where the picture and eye and brain stats were supposed to be was badly fuzzed, so much so that the computer couldn't rectify it. Changing an ID cube was a tricky business, only an expert could do it and have it pass undetected, but wiping a portion of one was relatively easy. A few minutes with a magnetic inducer and a simplewit computer and anybody with even a little programming skill could do it. Few did, because a damaged cube wouldn't get you very far. In this case, however, it only had to pass this one harried and busy woman. Bork had done the work himself.

"This cube is damaged," the woman said. The anger peeped through her forced politeness.

"Really? Gah, it was fine when I used it yesterday. Musta been hit when I fell off the hovertruck this morning."

The woman looked up at Bork, then back at the bad readout. "I can't give out messages to somebody with a damaged cube."

Bork counted to three mentally. "Uh, right, I can understand that. What do I do?"

She shook her head. He could almost read her mind: I don't have time for this shit. "You have to go to the nearest Republic ID Center and get it replaced."

One, two, three, and, "Will that, uh, take long? I really

need this message. I mean, I'm me, you know?" He nodded
at the partially fuzzed holoproj.

There was no guarantee it would work, but the psychol-
ogy of it was sound enough. Surely this giant dooze was
who he claimed to be? He didn't look or act as if he had
enough brains to tab his tunic by himself, and he was
holding up the line. More, he had the look of somebody
who would stand happily there and hold the goddamned line
up all day!

The woman made her decision. She rattled off a message
number, said, "Hardcopy," and pointed at the line of
printers next to the far wall. "Over there," she said, pulling
the ID cube from her machine and all but throwing it at
Bork. "And get this cube replaced before you come in here
again!"

Bork smiled and nodded. "Yes, fem," he said. "Sure
thing. Thank you very much."

Bork moved toward the printers.

The Siblings' compound had changed little that Khadaji
could tell from from the air. They had sent their own lighter
to transport him and Veate from the starship; that was new.
As the transport, empty save for the two of them and the
crew, fell from space toward Manus Island, the air was clear
enough of the usual tropical clouds so that he could see the
place fairly well. From high orbit, it looked like a hook-
nosed fish with tiny turds dribbling from its tail. As they got
closer, the details of the buildings and fenced compound
came into view. They had built their own landing pad inside
the fence. Three robed figures stood next to it, watching the
lighter come down.

When the door slid open, Khadaji and Veate walked
down the ramp to where the three siblings stood waiting. It
was summer here, hot and humid, and the smells of flowers

and molds and organic decay filled the air. No two planets ever seemed to smell exactly the same, Khadaji thought; even if the climates and gravity were virtually identical, each world had its own distinctive scent. The cloudless sky allowed the sun to lay its hot fingers on the open landing pad, and more heat reflected up from the stressed concrete. It was like opening an oven door. Despite the shrouds, which covered everything but the wearers' hands and a strip that exposed the eyes, he knew which one was Pen before they reached the trio. Pen had taught him the Ninety-seven Steps, had been his friend as well as teacher, and had put him on the road to his destiny with the Confed. And like as not, the siblings were cooler under their clothing than he was under his. He had worn the shroud for a time, a special dispensation, even though he had not technically earned the right to do so. The cloth was almost alive. It had been a long time ago.

Khadaji chuckled as he thought about it. He had thought he was in control, dealing in complicated and twisted criminal and political tactics, running the show, when in fact he had been more like a fly in Pen's web. Circuits within circuits and he still wasn't sure exactly who had been responsible for what.

"Welcome, Emile," Pen said. He waved at the other two siblings. "This is Moon, and Spiral."

Khadaji nodded. "This is Veate. My daughter." Still had a strange ring to it, to say that.

"We've met," Pen said. "Welcome, Veate."

"Shall we go where it is cooler to talk?" Moon said.

"By all means," Khadaji said.

"We've cleaned up the damage," Spiral said, "but I've asked Diamond to give you a little presentation about the explosion."

They were in the office of the Elder Brother, a job that Moon, Spiral and Pen had all held at one time or another. It seemed larger than the last time Khadaji had seen it. Probably it was.

"Diamond?" Khadaji said.

The edges of the three siblings' eyes all crinkled, an action that Khadaji knew to be smiles. He also knew the significance of the name. In the order, each student gave up his or her old identity when enrolled. A traditional nom de ordre was sometimes passed along, but only one person had any given tag. There was only one "Pen," one "Moon," and so on. Once they died, the names could go back into the communal pot to be reassigned. The original Pen had been one of the founders of the order, as had Diamond. For the siblings to give someone either of these designations was considered a vote of confidence.

"Yes," Pen said. "He's got great potential."

After a few more minutes, a half-shrouded student arrived. The system of clothing used by the siblings was such that past a basic starting point, each student had to earn his or her way to a complete outfit, much like a martial artist had to earn rank pins.

Diamond carried a small case, which he opened, after being introduced to Khadaji and Veate. He was a young man, Khadaji saw, and he had to pull his attention away from Veate, much as a man might shake himself out of a drug trance. Khadaji grinned slightly. Oddly enough, he had not felt anything hormonal when he and Veate had met. The pull of an Albino Exotic was usually very powerful. Maybe because she was his daughter?

Diamond said, "The bomb got past our security because when it came in, it wasn't a bomb."

Khadaji glanced at Pen, who remained silent. Listen to the boy tell it, Emile, the older man seemed to say.

"When we received the materials for the planned construction, they were, of course, scanned at the port. A second scan took place when we brought them into the compound."

Diamond removed a projector and a controller from the case. He clicked an inducer and the air over the desk lit with a three-dimensional representation of the exhibit that had blown up inside the compound's museum.

Khadaji sucked in a quick breath. It was the office of Marcus Jefferson Wall. The late and unlamented Factor Wall, who had in fact been the real power behind the Confed's puppet president during the final days before the end. Khadaji had never been inside, but he knew the place. He had sent the young-old woman who had killed the Factor with a poison spew to which there had been no antidote.

Diamond clicked the control and got a macro image of one of the exhibit's three chairs, a custom orthopedia. He pushed the viewpoint in closer.

"These are computer records of before the explosion, of course," Diamond said. "The plastic of this one was the culprit. An oxidation explosive. The color is a giveaway, see there?"

Khadaji nodded. Very clever.

Veate said, "Oxidation explosive?"

Diamond turned to her, obviously happy to have a chance to explain something—anything—to this beautiful woman. "Yes. You see, the plastic as it is created is inert. It won't show up on a sniffer or scanner because it is harmless. But a number of substances oxidize, that is to say, they combine with oxygen in the air in a chemical process, like rust on unprotected iron or steel. Actually a process similar to fire, but much slower."

Veate was not a chemist but neither was she inept. She could feel him struggling to control the attraction he felt for her, and as she had done so many times before, she altered her position slightly, roughened her voice a hair, and deliberately became more provocative. Testing his control against her attraction. As it had always done before, she felt it start to overcome another's resolve. He was partially covered, but Veate could feel his sexual heat rising. But her voice was cool again, the attraction toned down when she spoke.

"And you are saying that the oxygen in combination with whatever was in the chair became an active explosive."

"Exactly. With proper mixing of the basic elements and a knowledge of how fast such a chemical process usually takes, one could time the explosion fairly accurately, plus or minus an hour or two. When enough oxygen had combined with the chair, it simply went off."

"That's a rather iffy way to assassinate somebody," Khadaji put in.

"Indeed," Pen said. "We have concluded that there was intent to cause mayhem, but no particular target among us—there was no way the would-be assassin could know exactly when the explosion would happen. It would be like shooting a gun and hoping your target would happen to run by in time to be hit by the pellet."

"Who?" Khadaji said, half to himself. "And why?"

"We don't know," Spiral said.

"And what has this to do with my mother's kidnapping?"

Moon said, "Of itself, there would seem to be no connection. But there are other . . . events that lead us to believe they are intertwined."

Veate looked at Khadaji. "They have a computer program that predicts the future," he said. "Among other things."

"That's not quite accurate," Moon said, "but integratic

projections do deal in probability theory. Given enough input, some of the extrapolations can be rather remarkable."

Khadaji laughed. "I will attest to that."

Veate blinked at her father.

"I'll explain it to you later," he said.

"At any rate," Spiral went on, "there are certain things we have been able to surmise." He looked at the young sibling. "Thank you for your explanation, Diamond."

The half-shrouded youth nodded and understood that he was dismissed. He left.

"You worried about security?"

Pen said, "Not worried, but perhaps more cautious."

"Your integratics blew a circuit on this one?"

"Not really," Spiral said. "We had not yet pinpointed the event but we had been alerted to the likelihood generally."

Khadaji considered that. "There's more."

"Yes. Juete's kidnapping is part of it. And there have been other events about which we have learned."

Pen said, "There have been attacks on several of the matadors. As nearly as we can tell, all took place around the same time as the kidnapping."

Khadaji's heart quickened. Pen was not playing fugue here, and he meant just what he said: not the bodyguards' clients, but the bodyguards themselves had been targets.

"No fatalities," Pen said, "although some injuries have been reported. You taught them well, Emile."

Khadaji digested this new bit of information. During the revolution which brought down the lumbering dinosaur that was the Confed, there had been a number of malignant fleas leaping from the corpse who would have gladly seen those responsible die a thousand times each. When wheels turned, those on top sometimes found themselves buried in the mud after things rolled to a stop. The matadors, the most elite bodyguards ever, had been the axle around which the galaxy's government had turned. They had enemies.

But—why now? It had been five years. And who among the fallen, if the most likely possibility held, would it be?

"What are you doing about it?" Khadaji asked.

Pen said, "The siblings are asking questions. All of our sources are being checked."

"And you have nothing so far." Not a question.

"Correct."

"Then I guess I'll have to poke around some on my own."

None of the siblings said anything, but Khadaji was sure that they already knew he would say that. He had studied the great political thinkers and theorists of human history and the convoluted minds who ran the Shroud made Machiavelli look like a simpleton. They not only knew, he was pretty sure it was *their* idea, on some level.

"I'd better give Rajeem a call," Khadaji said.

"Rajeem?" That from Veate.

"Rajeem Carlos."

She turned to look at him. "You know the President of the Republic well enough to address him by his first name?"

He couldn't help but grin. Apparently his daughter's studies hadn't told her everything about him. "Sure," he said. "I got him the job."

FOUR

DIRISHA THE WOMAN stood in the terminal of Dirisha the planet's main spaceport, waiting for Bork to arrive. The shuttle had already landed and the passengers were streaming into the terminal. There was a gap in the flow of people and then Bork moved into view, alone. A respectable distance was left vacant behind him, as well.

Dirisha smiled. Good old Bork.

He looked much the same as when she'd seen him last, more than four years ago. The black hair had maybe a little more gray in it—she had no idea how old he was; he could have been forty, fifty, sixty?—but he still looked as if he could pick himself up with one hand, with muscle left over. That last visit he had been wearing a plain coverall and no weapons. Now, he wore the orthoskins of a working matador and a pair of spetsdöds. He had a single bag, hung from a strap over one shoulder, leaving both hands free, and his eyes were alert, scanning, weighing, measuring.

Dirisha understood. She, too, wore the dark gray orthoskins, spun dotic boots and bilateral spetsdöds that identified the members of their trade. Even in the freer

54

atmosphere of the Republic, it was not common to see people wearing visible weaponry, save for uniformed cools or guards or military. But the matadors were licensed to carry their nonlethal spetsdöds anywhere in the galaxy by a special commission from the President of the Republic himself.

Dirisha's smile continued as she thought about Rajeem. She hadn't seen him in nearly five years. They had been lovers, back when she'd been assigned to guard him, but he'd been fairly busy since he'd become President. She'd planned to look up him and Beel after he retired. The three of them had been good together and she wanted to introduce them to Geneva.

"Hey, Dirisha!"

"Hey, Bork."

He moved forward and they embraced. Even with his restraint, she could feel the power radiate from him as he lifted her from the floor as if she were weightless.

Bork put her down.

Yes. Everybody who'd survived had come a long way. She and Bork, while never intimate, had been friends a long time. All the way back to when they'd been bouncers together in the Jade Flower on Greaves. Working for Emile. She and Bork and—

"You hear from Sleel?" Bork said.

Sleel. The other bouncer and later a matador and subversive as she and Bork had been.

"No. He was living in Evets City, on Thompson's Gazelle, last I heard. I called but got no answer. I sent a find-him message and that came up dry, too. You remember Pawli, from school?"

"Sure. Guy who took six weeks to get the last three steps on the pattern."

"Yeah, well, he's working for a big-time jeweler on

Thompson's Gazelle and he's going to try to run Sleel down for us."

They turned and started for where Dirisha had parked her rental flitter.

"You think he's okay?"

"You know Sleel. It'd be hard to surprise him."

Despite what she'd said, Dirisha was worried. Sleel was always trying to prove he was the toughest man in the galaxy, and he would walk barefoot through a nest of firebugs if he thought that would make the point to somebody.

"How about Geneva? She almost well?"

"Getting there. A few more days and she'll be up and about."

"That's good."

They reached the flitter, parked in a no-park zone, and Dirisha pulled an electronic sniffer from her belt pouch and pointed it at the vehicle. The sniffer was a combination wide-band transceiver and olfactory sensor. It would scan and pick up most transmissions running from VLF to SHF, so if the flitter had been bugged since she'd gone in to get Bork, it would probably squeal. Too, the sniffer put out a pulsed series of common electromagnetic wavelengths running from about 25 kHz up to 30 GHz and had a feedback circuit so that if something on the flitter was receiving, such as, oh, say, an RC bomb, the sniffer would see that, too. Finally, the little gadget's microbrain could recognize a couple dozen explosives by using no more than a few stray molecules.

The sniffer pronounced the flitter free of tampering. Dirisha and Bork moved to verify that visually. After another minute, they were satisfied that the aircar was clean. This was all standard operating procedure when protecting a client, only now neither of them had clients, save themselves.

The drive to the medical center was uneventful.

Nobody attacked them on the way into the building.

Dirisha nodded at Starboard where he sat outside Geneva's door. She and Bork went inside.

"Hey, blondie," the big man said. "You having fun inside that box?"

Geneva smiled from within the Healy. "Hi, Saval. Good to see you."

Geneva wore a purple silk robe that contrasted nicely with her pale skin and hair. Dirisha said, "At least she dressed for your visit, Bork. She's been rolling around naked in there for most of the past week."

Bork managed a small grin.

Dirisha said, "Okay, I held off asking until brat here could listen in. What's the scat on your end?"

Bork looked away from the Healy at her. "Not much. The message I got was nothing more than a bank code. Supposedly if I was made dead, the account would trigger and pay the killers."

"How much?" Dirisha asked.

"And how would the bank know you were dead?" Geneva added.

"Ten thousand standards, and I don't know how. Maybe the bank's comp is tied into the mortuaries or something. I had the hitter's ID but the bank's comp never even got around to asking why it was damaged; it kicked it right out with a no-pay signal."

"So whoever set up the account must know you're alive."

"I figure. Must know you and Geneva made it, too."

"Yeah, I checked things out here. Dead end."

"How do we get into the bank's comp?" Geneva asked. "That's the next step, right?"

"Makes sense," Bork said.

Dirisha's com chimed on her belt. She pulled the light pen-sized unit from its case. "Yes?"

The voice from the com was clear, if somewhat futzed by the small speaker. "Dirisha, it's Pawli. I found Sleel."

Here was Pawli, via White Radio, tied into the local comnet, and taking almost no time lag to speak across light years. Amazing.

"Is he okay?"

"If you can call being put in prison for a fifteen-year sentence okay, then, yeah, I'd say so."

Dirisha looked at Bork.

"At least we know where to find him," Bork said.

"What's the story, Pawli?"

"Sleel claimed he was set up, that he was innocent of the original charge."

"Original charge?"

"Yeah, well, you know Sleel. He didn't go along willingly. And it happened pretty fast. He was arrested, charged, tried and shipped off a lot quicker than the ordinary run-of-the-rocket felon."

"*Was* he innocent?"

"My guess is yes. The evidence looks real shaky. Sleel is a lot of things, but not a liar. I'd trust him with my money."

And I have trusted him with my life, Dirisha thought. She said, "How long has he been in jail?"

"Not long. A week or so."

Dirisha and Bork and Geneva exchanged glances. He would have been getting into trouble about the same time whoever it was had started shooting.

"Get whatever else you can and download it into a message for me, would you, Pawli? I appreciate it."

"No sweat."

"And Pawli, watch yourself."

"Something up I should know about? I got a buzz from the Villa about the action."

"We don't know for sure what it is yet," she said, "but sleep with one eye open for a while, deuce."

"You know it. Thanks, Dirisha."

She holstered the com. "I've got three sets of dentcoms coming," she said. "That okay with you two?"

Bork and Geneva both nodded.

"What is the latest count from the Villa?" Geneva asked.

"Nine attacks altogether. None on the school, yet. Got two walking wounded, new matadors, after our time. Plus, Rimo is camped inside one of these"—Dirisha tapped the lid of the Healy—"and Becca L'evel is nursing a broken arm and a couple of cracked ribs. Nobody killed yet."

"Not to downgrade how good we all are," Bork said, "but that seems kinda odd, doesn't it?"

Dirisha nodded. Yes, it did. The matadors and matadoras were as sharp as they came, with trained reflexes and years of practice. Ordinarily for one to get wounded would be a fairly big deal. But if somebody knew who they were and had enough stads and organization to have nine attacks all pulled off at once, then it seemed strange that they hadn't done a better job of it. Nobody was invincible, and nine attacks had been thwarted with relatively minor damage, all things considered. Bork was right. It was true that less skilled men and women would probably have been killed outright, and if the bodyguards who'd been attacked hadn't fought back, surely they would have been dead, too, only—

Why did she get the feeling that the attackers hadn't been warned about how dangerous their targets were?

Something, Dirisha decided, didn't add up.

Here was one more piece of the puzzle to drop onto the

table, and there was already more than enough clutter there.

"What now, Dirisha?"

She pulled herself away from her thoughts to regard Bork. Geneva also looked up from within her tiny room at Dirisha. There they went again, automatically putting her in charge. Geneva was faster and a better shot; Bork was probably three times as strong, and yet, both deferred to her, as they had in the past. Face it, Dirisha, you're elected team leader again. Damn.

"I guess we'd better find out who wants to give us grief," she said, "and make sure they get it from us first."

"How?"

"We need to get into the bank's computer. And maybe do something about Sleel."

"You have a magic wand?" Bork said.

"No, but I have a powerful friend. Maybe we should give him a call."

It wasn't only that Truck was big, strong and violent that had made him the man in charge inside the east wing, it was that he was too stupid to know when to quit. He was out of his league now and didn't realize it. Yeah, he was hard and Sleel respected that, but he lost big points when it came down to brainpower.

Truck stood in the exercise room facing Sleel. They were alone, and the cameras normally set to observe the room were temporarily malfunctioning—Truck had a flatpack confounder running. Sleel didn't ask him how he'd come by the scrambler.

"You suckered me the first time," Truck said.

"Look," Sleel said, trying to be reasonable, "I just wanted to make a point. I don't want your job or your perks, I only wanted to be sure you got my message. Don't bother me and I won't bother you. Simple."

"You made me look bad."

You made yourself look bad, Sleel thought. But he was still trying to keep things calm, so he said, "Yeah, and I'm sorry about that."

"You're gonna be a lot sorrier." Truck clenched his fists tightly and slid into a left side stance, feet held wide apart and parallel. It would take a *real* truck to knock him down from straight on, Sleel thought. And he's gonna kick me, you can bet your ass on that. Some kind of striking style, probably real snappy and muscle-driven.

Last chance. "Look, Truck, you don't want to do this."

Truck screamed, a guttural rumble, and moved. He cross-stepped in, then whipped his leading foot up and thrust it at Sleel's groin, heel first, his foot and toes pulled back. His supporting leg straightened, heel aimed at his target. A classic crossover sidekick, full of power, but you could grow trees waiting for it arrive.

Sleel watched the booted foot come at him. It seemed to be moving in slow motion. At the point when Truck was committed to the strike fully, Sleel twisted, stepping outside of the kick, and threw the Second Variation on Cold Fire Burns Bright. His timing was a little off, he noted, as he dropped onto his side and did the hook-and-thrust with his own feet and legs.

Despite the small error, Cold Fire did its job.

Sleel broke the big bone in Truck's supporting leg just above the knee.

Truck collapsed, his face clenched in pain. He rolled, tried to stand, and the broken leg wouldn't support him. He yelped once and fell face down. It was a simple fracture, no bone showing, but somebody was going to have to inject a blob of orthostat glue into the crack and set it before old Truck here was going to do much walking around without screaming in pain every step.

"Fuck!" The big man's voice was muffled because his mouth was against the floor.

Sleel squatted, well out of Truck's reach, and said, "Okay, here's how it went. You forgot to set the safeties and you dropped a barbell on your leg and hurt it. I helped you get to the medex and you decided that I was an all-right guy and to let our hard feelings from before pass."

"Fuck you!"

"Or," Sleel continued as if Truck hadn't said anything, "I break the other leg and both arms and you lie there on the floor until somebody notices you're missing or gets the cameras working again."

Truck lifted his face to glare at Sleel.

"And after you get well if you try me again, I put out your lights permanently."

Truck swallowed, his eyes widening a little. "Nobody is gonna believe some snakeshit story about dropping a fucking weight."

"Who is going to call you a liar? I won't say any different. You spend a couple days letting the glue set and the swelling go down and it's back to business as usual."

"What do you get out of it?"

"I get left alone."

Truck considered his position. Sleel could almost see the wheels turning slowly inside the man's head. "That's it?"

"That's it."

Truck pondered on it a few more seconds. "Okay," he said finally.

"Come on. We'd better get you to the medex. How much weight was on that bar, anyway?"

Truck managed a tight grin. "Two hundred and fifty kilos."

"That's pretty heavy, Truck. Next time, maybe you should use the safeties or a spotter."

"No shit."

There was a tense second when Sleel helped Truck to his feet. If the man was going to try something, it should be now, but he merely leaned against Sleel and allowed himself to be half-carried to the exit. All things considered, this had worked out well. He'd have hated to have to damage the man any more. He'd have done it, of course; once you said you would then you had to if you got called on it, but it was better this way. There were other people on this planet more deserving of his efforts than simpleminded Truck here. The people who'd funneled him into this situation were at the top of the list. Those poor suckers didn't know who they were messing with.

Sleel felt almost sorry for them, knowing how bad it was going to be when he got out and found them.

Almost sorry, but not quite.

FIVE _____

"IT SEEMS AWFUL easy that we can just walk in here," Veate said.

She and Khadaji were entering the Presidential Office in Brisbane. The structure was four stories tall, with what looked to be almost featureless tan synstone walls broken occasionally by windows.

The door slid back to admit them into an entryway.

"Where are the guards?"

Khadaji laughed. He said, to no one visible, "Give us a moment, please." With that, he led his daughter back outside onto the approaching walkway and maybe ten meters away from the doorway. The day was slightly overcast, the air a bit muggy, and the smell of the dark green hedge that surrounded the building had an aromatic, almost mintlike scent to it.

"Good security doesn't have to be obtrusive," he said. "See the hedge?"

"Of course."

"I'm not patronizing you. Look at it more carefully."

Veate took a few steps across the neatly manicured lawn

64

and stopped near the hedge. It was taller than she by half a meter and it surrounded the entire complex save where it was broken by metal gates at the walk- and driveways. After examining the growth, she turned back toward Khadaji. "It's got some kind of sticker in it."

"It's called densethorn," he said. "Genetically engineered as a living wall. It can withstand a fairly hot flame for several minutes without burning; it'll char, but it will also give off a cloud of thick black smoke that stinks like you wouldn't believe. If you should try to push your way through it, you will find yourself cut or snagged on the barbs so that you can't move—the thorns are like fishhooks; they go in easy but are hard to take out. The branches have a tensile strength that allows them to be bent more than double without breaking. And the root system makes digging through it a real chore."

Veate walked back to stand next to Khadaji. "I'm impressed. Except that even a bad pole-vaulter could hop the hedge easily, and it would be no barrier at all to a flitter, or somebody in body armor." Did he think she was some backrocket child to be awed by a sticker bush? If this was all that was guarding the President of the Republic, then the Republic was in trouble—

"There are six photomutable gel cameras mounted on each wall of the building," Khadaji said, "and six more on the roof. You can't see them; they are built into the structure itself. You can see the missile hutches, there, those little round humps that look like spotlights at the base of the wall. There are more on each side and on the roof. Any vehicle that comes over the hedge or enters the airspace here gets spiked by a shower of doppler lances that can go through heavy armor like a rock through thincris."

Veate said nothing.

They started back toward the doorway again. "There are

permanent weatherproof sensors under the walk and lawn. The security computer can pinpoint an intruder to within a centimeter and if they don't feel like heating up the tracking lasers, the grounds are covered with overlapping zap fields."

"How do you know all this?"

He grinned. "The windows are two-centimeter-thick denscris and proof against just about anything you can reasonably throw at them from short range. The synstone walls are backed by ferrofoam plate that will stop small arms fire and the odd portable AP rocket that might come to visit.

"The door through which we have just passed is carbonex and you could hit it with an axe or shoot at it with a heavy rifle all day and it would simply absorb the impact of the blade and bullets. The door is covered by cameras, weapon and poison scanners, fluoroproj and I suspect a few other assorted sensors that have probably been invented since I was here last. We were checked and matched against the computer's records and if we hadn't passed, like as not we'd be lying on the floor out cold; there's another zap field in the entryway."

"How *do* you know all this?"

"I designed most of it."

That got to her. "He trusts you that much?"

"I hope not. Like I said, I expect there are other goodies here I don't know about."

Khadaji led his daughter to an elevator and touched a flat panel on the wall next to it.

"The control is a fingerprint sensor," he said. "Another little check for anybody clever enough to get past the door."

"Amazing." Veate looked around. "Doesn't look as if anybody is home."

"This floor is usually empty," he said.

The elevator arrived and they entered it. The manual control panel showed the President's floor as "3." Khadaji said, "Emile Khadaji to see President Carlos."

The elevator began to move, but Veate's sense of balance and acceleration told her it was dropping.

"We're going down," Veate said. "I take it that the President's floor is not three?"

Khadaji was pleased. "Right. Anybody who goes to three finds himself in a cage, as sturdy as they come. Rajeem's real office is underground, I'm not sure exactly which floor or how far down myself. Voice analysis makes sure nobody goes there who doesn't belong."

"I stand corrected about security," Veate said.

After what seemed a long time, punctuated by periods of slowing and brief halts, the elevator came to a stop and the door opened.

A young matadora stood in front of the elevator, a woman in her mid-twenties, Khadaji judged, dark hair cropped short in a working cut. She was dressed in standard orthoskins and gear. She was expecting them, knew who they were, and even so, Khadaji saw her eyes widen and the faint glimmer of a smile appear.

As he and Veate stepped out into the hall, he saw the second matador, a man of about thirty, standing to their left. The man appeared relaxed, but the position of his hands showed that he was ready to start shooting.

Sharp, both of them. Khadaji liked that.

The woman in front of them said, "It's a pleasure to meet you, sir. And fem."

Khadaji nodded. "And you are . . .?"

"Beryl li Rouge," she said. "That's Tam Staver to your left."

Khadaji looked at Staver, then back at Rouge. "The pleasure is mine."

"If you wouldn't mind?"

"Of course not," Khadaji said.

While Staver watched, Rouge pointed a small scanner at Khadaji and then Veate. "Clean," she said.

The word had no effect on Staver's alert pose.

"This way, sir."

Rouge moved ahead of them, with Staver behind, and they walked down the hallway and around a corner, stopping at the third door they came to.

"President Carlos is looking forward to seeing you, sir. And to meeting you, fem."

The door slid open. Before he moved, Khadaji said, "You and Staver move well, Rouge."

The young woman grinned and her face flushed a little. "Thank you, sir."

Khadaji stepped into the room, Veate behind him, and the door slid shut. The room was fairly large, had a couch and several chairs facing a large, carved desk of some dark wood. There was a door next to the desk, closed. They were alone in the room.

Veate said, "What was *that* all about? She looked at you as if you were Jesus or Chang come back to life. When you told her she moved well, she *blushed*!"

"She's a matadora," he said. "Trained at the school I started on Renault. My, ah, reputation there is somewhat high."

"Oh, that's right. The Man Who Never Missed. Inspiration for the whole set-up. I guess it would be like meeting a god from mythology for her, wouldn't it?" Her voice was dry, but he heard the undertone. Was it contempt? Or just amusement?

"It was a tool," he said. "Nothing more. The enemy was a giant; we needed somebody who could rally the small folk to slay him. At my best I was never half as good as the story."

She looked at him, and he saw surprise in her face.

Before she could speak, the door next to the desk slid back and Rajeem Carlos stood there. Next to him was Jarl, his personal matador. Disguised as Pen, Khadaji had trained Jarl. He nodded once to his student, who returned the nod, but looked no less alert for it. Good. The two out front were new; Khadaji hadn't known them personally or that they were on Carlos's staff, but Jarl was almost like family.

Carlos looked much as Khadaji remembered him. Tall, athletic, blue eyes, a light complexion. There was more gray in the red hair, more wrinkles around the eyes, but the last five years had been kind to his looks, at least. He wore a blue thinsilk monosuit and kung fu slippers.

Carlos moved toward Khadaji, a wide smile deepening the lines next to his eyes. Jarl stayed next to the door, watching and listening.

"Emile. It's great to see you!"

The two men embraced warmly. Khadaji noted that the President of the Republic managed to find time to continue working out; there was still muscle under the clothes and little fat.

Carlos broke the hug and looked at Khadaji's daughter. "And you are Veate?"

"Sir," she said. She was nervous, but her poise was solid. She was, after all, an albino. Being a good actress came naturally.

"I am very pleased to meet you. You are the image of your father."

Khadaji stared at his old friend. Had his eyes gone bad? Veate looked nothing like him.

"Come, sit," Carlos said. He gestured at the two form-chairs in front of the desk. "Something to eat or drink?"

Khadaji shook his head, "Not for me."

"Nor me," said Veate.

As Carlos moved to sit behind the desk, he said, "I'm sorry about your mother. Pen called me as soon as he heard. I have my best team of Republic investigators looking for her."

"Thank you," Veate said.

"What else, Rajeem?" Khadaji asked.

Carlos measured his old friend with a glance that held within it a calculation not there when last they had been together. Khadaji saw the look and understood how the years had affected his friend. Some of the idealist he had been was now replaced with a portion of cynic.

Before Carlos could speak, Khadaji said, "Are we going to play fugue, President Carlos? Or something worse?"

The measuring look vanished, and Carlos's smile, small though it was, returned. "Apparently you have not grown fat and stupid in your retirement."

"Have your men found me in the five years since I left?"

"No."

"And when did they start looking?"

Carlos chuckled. "About a month after I took office."

"Do you still trust me?"

"My advisors all say I should not. That you have been gone too long to know who you are anymore. That whatever help you might have been before, there is no way to be certain you are the man you were."

"Are any of us the men we were?"

"My advisors mean well, but they are paid to be suspicious. I trust you, Emile. Knowing you were out there somewhere has kept me honest these last few years. If I had been corrupted by the power, you would have come back to remove me, wouldn't you?"

"I would have tried. But I wasn't too worried about it. I trust you, too, Rajeem."

"There was an attempt on my life a short time back," he said. "My ship was sabotaged. It was cleverly done, more clever than the usual would-be assassin. My technicians have not yet figured out how it was accomplished. Beel was with me. The entire ship was at risk."

"And your advisors thought that I—?"

"As I said, they are paid to be suspicious. I did not think it was your style; besides, I haven't botched the job that badly, have I?"

It was Khadaji's turn to smile. "No. I'd give you a passing grade."

"I thought so. I advised my advisors that had you been the assassin, I would certainly be dead. At about the same time, there were several attacks upon some of your students, on different planets. This could hardly be coincidence, and the coordination needed involved careful planning. Juete was kidnapped. It takes only a casual look to see these things are all connected in some way to Emile Antoon Khadaji."

"Agreed, though none of it was my doing."

"So I believe. But something most unusual is happening and we don't understand what. Or why."

Khadaji was about to speak when a soft chime sounded in the room.

Carlos frowned. "I was not to be interrupted," he said.

A voice from a hidden speaker said, "Sorry, President Carlos. You have an offplanet com request from someone on your short list."

Carlos's frown deepened. To Khadaji, he said, "There are only seven people on that list—my wife and children, you, and three others." He raised his voice. "Put the call through."

After a few seconds, a woman's deep voice said, "Hello, deuce."

Khadaji and Carlos spoke at the same time:

"Dirisha!"

Dirisha and Bork leaned against the Healy.

"Amazing," Geneva said, from within her medical hutch. "He was there with the President when you called."

"Maybe not so amazing," Bork said. "The boss always had a way of getting into the middle of things."

Dirisha shook her head. Bork was a master of understatement. She said, "They didn't say what was going on, but something else is happening. For Emile to pop up after vanishing so long ago is passing strange."

"And with a daughter," Geneva said. "I never knew he had a family."

"Mostly nobody knew much about him at all," Bork said.

"Anyway, Carlos knows about what happened and he's arranging for the bank's computer operators to smile on us."

"What about Sleel?" Geneva asked.

"He's going to see what can be legally done. He can't just snap his fingers and make them let Sleel go. One of the first things Carlos did when he took over was to cut out about nine-tenths of the power the old Confed leaders had. He can't pardon anybody without a lengthy process, subject to review by a panel of planetary and galactic judges. It could take six months, maybe as long as a year."

"I wouldn't bet money on Sleel waiting around," Bork said.

"Nor would I," Geneva added. "Sleel can be very single-minded."

Dirisha laughed. Sleel had tried for years to get her to sleep with him and there had been times when she had been tempted. On some level, he was a loveable rogue. "*I* never gave in, brat."

"It was before I knew you," Geneva said.

"Did I say anything?"

"You were thinking it."

"We could bust him out," Bork said. "Sleel is a good man to have around when things get fuzzy."

"Bad idea," Dirisha said. "We're on the side of law and order these days, remember?"

"Yeah, but whoever is after us is probably also still after Sleel, too. He's pinned down in a place where he's easier to get to, and he's unarmed."

Bork was right. Dirisha didn't think whoever had set his or her sights on them would have been careless, and the bank's computer probably wouldn't give them much to go on. Whatever had been cause enough for them to start shooting probably hadn't gone away and there was no reason to believe they would stop after one round.

"All right. Maybe we ought to pay Sleel a visit and see if there's anything we can do. They'll let the brat out in a couple of days; Sleel will probably be okay until then."

"Sounds good to me," Bork said. "Bet Sleel'll be glad to see us."

"I wouldn't bet my ass on that," Dirisha said.

SIX _____

THE SHIP WAS a milk-run passenger liner, one of the squarish, no-frills transports built at the height of the Confed's reign, designed to move people efficiently, but with a minimum of luxury. It was a cut above a troop transport, but not a wide cut.

Bork sat at a table in the dining room, eating some kind of overcooked dark fish, staring into nowhere. A woman had laughed behind him a few minutes ago and something about the sound of her voice had called up a memory of Mayli. He chewed on the two together, not tasting the fish but unable to avoid the sourness of his recall. This biz with somebody trying to kill matadors had taken over and Bork found himself surprised to realize that he hadn't thought about Mayli much since it had begun. Maybe that meant something.

He finished the meal and looked around. He'd been distracted, had lost touch with what was going on in the restaurant, and that was bad. Inattention could get you killed. If he was going to stay alive, best he sharpen up some. He didn't want to make a stupid mistake and maybe put Dirisha or Geneva in danger. He owed them attention.

There was a gym somewhere on the ship. He'd go and move some iron around. He usually felt better when his blood was pumping after a good workout.

In their small ship cabin, Dirisha trailed her hand lightly over the mostly healed wound on Geneva's naked chest. Like the blonde, the dark woman was also nude—save for the spetsdöds they both wore.

"Hurt for me to touch it?"

"Nope. It's a little tender if I move wrong, but that doesn't hurt at all."

Dirisha slid her hand down her lover's body, gently scratching with her fingernails.

"Mmm. That feels even better."

Dirisha moved her hand yet lower. After a moment, Geneva's breathing deepened. "Ah, yeah. Right there."

Dirisha eased herself downward, sliding carefully over the sheets. In a moment, she was in position, and she replaced her gently probing fingers with her lips, then her tongue.

"Oh, yes!"

Dirisha lifted her face from the blond pubic mound and the warm saltiness there and said, "You tell me if you start to hurt anywhere."

"Hurt? It doesn't *hurt*! Do it some more!"

Dirisha laughed and bent back to her task.

It took only a minute before Geneva arched upward and pressed herself hard against Dirisha's mouth, the small spasms clenching and releasing and pulsing through her lips into those of her lover.

"You were ready for that. I hardly got warmed up."

Geneva slid her hands down and into Dirisha's hair, to

rub her head. "I've been ready since we were splashed. It's your turn. Move around."

"You sure you're up for it?"

"I'm sure."

"Well, okay. You talked me into it."

Both women laughed.

Lying quietly next to each other, the two women talked.

"That's the best it's been in a long time," Geneva said.

"Yeah. Nothing like a little danger to spice up your love life."

"That's true."

"I was joking, brat."

"I know. But you're right, you know. We've been getting stale lately, Rissy."

Dirisha propped herself up on her elbow. "You complaining here?"

"No. Of course not." Geneva moved to kiss the other woman's nipple. She leaned back, smiling. "It's just that we've been coasting for a while. Our lives haven't been *about* anything."

Dirisha nodded. Geneva was right. She usually was about such things. They had gotten stale. When they'd been on the run from the Confed, with death maybe lying in wait around any corner, they had never been more alive. When each day might be your last, it made a big difference. You couldn't maintain that stance forever, of course; the stress would eat you alive, but putting yourself at risk did bring out your best—or your worst.

"Well. It doesn't look as if we are going to be coasting much in the near future."

"It feels good, doesn't it?"

"Yeah," Dirisha admitted. "It does."

• • •

Sleel felt the killers start to line up on him before he was even sure who they were. He wasn't much on mystical shit, but there was something in a man's moves that gave him away when he was planning to do you.

It didn't take long for him to pinpoint the sources.

There was a woman guard in the cafeteria. She had the standard-issue shockstik visible, but she could have a hidden weapon; they didn't check guards as closely as they did prisoners.

The second hitter was a short-timer who'd been supposedly transferred in from another lockup, a dark man with a lot of thick hair and a beard. He was a squat and thick mue with callused hands and knuckles, and he moved with a rolling gait that indicated more than a little training.

The third and final assassin was an assistant medex who'd started work two days after Sleel arrived. He'd met the man, a tall and thin local, when he'd helped Truck to get his leg repaired.

Sleel spotted the first two on his own. It was Truck who had given him the third. Once again, it was when they were alone in the exercise room.

"How's the leg?"

"Better. Listen, you got trouble."

"Yeah?"

"Yeah. The new bonegluer wants to see you belly up."

"How do you know?"

"He told me. Figured I'd be likely to give him a hand, if maybe he needs it."

Sleel regarded Truck. "Why tell me?"

The bigger man grinned. "I don't much like you, but you're one of mine. We settle our shit face to face. I can't have anybody moving in from outside to fuck with me, now can I?"

"You're all right, Truck. I owe you."

"So leave me something in your will, Sleel."

In his cell lying on his extruded bed, Sleel thought about how he was going to handle it. This whole thing was a set-up all the way, and it looked as if he might not survive things here. He could take out the three who were targeting him, but that would only delay things some. They'd move on him again, and maybe next time he might not figure the hitters soon enough. It was time to leave this place, past time.

Dirisha had no hesitation in calling Rajeem again. He was glad to hear from her, she could see that on the augmented White Radio pix. They'd finally figured out how to get the color right, so that Rajeem's face looked natural on the holoproj in the hotel.

"Emile left his code for you," he said. He gave her the number. "Call if you need him. He's going to Vishnu to look for Juete, you can reach him there in a few days."

"Thanks, Rajeem. What about the visit to Sleel?"

"Arranged. I've instigated the pardon, but it will take time. A temporary parole of sorts might be worked out; my people are trying to contact the local judge. He can grant it, if he chooses."

"Maybe if we spoke to him?"

Behind her, Bork and Geneva grinned at each other.

"Hold off on that until my people see which way the current flows. He could be an honest man just doing his job."

"All right."

"I've got to go, Dirisha. Matters of state call."

"Thanks for the help, Rajeem."

"Any time, lovely lady. Remember the rabbit at the Perkins's estate?"

Dirisha laughed. Light years away, she felt the pull from him. They had been good together.

She cut the connection and turned to look at Bork and Geneva.

Geneva said, "What is a rabbit?"

"The first time Carlos and I made love," Dirisha said, "was triggered because a small creature, a little mammal about so big"—she held her hands apart to indicate the size of the animal—"hopped out of the bushes and scared the piss out of us."

"So you, ah, relieved your tension by screwing your brains out, eh?" Geneva smiled at her like a mother at a bright child.

"Stop that, brat. I'm not cute."

"Oh, yes, you are. You should see yourself."

"I'm going to swat you."

"Eek. Bork, save me."

The big man shook his head. "You two been married too long."

Dirisha said, "Enough of my sordid past. Let's go see Sleel."

Of the three stalkers, Sleel considered the mue prisoner the most dangerous. The guard and the medex theoretically had more real power, but they were bound to avoid being too obvious in front of witnesses. Prisoners had all kinds of reasons to lie about things, but a brain scan could pull truth out of a psychological morass, and electropophy gear was getting better all the time. Maybe his killer would worry about being caught if he or she got too rash. This was not a great comfort to Sleel. Dead was dead.

The mue, on the other hand, might have little to lose were

he a legitimate prisoner. He could be serving full life and they couldn't add more time to that. An argument could turn into a fight, and who cared what a prisoner's reasons were for killing another prisoner? He didn't have to be as careful as the guard or the medex would have to be; he could move at almost any time. Unless maybe Sleel moved first.

Having made his decision, Sleel got up and went to find the mue. He had a few minutes before he had to start work. Better *he* should pick the time and place to get this done, and the sooner it happened, the better.

The mue was finishing breakfast when Sleel found him. They couldn't face off here, of course; Sleel didn't have any desire to be chem-bound and stuck in isolation while waiting to be tried on new charges of murder. If he let the mue get in a few shots first, he could claim self-defense, but given his last encounter with local justice, he had a feeling that might not be wise. No, he would do this privately. Call the mue out, arrange a place where nobody would be watching, and do it.

That he might lose was not a real possibility to him.

The mue felt him coming. The man on the mue's right and the woman on his left also noticed Sleel's arrival, and they found other business to which they suddenly had to attend.

The mue's vapid look didn't fool Sleel. The mue was a killer, Sleel could feel it in his bones, and the universe would be a better place without him.

No point in pretending or dancing around it. Sleel said, "In the exercise room, twenty-three hundred."

The mue didn't bother to act surprised or innocent. "I'll be there."

"Prisoner Sleel," came a guard's voice from behind him. Sleel didn't turn away from watching the mue. "Yeah?"

"Go to the visiting rooms. You got company."

Sleel stepped back until he was outside of the mue's range, then glanced at the guard. "A visitor? You sure you got the right guy?"

"I'm sure. Go. Now."

Dirisha felt naked without her spetsdöds, and she was sure that Bork and Geneva must feel the same way. License or not, such weapons were not allowed in prison. She understood why, but she didn't like it. All three of them could walk the sumito patterns, and before she'd ever studied with Khadaji-as-Pen, Dirisha had been an expert in a handful of other arts, so she was hardly defenseless, but still . . .

The room was split in half by a floor-to-ceiling energy wall, invisible to the eyes, but crackling with enough voltage to stir the hair on her head and backs of her arms. The field was marked with bright red stripes on the floor and walls and ceiling, warnings in six common languages printed continuously next to the painted lines. To step across those warnings and lines would be to know the joys of a narrow-gauge zap field and the nasty headache that followed the fifteen minutes of unconsciousness. You could see and hear through it, but you couldn't move through a zap field without a fully insulated groundsuit. Assuming you could pry such a suit away from the military sub rosa units who were the only people legally entitled to own them, you certainly couldn't smuggle it into a prison, since anybody wearing such gear looked pretty much like an overstuffed orthopedic chair. And since the three had been scanned thoroughly, there weren't any weapons going to be tossed across the lines either. They'd been left alone, but Dirisha knew the room was hardwired for video and audio and all conversations were recorded. The legal clean-rooms were supposed to be different, of course, but Dirisha trusted that about as far as she could pitch Bork one-handed. And even if somebody were stupid enough to try to breach the zap-field wall, alarms would start screaming to high orbit the instant it happened.

There were tables and chairs on both sides of the room, but Dirisha and Geneva stood, and Bork leaned against the wall next to the door.

Across from them, on the prisoner side of the visiting room, a door slid open and Sleel, wearing prison-issue coveralls, sauntered in. Despite his situation and his clothes, he managed to look as if he owned the place.

He was glad to see them, Dirisha could tell, but he would have cut off his arm with a dull knife before admitting it. He smiled and shook his head. His bald head.

"Dirisha. Geneva. Bork. What are you doing here?"

"Nice to see you, too, Sleel," Dirisha said.

"We heard you changed your address," Bork said. "We thought we'd drop by and see your new place."

Sleel slouched into one of the chairs and waved one hand. "I'm planning on having it redone; it's a mess right now."

As usual, it was Geneva who went past the shit and spoke from her heart. "How are you, Sleel?"

For a second, the mask slipped and Dirisha saw worry on Sleel's face. Then the cock-of-the-galaxy grin came back. "Hey, I'm fine. Getting fat from all the carbohydrates."

"There's been some interesting developments lately," Dirisha said. "In the family."

She and the others could play fugue, though none of them were real experts at it. Anybody who really knew the between-the-lines talk would be able to follow their conversation easily. Dirisha was hoping the prison officials wouldn't bother to find an expert to listen to the hours of recordings from the visitors' rooms. What she'd just said to

Sleel, each knowing what they knew about the other, could be translated more or less to, *The matadors have had some trouble*.

"That's nice," Sleel said. *Oh? What trouble?*

"Yes, business is really booming. Pretty soon we won't need any clients, we'll have enough work of our own to keep us busy full-time." Dirisha moved her hands, adding meaning to the words with her gestures and her expressions. *Direct attacks on us*.

"Really? Sorry I'm missing it." *It have anything to do with me being here?*

"Ah, well, you aren't missing much." *Yes. You being here is part of it. Watch yourself.*

Geneva broke in. "Rajeem sends his best and says he hopes to see you soon. Might be a while before he can manage it." That one was a bit of a stretch. Dirisha couldn't see what hand motions the blonde used, but she realized that Sleel understood the main thrust. *President Carlos knows you are here and is trying to get you out. It will take some time.*

Sleel chuckled. "Tell him I'll drop by soon as I'm out." *I am going to escape. I can't wait. Something has come up in here.*

Dirisha knew that for Sleel to indicate something was amiss meant things were bad. She made a quick decision.

"I don't think I'll be able to do that for a while; we've got some legal business to clear up here first." *Sit tight, Sleel. We'll see what we can do to get you out.*

Sleel shrugged. "No problem." *Hey, I can take care of it myself. I don't need your help.*

Bork moved away from the wall. "Hey, Sleel. Fuck you."

Dirisha and Geneva both laughed, and even Sleel couldn't stop his smile. Anybody monitoring the conversation or listening to the recordings later would have to wonder what that non sequitur was all about. Dirisha didn't need fugue to understand Bork's statement, though, and neither did Sleel.

"You ain't that big, Bork."

"Sure I am. Besides, you owe me a uniform."

Sleel sighed. Bork had saved Sleel's life when they'd taken over the broadcast station on Mason. Sleel's arm had been blown off by a rocket and Bork had scooped him up and staunched the blood flow by jamming the wound against his own chest. He'd joked later about the ruined uniform. Now, he was calling Sleel on the debt.

Dirisha watched him. Sleel was stubborn, but he had a sense of honor. "Okay," he said.

"See you soon," Dirisha said. "Take care."

That was basically it. They had to find the judge who had put Sleel here, despite what they'd told Carlos. Sleel was in trouble and he needed help. Fast.

SEVEN _____

ABOUT AN HOUR before he was due to meet the mue in the exercise room, Sleel headed that way. Things were relatively lax inside the walls, insofar as personal time. You could schedule what you wanted pretty much when you wanted, as long as you did your assigned chores without raising heat. Nobody inside was going anywhere, in theory, and the guards had photomutable eyes all over the place. How much damage could you do before you were spotted? seemed to be the prevailing philosophy. While there existed electronic devices that could have pinpointed every inmate around the clock, up to and including their heartbeats and respiration rates, nobody cared that much. As long as you stayed inside.

Sleel had borrowed Truck's confounder, so that a couple of the cameras and recorders would be fuzzed until after his business was accomplished. Nothing made by any man was so foolproof that some other man couldn't figure out a way around it.

Sleel himself was big on honor, but he'd been around long enough to know that not everybody else was, and only a stupid man would trust somebody who wanted to kill him. The mue might or might not think he could take Sleel, but if he had the slightest doubt and even a rudimentary brain, he would cover his bets. Just as Sleel was about to do by showing up early.

When he arrived, he activated the confounder. He only had a minute or two at most before somebody would come to check the cameras. If the eyes cleared before the guard could stir him- or herself enough to go see what the problem was, then they usually wouldn't bother. Things screwed up sometimes and only some kind of officious fool went running every time some monitor hiccupped. It was human nature to avoid unnecessary work.

In the exercise room, Sleel moved to the stacks of weight circles. These were cast ferroplastic rings that weighed less than a kilo each. Slip a pair over the ends of a barbell or dumbbell and step into the mag field, however, and the bar would weigh anything from the four or five kilos it was in realgrav up to the limits of the field, about a thousand kilos. All you had to do was adjust a dial, and you could work out without ever changing a weight, increasing or decreasing the resistance in half-kilo steps. If you took the time to set the safeties, you could hoist the barbell up over your head and drop it, and the field would sense and slow the weight's fall enough so you could get out from under it.

Sleel tucked two of the circles into his hip pockets, one on each side. The fabric sagged, but that was okay.

He set a bar loaded with two more circles up onto the benchpress rack, then bent and undid the buckles that held the bench in place. He dialed the field to maximum but did not activate it. Using yet another pair of the weights, he propped the benchpress station on them so that it was leaning slightly backward. With the light weight on the uprights it didn't much matter, but if somebody were to, say, suddenly drop a thousand kilos onto the uprights by activating the field, well, that bench was going to do what a spoon lying on the edge of a table did when you slapped it smartly—take off like a rocket with bad attitude jets.

Sleel looked around. He didn't think he'd need any of this; the mue might be a hard elbowsucker, but that didn't mean shit. Still, it was a basic exercise to make sure you didn't come up stupid when you could avoid it.

He left the exercise room, flicked the confounder off so the cameras would clear and show the room was still empty. Maybe somebody with a real good eye would notice the weight on the bench, but Sleel didn't think he'd have to worry. Anybody with that sort of talent wouldn't be playing simadam on a bank of cameras watching empty rooms in a backrocket prison.

He stood outside the door and waited.

It had taken most of the afternoon to locate the judge who had put Sleel in prison. The man had taken a short vacation and gone on the locally infamous Smoketown Pub Crawl with a busload of other tourists. The judge, it seemed, was not averse to the pleasures of the flesh, for the Crawl consisted of a guarded run through some of Smoketown's worst pits, and included drinks, meals, guaranteed-disease-free prostitutes, and transportation both ways. Cheap thrills without any real danger.

In the night, Dirisha, Geneva and Bork headed toward Smoketown in a rented hi-mach flitter. Bork worked the controls. The local sun had gone down on this part of Thompson's Gazelle and the darkness was thick with stars and city glows both ahead and behind. It was a pretty planet after dark.

"So, what exactly do we say to this guy to get him to let Sleel out?" Bork asked.

"Whatever it takes," Geneva said. There was a coldness in her voice that chilled Dirisha. Sometimes the brat could display a resolve that still surprised the older woman. She'd risked her life to make a point when first they'd met at Matador Villa years ago, and Dirisha sometimes wondered if she knew the blonde as well as she thought. Whatever it took, yeah, that was no problem for Dirisha, who had killed men, women and mues when she'd walked the Flex, but sweet little Geneva?

Then again, Sleel was family. Not a chromosome-brother but closer to all of them than any of their own, if Dirisha read it right. There weren't any of them who hadn't risked their asses for each other at one time or another. It had been a while, but the feelings were still there. Somebody out to kill you and yours had a way of bringing out a certain resolve, sure enough.

Smoketown was a port city, and it seemed to exist to show travelers an interesting, if not always good, time. Eateries, pubs, small casinos, trullhouses, the basic desires all there to be sampled, if you had the stads. Dirisha had grown up in a place like Smoketown, and her distaste for such had not abated much in all the time since she'd left. Her last visit to the planet of her birth—she could never bring herself to call it "home"—had ended with Geneva being blasted, and that didn't serve to endear it any, either.

"We got the itinerary?" Bork asked.

Dirisha gave him the code number and he input it into the flitter's comp.

"It's almost twenty-three," he said. "According to this read, they'd be at someplace called The Electric Eel about now." Bork manually tapped the coordinates into the system and locked the flitter into the local traffic grid.

Over his shoulder, Dirisha saw that the ETA was three minutes. She took several deep breaths to calm the sudden rush of hormone jitters. The adrenaline surged, even after all the years of training and meditating and facing down Death in all his guises. The high cortex might rule, but the lizard brain and the mammal body were in accord otherwise and they went along but reluctantly.

Come on, Dirisha told herself, talking to a judge was not dangerous.

You lie, the lizard brain said.

You always lie.

The mue showed up, grinning, and Sleel saw from his attitude that he thought he had some kind of edge. A weapon, maybe, or some knowledge that he could use to best his opponent. It practically poured off him, and Sleel was suddenly glad he'd set things up in the gym earlier.

Sleel triggered the confounder again. He stepped into the exercise room well before the mue arrived, moved back far enough to give himself plenty of room, and waited.

The mue came through the door carefully, ready for an attack. He relaxed a little when he saw where Sleel was.

"Let's do it," Sleel said.

"What's the hurry, dead man? You got a later appointment?" The mue circled to his left, and Sleel automatically moved to keep the distance precise between them, circling to his left.

"Somebody will come to see why this room is offline in a couple of minutes."

The mue chuckled. "Not gonna happen, pard. Nobody is gonna come this way for a long time."

Sleel considered what the mue said. If it were true, that meant he had a friend in the shop. Given that a guard and a medex were also in the get-Sleel parade, that wasn't unbelievable. It wasn't good that there was maybe another problem that he had to look out for, but it *was* good that he knew it was there.

Sleel's problems, however, were only beginning.

The mue pulled what looked to be a regulation shockstik from his coverall and held it up. The stik was the general size and shape of a cool's riot baton, a slightly flexible hard plastic conductor rod half a meter long, wired to deliver an electric charge. The stik was activated by gripping it tightly on either of the insulated ends, and from the mue's movement, it was apparent he knew exactly what he was doing with it: the stik made a popping noise as it clicked on and hummed to life. It was a double threat, since it could be used lit or not—it made a dandy club that could shatter bone without power; activated, the slightest touch of the charged section would put a muscle into a hard spasm. Rake a man's belly and he'd double up, unable to move for as long as maybe a minute. Hit a hamstring, and the heel on that leg would jam itself against the buttock above it. Any touch on a major muscle would make moving freely very difficult indeed.

As the grinning mue stood there waving his new toy, the medex arrived. He, too, bore a shockstik and an accompanying shitty grin.

But wait, Sleel. What's this you see?

The new guard stepped in behind the medex and it was three villains and three stun wands to complete the set.

Sleel backed up a few steps, watching the trio carefully. He stopped when he reached the benchpress rack.

"I suppose you're wondering why I called you here," Sleel said.

"To the left," the mue said to the medex. To the guard, he said, "You take the right."

Sleel managed a tight grin. Nice to know who was in charge. For just a second, he felt fear dance with cold feet

somewhere inside him. Then he took a deep breath and let
the fear flow out with it. Win or lose, he would go down
swinging. And he fucking wasn't going to lose.

Slowly, the three assassins began to move in.

The Electric Eel was a small pub, with about three dozen
customers standing at the bar or seated at tables about the
room. The air was heavy with flickstick smoke and its scent
of burned cashews, and thickened a little with the damp-
hemp smell of Leaf. It was a quiet crowd, drinking or
smoking or otherwise ingesting assorted intoxicants and
talking among themselves. Mirrors behind the bar made the
place look larger than it was.

The tour group of seven men and two women was
collected at three tables near one corner, easily identified by
the pair of hulking uniformed guards who stood nearby,
arms crossed and attitudes daring anybody to bother their
charges all too apparent. Both guards looked as if a few
sessions with a plastic surgeon's laser wouldn't do their
faces any harm, Dirisha thought.

The black matadora sat at a table nearby with Bork and
Geneva, sipping at chilled glasses of splash and trying to
look uninterested in the tour party.

Dirisha glanced past Bork at the two guards. Both had
muscle, though neither was quite as large as Bork, and
doubtless both had some rudimentary expertise in one
martial art or another. Probably both were armed, though no
weapons were visible, just as she and Bork and Geneva had
removed their weapons and tucked them away. She doubted
that these two ordinarily got much of a workout on this kind
of run.

"You want me to take out the guards?" Bork asked.

"No. Let's hold off a bit. You see the judge?"

Geneva said, "The gray-haired one, in the jumpsuit, two from your left end."

Dirisha nodded. "Looks better in his computer holo than he does in person, don't you think?"

"They *paid* to be brought here?" Bork put in. "Me, I'd ask for my money back, if it doesn't get any more exciting than this."

"Maybe the tender does a strip or something later," Geneva said.

Bork glanced at the man mixing drinks behind the bar.

Dirisha had noticed him when they'd arrived; he was white-haired, couldn't be a day under seventy, and she probably outweighed him by ten kilos. He looked like an ad for somebody's kindly grandfather. He moved pretty well, though, and Dirisha felt pretty certain the man had some kind of extensive training. Walking the Flex gave you the ability to see that in somebody, and she'd bet stads the tender was not so innocuous as he attempted to appear.

"I wouldn't pay to see him naked," Bork said.

"The evening is early," Dirisha said, grinning. "Who knows what might happen before it's done? The tour might get its money's worth yet."

No sooner had she said this than the judge got up and moved toward the fresher.

"Ah. Looks as if the judge is about to pay his respects to the toilet. One of us should maybe join him there, you think?"

Bork started to rise.

"Not you, Bork. You look like a planetoid; the guard can't help but notice you if you change orbit. We need somebody who looks a bit more harmless, in case they are watching."

"That's me," Geneva said. "You're as bad as Bork; if

you get up, half the men in the place will have to check to see if their testicles are in place."

"You wound me, brat."

"Come on. The way you swagger, guys'll start spitting on the floor and trying to lower their voices when you pass. It'll be an awful scene."

Geneva stood, smiled sweetly at her lover, and followed the judge into the fresher.

"I don't swagger when I walk, do I, Bork?"

"Uh, swagger?" He looked uncomfortable.

Dirisha laughed.

After a couple of moments, the judge and Geneva came out of the fresher. They had linked arms and Geneva was smiling and laughing, as though the judge had just made some witty remark. Dirisha saw the blonde squeeze the judge's arm and say something quietly to him, and it looked harmless, unless you could see the judge wince slightly and pale. He smiled and nodded as if he were having a wonderful time.

The two of them walked back to the group, where the judge smiled even more and spoke to one of the guards. The uniformed man leered and shook his head. Dirisha couldn't hear the dialog, but she could guess the gist of it: I'm going to be leaving the tour here for a while, the judge would be saying. I'll meet you at the rendezvous in the morning.

The guard's look at Geneva was admiring enough, and since she wasn't wearing her spetsdöds and the thinskins she wore hid very little of her shape, he was probably thinking that the judge had managed to pull off a neat trick to come up with such a shapely twat as this one.

The guard bought it, for the judge and Geneva headed for the exit. Dirisha almost shook her head. Stupid guard was sure wasting somebody's money.

Bork and Dirisha stood and walked to the exit.

Outside, the judge was beginning to worry, and he was voicing it to Geneva when Bork and Dirisha left the pub.

"You can't do this!"

"Sure I can, I already *did* it."

Dirisha grinned and reached into her jacket pocket for her left spetsdöd. She stripped away the backing from the plastic flesh and seated the weapon on her left hand, adjusting the thing before the flesh set. She was reaching for the right-hand weapon when the two guards emerged from the pub.

Not so stupid after all, maybe, Dirisha thought.

The judge saw the guards. "H-help—!" he managed, before Geneva's nerve pinch on his arm caused him to shut off his appeal in a yelp of pain.

Dirisha thought about the best way to handle things. Bork glanced at her and she nodded at him. He moved to flatten the pair.

When they saw Bork coming, the guards stopped. Maybe they were a lot brighter than she'd given them credit for, Dirisha thought. One dug for something on his belt, under his jacket at the small of his back; the other was already swinging a stubby short-range hand wand up from where it had been hidden in a belt holster. Weapons changed things.

"Bork, down!"

The big man dropped flat instantly. Dirisha raised her left arm and the spetsdöd spoke twice. Each guard caught a dart, the first one at the base of his neck, the second one on the chin. The one who had cleared his hand wand triggered it as he fell, but the pulse only patterned the dust on the walk harmlessly, forming complex geometric designs from a psychedelic dream. The patterns were destroyed when the guard fell on them. The second guard fell on top of the first one. The shocktox in the darts would keep them out for fifteen minutes.

"What say we lift?" Bork said as he came to his feet and brushed the dirt from his chest.

"Sounds good to me," Dirisha said.

"This is . . . this is kidnapping!"

Geneva smiled at the judge. "Very good, you get points for that. But don't forget assaulting those two. And maybe later, even homicide. Let's go."

The four moved toward the flitter.

When Sleel had been a boy, there had been an ancient game of skill called "Wink." It was played with small plastic disks, one of which was used to propel another by pressing the edges sharply against each other over a hard surface. The one lying on the table would snap up in response to pressure from the one in a player's hand, and the object was to try to aim the snapped disk so that it landed in a small cup some distance away.

As the three assassins moved in to kill him, Sleel reached over and flicked the switch on the benchpress field.

The bar, which weighed only a few kilos on its own, suddenly became as heavy as if ten men had leaped on it. The unsecured bench, propped as it was, did just what Sleel had intended. It popped up from the floor at an angle and spun and twisted through the air.

And slammed smack into the woman guard. She was quick; she saw it coming and managed to raise her shock-stik, but it was a futile gesture. The bench was too fast and too heavy and one of the legs hit the woman in an uppercut under the chin. Her head snapped back, her neck broke, and she collapsed bonelessly, certainly paralyzed and likely dying of massive shock.

Before the other attackers could do more than blink, Sleel pulled one of the ferroplastic circles from his pocket and slung it at the mue, figuring him to be the more dangerous of the two. At this range, he couldn't miss, and the weight was heavy enough to knock the mue senseless when it bounced off his head.

Unfortunately, Sleel had forgotten about the field. The ferroplastic started out fine, entered the still-working field, and was spun and jerked down against the floor, hard. Sounded like a hammer swung by a giant when it hit. Damn!

Sleel darted to one side as the mue jumped in, shockstik leading. No problem; he avoided the strike, spun around, and reached out to upend the mue—

Suddenly Sleel was snatched violently off his feet.

What the fuck? The medex was three meters away—!

The mue recovered from his swing and turned.

The weight, the other goddamned weight—it was still in his pocket! He was stuck to the floor like he'd been nailed there!

Sleel twisted as hard as he could. His coverall ripped and he pulled away from the weight holding him down, only he was a half second too slow. The shockstik was coming down as his head—

Sleel raised his arm. The stik hit him on the outer edge, just below the wrist. His hand clenched tight with the charge and the bone snapped under the force of the strike, but he was rolling, out of the way and toward the medex—

The medex was slow; he tried to hit Sleel on the floor, but it was the matador's foot that found the man's belly, knocking him backward and into the wall.

Sleel came up, twisting, and jumped to his right as far as he could. The mue sailed past, swiped at him with the stik, but missed him by a meter. Sleel turned. Stupid mistake had almost got him killed. He was glad nobody was around to see it.

As the medex tried to get his wind back, Sleel slid in and

thrust his good elbow into the man's throat, crushing his windpipe. The medex wasn't going to be breathing through that throat anymore unless somebody cut him a new airhole. The man gagged and fell, both hands clutching his ruined larynx.

The mue made his run. Sleel twirled, ducked, and came up. The broken bone in his left arm grated and the throw was off, but the mue did a lazy half flip and slammed into the wall, head down. He slid, hit on top of his head, and peeled back from the wall. He was tough; he shook it off and came up, but too late. Sleel had snatched up the medex's weapon and now he moved in with the stik cocked by his right ear. He snapped his arm down, hard, and hit the mue squarely on top of the head.

The stik broke. So did the mue's skull.

Five full seconds passed while Sleel waited to see if anybody was going to get up and come at him again. Nobody did.

He slowed his breathing and checked out the trio.

The woman was dead. The mue was dead. The medex was about to be dead. You're getting old, Sleel. Five years ago none of these balloos would have touched you. Course you wouldn't have been so stupid as to leave the field on, either, and fuck yourself up that way.

Sleel wiped clean the broken stik he held and put it into the medex's hand. He turned the benchpress field off, and walked to the exit. Let whoever found these three figure that they killed each other. The matadors didn't hold with killing, but the way Sleel figured it, when someone tried to take you out, they lost their breathing rights. He'd worry about his conscience later. At least he'd be alive to worry about it.

The rented flitter sailed through the ocean of night, Bork at ease with the manual controls.

To the judge, Geneva said, "Do you know what Spasm is?"

The man shook his head.

Geneva took the magazine out of her right spetsdöd. She paused, then pulled another magazine from her pocket, carefully clicking the replacement into place. She said, "Spasm is the old military load for this." She held the weapon up in front of the man's face. "It puts you into tetany, all your voluntary muscles locked, for six months. Can't move, can't eat, you have to be taken care of in a hospital until it lets go. No antidote; it's some kind of bioelectric virus, I think. Keeps replicating itself, incurable until it dies on its own."

Dirisha watched the judge break into a sweat.

"Of course, it's banned now. Spasm is. The Republic won't allow its use. Says it's barbaric."

"The trial was legal! The evidence—!"

"Was faked," Geneva said. "Let's assume for a second that you are an honest man and didn't know that. Not that I believe that, but just for the sake of argument. It doesn't matter. Our friend is going to be released on your order; that's the end of the program here."

The judge licked dry lips.

"Spasm is illegal, but you know how the black market is. You have enough money, you can get just about anything you want." She pointed her right spetsdöd at the judge's face. Her smile was that of a saint, of an angel, so sweet was it.

Dirisha suppressed her own smile. The brat must have been a cat an incarnation or two back.

"Wait!" the judge said. "Wait!"

EIGHT _____

THE WARNING CLAXON hooted as the outer gate of the prison
slid open. Sleel, bald, dressed in his prison coverall, stood
there with four armed guards boxing him. There was a
pregnant moment; then Sleel ambled away from the guards,
as if he were on a stroll in the country.

In the flitter across the street, Dirisha shook her head.
Now *that* was a swagger.

"He's hurt," Bork said.

Dirisha saw what Bork meant. To somebody without
their training, Sleel would have looked normal enough, but
to the three of them, the matador was splinting, holding his
left arm tighter than he should have been.

"He's alive," Geneva said. "That's the important thing."

Sleel arrived where the flitter was parked.

"Hi, soldier," Dirisha said. "New in town?"

"How much you charge?" Sleel said.

The flitter kicked up road grit as the fans came online and
lifted the vehicle. Bork put into a tight turn and kept it on
manual, heading straight for the port. The judge wasn't

likely to be a problem for another day or two, but they wanted to be offworld as soon as possible, just in case.

"I forgot to compliment you earlier on your great haircut, Sleel," Bork said. "Oh, and what happened to your arm?"

"I ran into a door."

"Really," Geneva said. Her voice was dry. "Lucky you're out of that place. The warden didn't want to let you go, you know."

"I'm good company," Sleel said. "I can understand that."

"I think maybe it had more to do with the three people who got killed in there last night," Dirisha said. "Seems a guard and medex and inmate somehow beat each other to death in the gym around midnight."

"Pretty tough workout," Sleel offered. "How did you manage to get me loose?"

"The judge who put you in changed his mind suddenly. And you're welcome, Sleel; think nothing of it."

Bork chuckled. "Geneva threatened to shoot him with a Spasm dart."

"I did not. I merely explained to him what Spasm was and what it did."

"Yeah, while loading a fresh magazine into your spets-död."

"Plain old shocktox. Not my fault the man jumped to a conclusion."

Sleel said, "Any chance of paying him a visit before we leave?"

"Probably not a good idea," Dirisha said.

Sleel raised an eyebrow.

Good old Sleel. He never let go. Dirisha said, "The judge is about two hundred klicks from here, in the middle of the Nyoka Game Preserve. He's manacled to a tree about as big as Bork's arm."

Sleel said, "Good. Maybe he'll get eaten by something before he starves."

"Probably not," Bork said. "The only big animals in the preserve are plant-eaters. Besides, we left him a penknife. If he works at it, he could whittle through the tree in a couple of days, easy. Or he could cut his own arm off maybe a little quicker."

"Your idea?" Sleel said, looking at Dirisha.

"Geneva's."

He looked at the blonde. "You might amount to something someday, kid."

"Forget the judge, Sleel. We've got bigger players to find." Dirisha pulled a case from behind her seat and handed it to him. "Why don't you slip into something more comfortable? You look like a trash collector."

Sleel opened the hard plastic case. Inside was a set of gray orthoskins to match those the other three wore, a pair of new spetsdöds, and a short block of shocktox ammunition magazines.

Geneva came up with a medkit as Sleel slipped the top of his coverall off. "That ulna broken?"

"Yeah. About eight centimeters above the wrist. Just cracked; the ends are lined up okay."

"Give it here."

Sleel extended his arm and Geneva put the medkit over the purple swelling. The machine hummed and clicked, and Sleel's face tightened as jets popped medication and orthostat glue through the skin and muscle.

"So," he said, "what's the scat?"

"Somebody doesn't much like us," Dirisha said. "We thought we might go find out who and maybe pay them a visit to find out why."

"I got nothing better to do," Sleel said. He was silent for another few seconds as he dressed. As he seated his spetsdöds, he said, "Uh, look, about getting me out. I, uh, well—"

Bork laughed. "Shut up, Sleel. You're gonna ruin your image, you're not careful."

Everybody joined Bork's laughter and Sleel's was the loudest.

It was good to have something worthwhile to do again, Dirisha thought. And these people around her to do it with.

Part Two
Soul of the
Beast

NINE _____

THE LARGEST COLLECTION of formerly extinct animals in the galaxy is located in a fifty-kilometer oval of exotic grass-land on a plateau in Old Brazil just east of Cuiabá, along the meandering Rio das Mortes. Many of the imported offworld grasses have gone to seed since the fall of the Confed, and the Planalto do Mato Grosso around the zoo has been mostly taken over by the giant variant known as *jatte riz*, with its unique layered structure that allows it to sometimes reach a height of ten meters.

The people have long memories, so it is said, and so it is, but the group-mind of the people is not infallible. Before he was killed by a poison spew during the revolution, Marcus Jefferson Wall had a particular fondness for the South American zoo and its herds of elephants, mastodons and Spandle curlnoses, and he had spent much of his spare time among them. His visits had not been common knowledge, but there had been more than a few who had known of Wall's fondness for the proboscideans. Somehow, during the tumultuous time of the revolution, the zoo had slipped through the cracks, had been missed by those attempting to smash flat every last bit of Wall's handiwork. Perhaps it was because the late Factor Wall had taken care to have the creation of the zoo and its operation far removed from his name. Or maybe it was because the herds of lumbering herbivores posed no threat to anyone and therefore remained unnoticed. Or maybe in the end the zoo was simply so far down the list that no one had yet gotten around to it.

No matter. The zoo was there, still run by the galaxy's foremost expert on the animals therein, an emaciated woman who had commanded the place since its creation. Operating funds from a special account were always sufficient to get things done. The revolution had not laid its angry grip upon the grasslands, and if the trunked animals living there noticed any change, it was not apparent. They foraged, they bred, they brought forth young, they passed on.

It was difficult to reach the zoo through the swamps by ground travel. It was easy enough to get to by air, but few made the trip. The odd scientist arrived now and then to study, academic zoological types who drooled over the exotic animals, but mostly the staff had the place to themselves. The tropical heat and frequent thunderstorms offered little competition to a Republic intent on rebuilding an entire galaxy. What use were clumps of oafish animals when billions of humans and mues needed proper governing? Yes, the people had long memories, but the people were now and then shortsighted. And sometimes, the people were simply blind.

In a building near the east bank of the River of Death, the air coolers hummed as they struggled to keep the inside at three quarters of the tropical day's temperature without. The place was sparsely furnished; there were chairs, tables, beds and a small kitchen, as well as a fresher with shower and toilet and sink. Adequate, if not luxurious.

Within the room were visitors. One of them was a colorless, average and easy-to-forget man called Tone. The second was a dark man with a long nose and thick muscles who went by the name of Cteel. The third was the Albino Exotic woman, Juete.

The fourth visitor was invisible.

And it was this fourth visitor who ruminated upon the zoo and its fate, and who listened at the same time intently to the conversation in the room. And who tended to several hundred other items of business simultaneously.

"You are free to wander about the grounds as you choose," Cteel said. "You will find sunblock in your quarters, as well as an umbrella-field and a dogheel cooler. Don't bother trying to escape. None of the vehicles will operate without a code only I know; none of the communication gear will transmit; none of the staff will come near enough to speak to you. You must be in your room by nightfall."

The Exotic woman inhaled slowly, inflating her chest and lifting her rather perfect breasts slightly under her dark thinskins. Her nipples hardened, easily visible through the cloth. She exuded pheromones, deliberately now, filling the air with a sexual call. No doubt she would be puzzled once again as to why the two men were not responsive. Albinos learned early of their ability to attract others and there were few who could resist the call when it was fully unleashed. Probably Juete had never met such a one, and her failure to lure either Tone or Cteel into an embrace or even a response must be frightening. It was her most potent weapon, and it had proved useless so far.

It would continue to fail; the two men were infected with a tailored olfactory virus specifically designed to counter the albino's hormonal signals. More, if either somehow lost control and attempted without orders to have sex with Juete, a series of interlinked viral-molecular charges growing in their hypothalami, cranial nerve clusters, and higher brain, would receive an ultrahigh frequency radio pulse. The explosions resulting would be tiny, but of sufficient strength so that an intensely painful death would follow. The best surgeons who had ever lived could not stop it. Both Tone and Cteel knew what would happen; it had been explained to them in great detail. Neither would be seduced and sympathetic to Juete, no matter how hard she tried. Not if they wished to continue living.

The fourth watcher knew the woman was frightened at her failure to sway them, for he had once been an albino himself. Had he lips, he would have smiled, but that was no longer possible. He was alive, after a fashion, but without flesh. He existed only as a viral matrix in a supercomputer that hung in high orbit over the Earth; half a dozen smaller computers on the planet supplemented the main one, and he had thousands of sensors feeding him. He was mind; he could think, he could act after a fashion, he could receive input. His multiple photomutable gel eyes were much sharper than any man's and they saw farther into the red and violet; his ears could detect sounds higher and lower than any ears born of natural life; he could hear radio, sense solar flares, could analyze Juete's organically generated perfume—but he could not *feel*, for he had no skin, no nerves, no muscles, no body. The fission furnace powering him would last for two hundred years, and he could survive on solar radiation indefinitely past that, if somewhat less actively. He could, in his present form, live virtually forever.

It had not always been so. He remembered his own death, for even that recording had been pulsed to the computer along with the others. He had all the major memories from his former being and they had been coded into electromagnetoencephaloprojic records that occupied and nearly filled the supercomputer which was to become his new self. His *essence* was intact, and though he had no body—yet!—into which he could focus himself, he was mentally the same as he had been before. He had the thoughts and desires and hopes and dreams of a man, albeit he was now certainly something other than man.

He had been, and was now again in his own unique way, Marcus Jefferson Wall, the man who had run the Confed at his pleasure. He had been brought low, assassinated by one he had once loved, and now he had enemies to repay and plans to bring to fruition. Death had slowed, but not stopped him. He grew stronger each day, his unwitting agents spreading his reach throughout the galaxy, and the time had come for retribution. And a fitting one it would be, too.

For it was not only the people who had long memories: the memories of Marcus Jefferson Wall were now and forever eidetic, and those who had given him the worst ones would pay most dearly for having done so.

TEN

WHILE THE President of the Republic had by his own desire far less power than had the leader of the Confederation, his wishes still received a great deal of respect throughout the galaxy. If you received a com from Rajeem Carlos asking for a favor, chances were probably good that you would at least seriously think about it before refusing.

Khadaji was not surprised, therefore, when doors seemed to magically open for him and his daughter upon the tightly regulated pleasure world of Vishnu. The gas giant Shiva blocked the sun now so that it was both shade- and spin-night, but the huge moon's civilization had been designed to run in day or dark, and myriad colors of generated light—neon, biolume, halogen, incandescent— kept the dark at bay wherever man or mue built their houses of joy. When they arrived at the casino where Juete had worked and lived, it could have as easily been midday, to judge by either the crowds or the illumination at ground level.

The casino owner would be dining on the story of his White Radio com from the President for a long time, and he gave Khadaji and Veate scan rings that would admit them anywhere they wanted to go. Anything for my friend Rajeem Carlos.

Khadaji and his daughter moved toward Juete's room. The young woman wore a set of plain, tan coveralls, tight clothing that disguised little of what she was. She had the build of an athlete, and he noticed once again how well she moved, with an easy grace. Where did those easy and balanced motions have their base? Was she a dancer? He assumed she could ski, from her story of where she had been when her mother went missing, but he realized how little he knew about her. And Veate had not been particularly forthcoming.

As for himself, Khadaji wore his gray orthoskins and spetsdöds, and the soles of his spun dotic boots were new, something called tackgrip shears. He could almost run up a wall, if he put sufficient force into it, and the soles would not slide a centimeter. During a normal walk, the soles would seem no more than standard flexoprene. He didn't have the matador patch on his shoulder—he'd taught them but never gone through the graduation ceremony himself—and the spetsdöds he'd worn virtually every minute for years now seemed strange on the backs of his hands. Still, he was obviously what he was, out of practice or not; he wore the clothes, he had the look. Probably he looked better than he felt.

The security din built into Juete's door came to life as the pair approached. It scanned them, then queried vocally:

"Veee-et-tay?"

"Yes."

"Kaahhh-dah-jjee?"

Khadaji grinned at the gravellike tones of the thing's voice chip. "Yes."

As the door slid open, Veate said, "The security system

functions just fine, but the vocals have always been like that, slow and stupid-sounding. It amused my mother so she never got it fixed."

"She would find that funny."

The young woman glanced at him sharply. "How would you know? You haven't seen her in more than twenty years."

"I can see her now," he said. "In my mind, and in your face. I lived with her; I loved her."

"You *left* her!"

"I really had little choice."

"Right. You had to save the galaxy, to become a hero, to be the Man Who Never Missed!"

He looked around the room, feeling the emptiness and at the same time feeling Juete's presence. This is where she lives, he thought. He turned back toward his daughter. "Does your mother hate me that much?"

She had promised herself she wasn't going to do this, Veate thought, that she wasn't going to lose control. Fuck it. "Yes!"

She was breathing quickly and her face was flushed, as flushed as it could get. Now he could feel the pheromonic pull she put forth for the first time. Had she been able to keep it from happening before? Or was it that strong emotion intensified it so? It had been that way with Juete. He said nothing. Years of meditation had given him the ability to resist a lot of things.

Her breathing slowed, her color faded back to its fragile, translucent white, and the hormonal attraction ebbed. When she had regained control, she said, "That's not true. She doesn't hate you. She never has. She said you asked her to go with you, all those years ago. After a fashion."

He sighed. "After a fashion, yes. I was young and stupid

and I tried to protect my ego and I insulted her. But she knew I wanted her, knew I loved her."

"How could you go, then?"

He drew himself back from the past, refocused his time-stare, and looked at the woman who was the image of her mother and the child of them both. He said, "Have you had many lovers?"

"What is 'many'? Ten? Thirty? Fifty? And is it your business if I have had a hundred?"

"Do you keep several going so that if one bores you another is waiting patiently in line to step into place?"

"Yes, of course."

He smiled. "Those last two words are more easily spoken by an Albino Exotic than anyone else, aren't they? It's taken for granted that you will have people fighting for your favor. It's who you are, isn't it?"

"You lived with my mother. You know that it is. We were genetically engineered to be sexual toys for the rich. We can't help what we are!"

"Certainly you can. There are albinos who take chem to suppress their pheromone output, use skin dyes and lenses, dress to conceal rather than reveal."

"Passing for tintskins, you mean. Denying their true nature."

"That's what I mean. You can change what you are. You don't *want* to change it. Neither did your mother."

"What are you trying to say?"

"Albinos take others' desires for them for granted. It is a given, like the sun coming up in the morning, a constant."

"Yes," she said. "It is. One of our few advantages and something we would be foolish to ignore. So what?"

"Your mother would not give that up for me," he said. "She knew what she was and she enjoyed it. I could only be a small part of her life, only another in the long parade of lovers who was interesting briefly, but not worth concentrating all of her love and energy upon."

"So?"

"So how can you be angry at me for doing the same thing that she did? I loved her more than she did me, but you would have had me give up *my* life to worship her. Where is the fairness in that?"

"She birthed your child," she said. "If she hadn't felt something for you, why would she have done that?"

"I don't know. If she had felt something for me, why is it I never knew you existed until you walked into my pub a few days ago? If your mother had not been kidnapped, would I have ever known I had a daughter?"

Veate closed her eyes. "I don't know," she said.

Khadaji moved to a table and picked up a hand mirror lying there. The mirror was an antique, set into a frame of some hard, dark material carved into an intricate likeness of a serpent coiled around the small circle of glass. The frame substance escaped him, some kind of plastic, and for a moment, it seemed familiar. Where had he seen it before?

"It isn't your mother who is angry with me, is it?"

She opened her eyes and stared at him. "I wanted and needed a father and you weren't there. You know how it is with my kind. The galaxy is full of dangers for us."

"And it's my fault that I didn't know you even existed?"

"Yes. It's your fault. You sent her money, but you never came back. Your revolution ended five years ago. You could have found her then. Why didn't you?"

It was a question he had asked himself more than a few times. He'd told himself during the revolution that it would have been dangerous for Juete to be connected to him. But after it was over, the danger was much less. He had gone to hide, but he could have called or even looked her up. Why hadn't he? He didn't have an answer. "I don't know."

He started to put the mirror back onto the table.

"Wait," she said, and he could feel a change in her, a sudden tension and alertness different than before. "I don't recognize that. Let me see it."

He tendered the mirror. "A gift from an recent admirer, perhaps. I would think that Juete would still have many."

"She does," Veate said. Her comment was matter-of-fact, and he heard the cruelty in it.

She looked at the frame, scratched at it with one short fingernail, then held it closer to the lamp on the table.

"What are you—?" He stopped, as he finally recognized the material. "Put it down," he said.

She put the mirror onto the table and the two of them moved quickly toward the door. Khadaji didn't relax until they were fifty meters away from Juete's room, and even then he was shaken. She had seen it first, he would have missed it altogether if she hadn't noticed, and such mistakes on his part could be fatal. He'd been away from it too long; he felt old, slow, stupid, he'd lost the sharpness he'd had when he'd been living on the edge. It scared him.

The mirror's frame had been made of the same substance as the oxidation bomb that had exploded in the Siblings' compound on Earth. A perfect match. Damn!

As they were heading toward the hallway's exit, half a dozen figures suddenly appeared from around a turning. Three of them wore full softsuits, gloves and helmets, and while the rest were unarmored, all six were carrying handguns. Khadaji knew in an instant they weren't friendly. There was no place to hide, no cover, and they were too close to run. The only advantage he and Veate had was that the six had apparently expected to trap them in Juete's cube, and their weapons were still holstered.

How could six armed men or women elude the hotel's security system, the cameras, the sensors?

"Behind me!" he ordered.

The first of the six saw them and reached for his weapon.

The supervisor of the bank was most helpful, primed as she was by the request from the Republic's President. Once Dirisha had presented her ID and had it verified, full access to the bank's computers was available.

Dirisha had what she wanted in a matter of seconds. The laser printer chirred quietly and spat out a flimsy.

Outside, Bork, Geneva and Sleel waited, standing next to the hopper they'd rented. The vehicle had hard plastic tires, three on each side, for riding around on the road system, but could make flights over rough ground or water, if you didn't mind paying for twice as much fuel. It was midmorning and the local sun was keeping the air temp around half that of body heat, so it was crisp out. A faint tang of fossil fuel hung in the air, something more common to frontier worlds than to the older, civilized planets.

Dirisha waved the flimsy at Bork. "Know where this is?"

He took the thin plastic sheet and looked at it. "Yeah. In Oldport, across the strait on the Big Island. Looks like the address is down in the Dogtown Docks."

"Sounds like a great place to have a good time," Sleel said.

"I never heard of the Perimeter Corporation," Bork said.

"Probably a dummy," Geneva said. "But these are the people who were going to pay to have you killed."

They looked at Dirisha.

"So get in the hopper," she said. "Let's go visit our friends in Oldport."

"Dogtown," Sleel said, shaking his head. "Great."

The docks in Oldport were constructed in the days when waterships were cheaper than hoppers or orbital boxcars.

There was still a fair amount of hovercraft ferry traffic back and forth among the five main islands to keep a few of the docks active, but many of the seafront properties had either been converted into storage or shops, or boarded up and left vacant.

Back when she'd walked the Flex, Dirisha had been beaten pretty badly on a dock on one of the Hothouse Islands on Aqua, and the sight of such places brought up unpleasant memories. As the four of them left the parked hopper in front of the address printed upon the flimsy, the air held that same salt-and-wood-preservative stink that she remembered as she lay curled into a broken-legged ball on that long-ago and faraway dock. The guy who'd damaged her had been worse off, but it hadn't been much consolation at the time.

The building was old, mounted on thick pilings that went down into the bay. The everlast coating had bleached to a pale green mostly, and was torn through in spots, revealing the dead-gray wood under it. The windows were cheap nonshatter plastic, scratched and eroded by salt spray, and caked with city effluvia. The whole place had a grimy look to it. Water sloshed below and sea birds *crawed* and sailed back and forth in the cool air. There were no vehicles parked anywhere close, save their own, and the building appeared quiet. No people around.

"Looks like a major corporate operation to me," Sleel said.

"Let's go," Dirisha said. "And don't let the look fool you. We don't know what's on the other side of the door."

"Yeah, it's probably a pleasure palace."

"You are so predictable, Sleel," Geneva said.

The four of them moved toward the structure's entrance. Sleel was likely right; the place was empty and another dead end. Still, they had to check it out.

Halfway across the street, Dirisha stopped.

"Hold up," she said.

The others looked at her. "I think maybe we need to get back to basics. We're taking a lot for granted here."

"You want me to check for another way in?" Bork asked.

"Yeah. I think we should all do that. But nobody goes inside yet."

"You know something we don't?" Sleel said.

"Probably not, but maybe we are being a little slow. Somebody did try to splash us all. What say we remember they are still running around somewhere? Let's pretend they are in there and know we're coming."

Five minutes later, the four were back on the street in front of the building. "What do we have?" Dirisha said.

Sleel said, "Two doors on the back, one a sliding cargo door big enough for a good-sized hovertruck."

Bork said, "Five doors on the sides, two on the left, three on the right."

Geneva said, "Two portals on the roof, but there are also half a dozen skylights I could pop off and wiggle through."

Dirisha thought about it for a second. "All right. Everybody waits here. I'm going up on the roof and in through one of the skylights."

"Why you?" Geneva asked.

"Because I'm harder to see in the dark. I might swagger but I don't glow like a halogen tube." She smiled and fluffed Geneva's short, almost-white blond hair.

"It was a joke, Rissy. And you're never going to let me forget it, are you?"

"I got a better idea," Sleel said. "Let me go. I mean, if there's company inside, I should get first shot at them, right? They only tried to kill you; they put me in prison *and* tried to kill me."

Dirisha laughed. "Can Sleel get through the skylight?"

"If he doesn't breathe too deeply, yeah. I dunno if his ego will fit."

"Funny woman."

"Okay, Sleel. Go."

Five minutes later the front door opened, and Sleel stood there holding something that looked like a crooked red boot in one hand.

"Looky here," he said. "Nobody home, but they left us a gift."

"Chang, Sleel, that looks like—" Bork began.

"It is," Sleel cut him off. "A tightbore guillotine bomb. There's one mounted over each door, including the two on the roof. Anybody coming to visit would be tokamaked, if they weren't clever enough to use the skylights."

Dirisha took the bomb from Sleel and examined it. "This is top-grade hardware," she said.

"Nice to think we're worth the best," Sleel said.

"Can we trace it?" Geneva said.

"I don't see why not."

"Should we check out the building still?" Bork asked.

"Very carefully. They might have left other little presents for us. Got your sniffer?"

"Yeah."

"Then let's go."

The three without protection were easy enough. He was slower than he'd been at his peak, but it was amazing how fast the adrenaline surge brought it all back. Khadaji fired both spetsdöds twice each and took out the three, two darts for the leading man, one each for the other pair. He'd stood still for the second that took, but he started running toward the remaining three before the first trio hit the floor. A softsuit would stop a whole range of projectile weapons, including a spetsdöd's dart. He had to get to the armored attackers for hand-to-hand and he had one hope of keeping them from blasting him before he could cover the distance.

He pointed his handguns at their protected eyes, extended his forefingers rigidly into full auto, and charged.

Five meters away. Four meters. Three. He hoped Veate had enough sense to turn and run while he had the attackers busy.

The first of the three softsuiters dropped his hands from his helmet and snatched at his weapon. Too slow—

Khadaji barreled into the figure and drove his elbow into the man's throat, hardly an elegant move, but effective anyhow. He twisted away from the falling man? woman? and stepped into the first moves of Bamboo Pond. The second softsuiter had managed to clear her weapon— definitely a woman, even the softsuit couldn't hide those contours—and was swinging it around oh-so-slowly toward him. She was in too much of a hurry and she triggered the gun—he heard the hard *twang* of a spring pistol—and the missile *thwiped* past to his left. As he drove his knee into her groin, a strike effective for men or women, he saw with his heightened perceptions the line of spetsdöd darts embedded across the protective plastic of her face shield, heard the impact of his knee and her grunt, smelled the sharpness of his own sweat. No time, no time! The third softsuiter was two meters away, he had his gun out, it was aimed right at Khadaji, he'd never get to him in time to stop the shot—

Another figure blurred into view.

Veate!

As he watched in that syrupy flow of time that often accompanies life-or-death battles, he saw his daughter snap her foot out, kicking the gun free of the softsuiter's grasp. The man jumped away and turned, dropping into a defensive posture, fists knotted, legs wide and bent.

Veate did not pause. She hopped forward, kicked with

her leading leg twice—fakes, both shots—and drew a left downward block from the softsuiter. She pivoted and swung the same leg around in a spring kick at the man's head. He jerked his right hand up wildly and blocked, but this kick was also a fake, without real power, and the foot was snapped back quickly, leaving the softsuiter with both hands wide of his body. Before he could recover, Veate set herself, both feet on the ground, and thrust a back kick upward from a crouch with her other leg, heel leading. Her boot caught the softsuiter square on the chest, and the kick was powerful enough to lift him from his feet, slamming him into the wall behind. As his back hit the wall, Veate stepped in and sidekicked, the edge of her foot taking the man on the forehead. The *clunk* as the back of his skull hit the wall was quite loud. He slid down, knocked senseless.

Veate turned to look at Khadaji.

He blinked. He was impressed. He didn't know the style, but whatever it was, she was very good at it.

"We'd better go find security," he said.

His daughter nodded, and let out a ragged sigh. "Yes. My mother would hate it if we let her room blow up."

As he moved ahead of her, Veate fought the urge to shake her head in wonder. He was good. He'd taken out five of the six attackers and she wasn't sure but that he could have gotten the last one if she hadn't. She'd studied fighting for three years, two hours every day, and watching him move made her feel like a cripple. He was better than Mother had said.

What else about him had changed since he'd been with Mother?

ELEVEN _____

THE HEAD OF the casino's security was abashed. That six armed intruders had bypassed the state-of-the-art wards was unthinkable. But obviously not impossible. As the apologetic leader had his guards haul the six injured attackers away, Khadaji told the man about the mirror bomb in Juete's cube.

"If you can get to it before it explodes," Khadaji told the security man, "sealing it into an inert gas cannister will render it harmless."

"Our EU is on the way," the security man said.

"Do you have a courier service?"

"Yes."

"I want the bomb sent to Earth." He gave the man the shipping coordinates for the Siblings' compound. "I'll tell them it is coming."

"The local authorities—"

"—are perfectly competent, I'm sure, but this is an interplanetary problem and I'm working on it for President Carlos. Get it to Earth and let me worry about it."

Veate watched and listened as the tone of command

washed over the security officer and cleaned away his doubts. Right. Somebody was in charge; that was all he really needed or wanted to know, it was obvious from his quick nod.

Her father was not only fast with a weapon, he could focus his will sharply to move people with words, too. Why was she surprised? This was, after all, a man who had once taken on an army by himself. A single security guard would hardly worry him. Still, it was one thing to know it in theory and another thing to see it in practice.

The guard hurried away to do his assigned chore, and her father turned back toward her.

"You move well," he said. "I don't recognize the style."

Her heart rate and breathing had slowed but the reaction to the danger had set in. She had defended herself before, usually from overzealous suitors, once from a would-be rapist, but never against so many armed men. Her father had done most of the actual fighting, but she had been a part of it. Her words spilled out; she always talked too much and too fast when she was scared.

"It's called Jalka sla Nio, the Nine-strike Foot. My instructor is Kaplanian, from the Nordic Complex. The name comes from the nine surfaces used to kick an opponent: the instep from the ankle to the base of the toes, the right and left sides, the ball, big toe, bottom flat, bottom heel, back heel, and the Rodiya jambe." She paused for air, then hurried on. "Actually, the Rodiya jambe strikes are done with the lower leg or knee and consist of another seven moves, even though they are all lumped together as the Ninth Surface."

She was babbling; gods, he would think that she had lost her mind!

Khadaji smiled at her.

Veate took another deep breath and allowed it to escape

slowly. "You're used to this," she said, waving at the now-empty hallway. "People with guns. I'm not."

He gave her a moment to relax. "I was scared, too," he said.

"What? Really?"

"It never goes away, the fear, not when your life is at risk. Each time is new, each time is different. You learn that if you keep moving, you can survive, but you don't ever really get used to it. It's like a serpent in your belly, cold, waiting to roil around and knot your guts. And I'm long out of practice."

She didn't say anything. The great Khadaji, admitting that he was afraid? That didn't go along with the image she'd grown up with. He was a man who was supposed to have liquid nitrogen in his veins, a man who had spat in Death's eyes so often that Death had gone blind trying to take him. Dammit, he wasn't supposed to be human! He was supposed to be arrogant, uncaring, and easy to dislike. She had spent years setting him up as somebody unworthy of her, and unworthy of her mother before her. And now, here he was behaving in ways she had never prepared for, never anticipated. She did not want him to have any redeeming qualities. He had deserted her mother, after all was said and done, and had never been the father she had needed.

Ah, said her little voice, *but what would have happened if he had known about you? Would things have been the same?*

He should have asked!

Ah. Of course.

"My mother has always had someone to protect her," she said. "Albinos need protection. I grew up watching her always relying on somebody. I decided I'd never put myself in that position if I could help it. Maybe if she hadn't depended on the casino's security, she'd still be here."

"No defense is perfect," he said. "No matter how strong or fast or clever you are, sometimes you come up short."

"That's funny, coming from you."

"I was good, but I was also lucky. It could have just as easily gone another way. Your mother was the target of somebody who was *very* careful and *very* good. I doubt that knowing how to fight would have helped her much."

"Maybe not. But I'm not ever going to surrender my welfare to anybody else's care."

"Good for you," he said.

They were so easy to fool that it was pitiful, Wall thought. There Cteel stood, a human echo of a computer ghost who had also been named for another, a man who had once been Wall's most trusted advisor. He'd killed the original Cteel, of course, because the man had betrayed him. Still, it amused Wall to have the name continue. And so now Cteel Three stood in front of the holoproj, hand reaching for the control, motionless to Wall's altered scan, frozen in that way a computer can almost stop the flapping of Chronos's wings. Wall now had the ability to split real-time into so many parts that the flight of a bullet became as the movement of viscous gel on a cold winter's day. He could brake time yet more, could live in his bioelectronic circuits the entire span of a man between two beats of a human heart. True, he did not spend much of himself that way, because while he was a computer, he had been born of woman, and he was in his own thoughts a man still. But every now and then, the ability to play God could not be denied.

Cteel, a statue, longed for the control, and Wall took a certain kind of joy, knowing he could keep the man that way virtually forever. The metaphysics of it were quite astounding.

Enough. I release you.

Cteel waved his hand over the heat-sensitive control and the holoproj blossomed to life. The man on the screen was rugged-looking, as muscular as Cteel himself and then some, with jet hair and emerald eyes, and an expression that brooked no resistance to his will.

Wall shaped a mental laugh, knowing that the image he created from photons and thought was the idealized image of Cteel's father, an authority figure to the nth degree for the man who cleared his throat now to speak.

"Commander," Cteel said.

"You have done well," Wall said. The voice was deep, quiet, but laced with power sonics that beat hypnotically upon the ears of any listener. Where he sat at the table nearby, Tone was compelled to turn and look at the fake man upon the screen.

They did not know, of course. All of his underlings thought Wall existed in the flesh. He gave different ones different images he imagined they would most respect or fear, and he was literally a man of a thousand faces. Or ten thousand times ten thousand, did he choose.

"Thank you, Commander. What are your orders?"

"Leave Tone to watch the woman. Go to the Toowoomba station and wait for a delivery. Be there by noon tomorrow."

"Commander."

Cteel reached up to cut the comlink. Wall turned his attention elsewhere.

He had constructed for his amusement a room with a skylight. Bright sunshine flooded down upon a cushion upon the floor of his room, and it was upon this cushion that the image of Wall as he had been five years past lay naked.

Before him, the honeysuckle-scented air shimmered as he brought forth one of his flowers. His flowers. Ah, yes. The girls, the perfect children, never more so than now, when he could alter them as he wished, to be anything he wished. God, indeed, to create with no more than desire that it should be so.

The air shimmered, and the girl came into being. She appeared, was short, petite, just on the budding lip of womanhood.

She was twelve. No, make that eleven and a half.

The image altered slightly. The tiny breasts grew a tiny bit smaller, the fuzzy pubic hair thinned to the faintest wisps of down. Yes. Better.

Blonde. No, brunette. Shining hair falling to her sweet and tight buttocks. Skin colored like thimblebee honey. Long lashes over sky blue eyes. All atremble, this newborn virginal child. Here. Now. His.

"Wh-who are you?" she asked. And the voice was of course perfect, high, nervous, but curious. Wanting to know more, much more. All those things that he, Wall, could teach her. Afraid, but drawn. In joy and pain she would learn, but the joy would more than mitigate the small pain and the tears would become only a faint memory. She would know pleasure to her depths and be ever thankful to him for the lessons, for he was the kindest of men, and gentle beyond compare.

"I am your friend," Wall said. "And you are my flower, come to lay your sweet petals on me."

The girl looked puzzled.

Wall raised one hand languidly. "Come over here, child. I will teach you everything you need to know."

He had her hesitate, the part of him that had built the fantasy. He could keep the two parts almost separate, the computer god and the naked man, almost, but not quite. It took some of his pleasure away from it. Although these flowers were more perfect than any he had known as a man, although he could make them be or do anything he wished, the anticipation, the wonder, the *mystery* was lessened here. He would trade the total control for the imperfections in the smallest part of a second, were that in his power. To feel the living skin against his own for real once again would be worth all that he could do in his most virulent fantasies.

And it was going to happen. Soon, he would be able to open the petals of a real flower once again. He was going to torture and kill his enemies, yes, of course, but he was going to start a new garden, and therein would be hundreds of young flowers, awaiting his gentle and caring hands. They had called him perverse when he wore flesh, but they were fools and did not know, could never know the truth of it. He gave his flowers joy, and lesser men envied and hated him for it. Fools, all of them.

As he desired, the girl overcame her hesitation and came toward him.

Marcus Jefferson Wall smiled, and reached up for her. Such a beautiful child. And so lucky to have found him.

"Sleel?"

The matador wore his know-it-all grin as he sauntered into the rental cube where the others waited.

"Found the guillotine seller," Sleel said. "I persuaded him to give me the name of the guy who bought them. I asked him real politely."

Dirisha said, "And—?"

"The buyer did his business by com. The arms dealer keeps recordings of all calls. He can traceback the callers, so I got an address. And look at this. The buyer did it on visual."

"That doesn't seem real bright," Geneva said.

Sleel pulled his belt computer and tapped in a file number. A quarter-scale holoproj lit the air.

Bork and Geneva moved closer as Sleel turned the unit so that the image above it faced them. The man on the screen was talking, though Sleel had not triggered the sound.

Dirisha felt a chill touch her. She knew the man on the holoproj.

So did Bork and Geneva. Bork got it out first, in an awed voice: "Massey?"

Sleel looked serious, unusual for him. He added the speaker's voice. It was Massey's voice, too. And it was impossible, not just impossible, but *fuckit* impossible, because Massey was bootsole cold *dead*. The last time Dirisha had seen him, he'd been floating in a haze of his own crystalized body fluids in Deep outside of the ship *Raymond Bartlett*. The best medics that ever lived could not bring a man back from vacuum rupture and hard freeze, and the exhaust of the escape ship in which Dirisha had been fleeing from the *Soldatutmarkt* spy would have cooked the body to a black crisp on top of that. No way could Massey be alive. No way.

So, unless the people they were hunting were capable of miracles like bringing back the for-sure dead, this had to be a trick. They must have known that we'd get this far, Dirisha realized. They've been too smart in hiding things to let this accidentally slip past. Somebody who knew about Massey, knew enough to build a fake image of him complete with the right voice to taunt them, was involved in all this.

Who? Why?

What did it all mean?

TWELVE _____

IT DIDN'T TAKE long to find out that the six who'd bypassed the casino's security were no more than relatively ignorant hirelings. Their leader had not met the man who wanted the job done, said job being to capture Khadaji and Veate, only seen him on the comlink's holoproj. What were they supposed to do with the pair, once they'd been collected? Wait to be contacted. How had they managed to get past the electronic safeguards in the casino? They didn't know; it had all been arranged by somebody. They could not say what they did not know, and it seemed that they knew little.

A few days after the aborted kidnapping, Khadaji received a call from Earth.

It was Diamond.

"I have the analysis on the mirror bomb," he said.

Khadaji nodded at the image of the younger man floating in the air in front of him. "Yes?"

"It was the same lot as the stuff that blew up the exhibit here, but timed differently. This one wouldn't have oxidized enough to detonate for another two weeks, at least."

"Odd," Khadaji said.

"Yes, isn't it. Here's something else you'll probably find interesting. If we assume that there was zero or minimal oxy content before the device was exposed to the air in Juete's cube, then my calculations indicate that the mirror was there about six days. Between one hundred and forty to one hundred and fifty-five hours, roughly."

"Put there well after Juete was kidnapped."

"So it would seem."

"Any way to trace the origin of the explosive?"

"We're working on it."

Khadaji discommed and leaned back in the form chair. Very interesting indeed. Somebody was playing games, and they were fairly convoluted.

A few hours later, he got a call from Dirisha.

"Hello, Emile."

"Dirisha. How are things on your end?"

"Kinda odd."

"There's the key word of the day. How so?"

She explained to him about their visit to the docks in Dogtown, and the holoproj recording of Massey. She transmitted a copy of the recording, and waited while he quickscanned it.

"What do you think it means?" she asked.

"I think it means somebody is playing with us."

"Yeah, what I figured. Who?"

"No idea. Where do you go from there?"

"We're all running down our sublevel contacts. Bork knows somebody who knows somebody in Black Sun."

"Take care."

"Of course. What about you?"

"I'm going to work the political end. Rajeem has lists of those fairly high up in the Confed who fell hard when it came down."

He felt another presence arrive in the room, behind him.

That would be Veate, coming back from breakfast in the casino.

"Keep us posted," Dirisha said. "How are things with your daughter?"

She was standing right behind him, but he didn't hesitate. Call it like it was. "A little strained. She's a pretty sharp kid, though. You ever heard of something called Jalka sla Nio?"

"New Nordic foot-fighting," Dirisha said. "A guy broke some of my ribs with it once. Long time ago."

"Veate is good at it. We had a little trouble here and she held her own. She's okay when things heat up."

"Nice to hear. We'll let you know if we come up with anything. Stay well, deuce."

"You, too. Discom."

When Khadaji turned away from the com, he saw that Veate was indeed standing there. She looked embarrassed.

"I didn't mean to eavesdrop," she said.

He shrugged. "You're in the middle of all this. Might as well know what the rest of us know."

Veate watched her father stand and move to the computer. He had been complimentary toward her when talking to the black woman. There was an easy rapport between him and Dirisha, a time-together thing, and on the face of it, nothing to be gained by telling the woman that his daughter was competent and clever. He had known she was there, of course, so maybe he was trying to curry her favor. She couldn't be sure.

There was an awful lot of all this she couldn't be sure about. Her father was liked by a lot of people, respected and trusted by them. Those things didn't go along with the image she wanted to keep of him.

• • •

Cteel arrived at the Toowoomba station, a small storage building in the middle of hundreds virtually identical with it on the industrial side of the city. The shiny gray plastic of the structure gleamed under the Australian sunshine, and the place smelled for some unknown reason of dust and rubbing alcohol.

As he was many places, Wall was also here.

It was not necessary for Cteel to go anywhere, but this was all part of Wall's game; he wanted those who were in his employ to think there was a network of living people involved in all this.

The holoproj winked into life as Cteel entered, and the image floating in the stale air was of a man Cteel had never seen.

"Yes?" Cteel said.

"The Commander has bade me to direct you to the Tiboburra Medical Center, where you are to collect a certain doctor, one Elbu ra Jambi, and his equipment and assistants."

"All right. Anything else?"

"The medic will be conducting a certain experiment at the zoo. See to it that he has the full cooperation of the staff and any items he deems necessary."

"Understood."

Wall dissolved the image, sending it back into his vast memory stores, and watched through his photomutable gel cameras as Cteel left the building. If Jambi's experiment worked, the timetable would be advanced considerably. If not, well, Wall had nothing if not time.

In any event, there were other things that needed to be done, and Wall set about doing them.

On Mti, in the student complex, a dissident group that thought itself a well-kept secret suddenly found in its electronic mail an offer of aid in the circulation of its literature of revolution. The students would be cautious, but in the end, they would accept the help.

Large monies were always well protected, and even Wall's abilities could be thwarted when one began speaking of electronic sums in the billions of standards. True, he put all of his energies into it, he could eventually bypass many of these wards, but it was not necessary. Not every organization was as careful as galactic banks and stock exchanges, and into a number of these less-guarded computers Wall could reach. And did. He had enough credit of his own, of course, but causing certain key businesses to either fail or succeed through his manipulations was part of his plan.

Causing union trouble was easy enough, since unions were almost always paranoid by nature.

"Are you sure about this?" the union leader asked.

"Of course I'm sure," said the image of a man who never lived save in Wall's projection. "The bastards are trying to break you. I'll upload the evidence and you can see for yourself."

"Thank you, citizen worker."

"It is my duty, citizen worker. No more."

"How much explosive we talking about here, pard?" asked the gunrunner.

"A thousand kilos of shapegel. Military grade."

"No problem, but not cheap, you know?"

"I am a reasonable man. We can negotiate, can we not?"

"Why, sure."

It amused Wall to use the tactics of his former enemy. He wondered if perhaps Khadaji himself wouldn't find it amusing as well. Of course, humor depended on one's relative position to the effect, but still, even Khadaji would have to see some irony in Wall's moves, had he but known who was responsible. Alas, he would not know, not until it was too late to really appreciate it. Much too late.

There were others to be called.

"Nobody sees Maro," the man said to Dirisha.

They were in a small pub called the Pregnant Pelican, on a back street near the water in the bad part of Dogtown, and that was saying something. The man across from her had insisted on meeting her alone, but Dirisha knew he had accomplices scattered through the meager crowd in the dim room. Dirisha herself had triggered her dentcom the second she'd entered the place, and her friends could hear the conversation easily from their hidden positions outside the pub.

The man across from her called himself Dub, and he was an oily-looking little character with stainless and platinum teeth plates carved into needle patterns. Depilated, he wore hair and eyebrow tattoos in a formal style popular on Vul maybe ten years past.

"Nobody sees Maro, huh? He invisible?"

"If he wants, yeah. And besides, he ain't even onplanet. He's got a lot on his mind, he don't come here often."

Dirisha had picked out two of the little man's muscleboys in the crowd. They might be hard, but they weren't very good, and too obvious to anybody with half her training. She figured Dub was good for at least one other to watch his back and she wanted to spot him before she made her point. So far, the third man had been more careful than the others, and she hadn't seen him.

"Then how do I get to him?"

"Through me."

"I worry that something might get lost in translation. Nothing personal."

Dub flashed his custom teeth, looking sharklike for his effort. "I'm like a recorder, fem. It gets passed exactly like it gets said."

Dirisha shook her head. Black Sun—they would rather be called "The Organization"—had been around for a long time. The name might have changed, but the criminal underground was the same. There had always been something like it and Dirisha figured there always would be.

She finally spotted the third watcher. The bartender. A good move, that, since he would be expected to keep his gaze roving over his customers.

Were there any more? She didn't think so. There was a quick way to find out. And if she were wrong? Well, life was risky, wasn't it?

"Look, Dub, supposing I impress him somehow. Think that'll get me in for a face-to-face?"

The little man shrugged. "I doubt it. Maro, he don't impress real easy."

Dirisha smiled. "Well, suppose we try?"

She shot the first two while she was still seated, the *whump!* of the spetsdöds loud in the enclosed space. Dub's eyes widened and his mouth gaped as Dirisha had to stand to get a clear shot at the tender, who'd moved to the end of the bar to serve another patron. She'd made it look as easy as she could, offhand; she hadn't even looked away from Dub for the first two, using her peripheral vision to find them.

As soon as the first shots went off, people started dropping to the floor, hunting for cover. A handful of weapons came out, but nobody still awake need worry about Dirisha and apparently nobody wanted to risk pointing a gun in her direction.

She settled back into the chair and waved one hand lazily at Dub. "Think that'll do it?"

"Y-you're *crazy*!" He kept his hands on the table, fingers spread wide. A wise move.

"Probably. But I've got some serious business to discuss and I don't want to filter it through a ferret like you. I expect Maro can find me."

"You are in deep shit, fem!"

"Not from you, friend. And I figure Maro is too smart to flatten me without knowing who I am and what I want."

Dirisha stood and walked away. She allowed herself to swagger a little as she did. What the hell.

Maro was pushing sixty, a lot of natural gray in his black hair, but he had a lean, hard look. He wore a plain silk jumpsuit, dark blue, and his hands were laced together on the otherwise empty desk as Dirisha walked into the office. He sat straight in the chair. His face was neutral, no anger or fear in it; he was simply watching her.

They were on the second floor of a business building, running to bland earth-toned carpet and walls, the kind of place that could have been the headquarters of almost any kind of operation. Dull, quiet, safe—if you bought the picture.

The guards had scanned and hand-searched her carefully, though they'd apparently missed the dentcom; her spetsdöds were gone, and she hadn't tried to smuggle any obvious weapons into the meeting. She was not, however, unarmed.

Maro leaned back in his chair and waved at the seat facing his desk. One desk, two chairs; those were the room's only furnishings. There were no tapes, no paintings on the wall, nothing else.

Dirisha sat. She also leaned back and propped her left

ankle on her right knee, her hands resting on her shin and boot.

"Why shouldn't I have you killed?" he said. His voice was calm, full of power, confident. "If I let somebody thump my people, it's bad for business."

"Nobody got hurt," she said. "And I don't think you want a war."

He smiled. "You think I'm afraid of your three friends listening in on your dentcom?"

Dirisha smiled. He'd prepared for this meeting with at least a little investigation. Good.

"No, I don't think you would be, though it would be a mistake to discount them."

"I can field an army against your three matadors," he said.

"We had a guy take on an army once; he did okay. And how many matadors do you think there are? You might be good enough to beat them all, though I doubt it, but a war would surely be bad for business."

"Point taken. What is it you want?"

"There's somebody giving us a hard time. We want to know if he's connected to your organization. If he is, we want to know why he's on us. If not, we'd like to ask you to help us find him."

"Let's assume for a minute that I don't know who planted the bombs at the Dogtown warehouse," he said.

Dirisha scored another point in Maro's favor.

"Why should I help you find him?"

"He's going to be bad for your business as well as ours. A lot of people are looking for this guy. A lot of rocks are going to be turned over. Some of your operations are under some of those rocks. No offense meant."

"No offense taken. And if I help you find this person, the heat gets turned down."

"No lower than it was before, but yeah."

He raised one hand and touched his chin lightly.

"I do biz," he said, "and what you have said makes sense. And I like your nerve. My people will be in touch."

Dirisha nodded. "Nice talking to you."

"You took a big risk coming here," he said.

"Not really."

"The room is wired for zap," he said. "Every part of it, including where I sit. The field is variable, state-of-the-art—it can be set to tickle me while at the same time it will fry whoever is across the desk. All I have to do is say the word. You're unarmed. No matter how fast you are, you'd never be able to get to me before you died."

Dirisha pulled at her boot heel, peeling from it a thin sheet of material that matched the color of the spun dotic. She raised it slowly so Maro could see it.

He blinked and sucked in a short, sharp breath. He didn't know what it was exactly but she could see that he knew what it was in general.

"Sönderstat," she said, laying the dark square onto the desk. "You can pound it, burn it, or eat it and it won't do anything other than flatten, smoke or give you indigestion. But if you run an electric charge through it or put it into a working zap field it will go boom. Even a hand wand might set it off. Piece that size would take out this room, rooms on both sides and maybe the one above and below it."

"Nice," he said. "My guards will be sorry they missed it."

"What you get when you hire second best."

"We'll be in touch," he said.

Dirisha stood. She was almost at the door when he said, "What about the other boot heel? More explosive?"

"Inactive biocell battery," she said. "Doesn't show on a scanner. Good for one shot of juice if you rap it twice."

"Of course. A pleasure to meet you, Fem Zuri. You ever need a job, look me up."

"Thanks."

Since Massey had been *Soldatutmarkt*, one of the elite troops run by the Confed, Khadaji thought that was a good place to start. The infamous spy-soldier group had been disbanded, those who weren't killed during the revolution, but some of the leaders survived. Khadaji had the names, and several of the highest-ranking survivors still lived on Earth. Perhaps he should pay them a visit.

This was more than just a kidnapping and attempted killings on the matadors, he felt. And whatever was going on was a lot more complex than first he'd imagined.

Best he find out what. Soon.

THIRTEEN _____

"SO WHAT DO we do now?" Sleel said. "Sit and wait?"

He and Geneva and Dirisha were sitting or standing near the mirrored wall of the gym, watching Bork do squats. The big man was naked, save for a sweatband, groin strap and half-fingered lifting gloves; the flexsteel bar across his shoulders was loaded with plates. Dirisha figured the weight must be about three hundred and fifty kilos, counting the bar. There was a rack behind him so that if he leaned back it would catch the bar, but that was the only safety.

Bork squatted, and muscles bulged and veins stood out all over him as he went down. He came up fast enough so that the flexsteel bar bent, and the weights bobbed up and down on the ends when he stopped at the top.

Geneva said, "You could use him to teach anatomy. He looks as if he's carved out of something; no fat at all."

"I could probably manage that much weight," Sleel said.

Dirisha and Geneva smiled briefly at each other.

Bork did another rep, his fifth.

"To answer your question, no, we don't wait," Dirisha said. "Maro and Black Sun may or may not be able to find out anything. While they are looking, we keep our own motors running."

"To where?" Sleel said.

"Earth."

Both Sleel and Geneva turned from watching Bork complete his seventh squat to stare at Dirisha. Sleel said, "Earth? But you said that's where Emile was going."

"He can't cover the whole planet by himself," Dirisha said. "He's running down old *Soldatutmarkt* leaders. We have another reason to go there."

"Yeah? What?"

"We need to see a man about a computer."

"What are you talking about?" Geneva said.

"Ever hear of Jersey Reason?"

Geneva and Sleel both looked blank. Bork arrived at that moment, wiping the sweat from his face with a towel. "Jersey Reason the thief?" he said.

"Ex-thief," Dirisha said. "He's retired these days. But he kind of keeps a hand in. An electronic hand."

"What *are* you talking about?" Geneva said again.

Dirisha smiled.

Many of the upranks of the *Soldatutmarkt* had been imprisoned after the Republic took power, and rightfully so. Some managed to disappear, to take new identities and new faces, and those who chose quiet and unassuming lives mostly got away with it. While the *Soldatutmarkt* had been full of cruel men and women, it had never become quite the arm of slaughter as had some of the more infamous elite armies of history. Some of the troops had been no more than good soldiers doing what they thought was their duty. Some of these men and women were known, though the Republic had not chosen to unmask and punish them. The Republic had its reasons for so doing.

As the boxcar dropped from orbit toward its destination at the Western Canadian station, Khadaji mentally reviewed the information he had been given about one of these ex-soldiers. He needed somebody who would not only be willing to talk, but also somebody who had been ranked high enough to have something worth saying.

Khadaji's quarry lived in a small bubbletown built about sixty years ago. About fifty klicks south of Liverpool Bay in what had once been the Northwest Territories, New Anderson lay twenty kilometers west of the Anderson River, just out of the eastern edge of the Eskimo Lakes. The main industry in the town was tempdiff power conversion. Back before the powersats took over supplying most of Earth's electrical needs, it had been deemed a good idea to try alternative methods of generation. Tempdiff technology had progressed to the point where it could produce enough juice to warrant the building of several Arctic stations. Deepdrills tapped into the Earth's natural body heat many kilometers below the surface, and that warmth and the cold air outside the town were artfully and precisely mixed to make power.

The technology was outmoded now, but New Anderson continued to pump its small sparks into the NoHemi Grid. One never knew but that a microwave sat could go down and even a few gigavolts might come in handy.

New Anderson was far from anyone likely to accidentally happen across and recognize a former *Soldatutmarkt* Section Chief, an officer equivalent to a Sub-Befalhavare in regular military rank.

"Looks cold out there," Veate said, snapping off her seat's holoproj.

Khadaji pulled his thoughts back into the boxcar.

"It is. Even the summers aren't real warm and it is winter now. Probably they have more snow on the ground than I did at the Red Sister."

Veate said, "I wondered at the name. How did the place come by it?"

Khadaji leaned back in his seat. "During the fighting at the end when the Confed was falling, I lost two of my people. Lyle Gatridge —everybody called him 'Red'—and Mayli Wu, sometimes known as 'Sister Clamp.'" He still felt a twinge of pain when he thought about it. He hadn't seen them die, but he'd set them on the path; it had been his fault, at least partially.

"Red was one of my first teachers, the man who showed me how to use this." He waved his left hand and the spetsdöd on the back of it. "Mayli was many things, and the most centered of all the matadoras. She taught us about love."

Veate did not speak, and Khadaji allowed his memories to flow again, recalling his friends. Red had also been Geneva's father, and Mayli had been Bork's lover. The death of the Confederation dinosaur had not been bought cheaply, even if it had cost nothing but those two. It had cost more. A lot of people had died and though not directly by his hand, they were piled high on Khadaji's karma.

He shook the morbid thoughts. The dead were dead. He had the living—Juete still among them, he hoped—to attend to, and that had to be more important. You could not bring back the past but you could still save the future.

Maybe.

Khadaji and Veate rented a flitter at the WC station, bought heatmesh and spare batteries for it, as well as hats and gloves, and took off for New Anderson. Between the WC station just outside Greater Vancouver and their destination were a dozen bubbletown settlements. Such places utilized Ben Lu generators, the cheaper version of the Ben Wah devices used on airless worlds to form a hardball force sphere around itself. A Ben Lu would shield against most precipitation and extremes of heat or cold, but did not greatly affect light or other electromagnetics. Khadaji was no physicist, but he understood that a Ben Lu effect was more like a wall of thickened air than anything else.

Two thousand meters below, the ground was covered with snow. As they flew over the first of the bubbletowns, they could see the perfect circle standing bare against the whiteness. The town within was visible through a dome only slightly fogged in a few spots. Veate said, "Why doesn't the snow stick to the bubbles? Are they heated?"

"As I understand it, the field vibrates in such a way that snow and rain are repelled, something like personal weather shields."

"Ah."

Two hours later they came within range of New Anderson. Khadaji allowed the town's traffic-control comp to lock them into a landing mode. Most of the power complex was apparently underground, although there were several large buildings that had a heavy industrial look to them visible up top. According to the infonet feed into the flitter's comp, New Anderson sported a permanent population of around two thousand, more than half of whom worked running the tempdiff plant, despite the dins and automatics. He guessed that merchants, children and assorted service people made up the rest of the town. There'd be pubs, stores, maybe gambling and prostitutes, as well as medical and dental facilities.

The only way Khadaji could tell they'd crossed the Ben Lu barrier was that the flitter's outside temp sensor showed an instant rise.

The flitter made a series of inward spirals and put down on a plastcrete landing lot, then taxied to an assigned parking slot near a small building. The com came to life.

"How long you gonna need the slot?"

Khadaji saw the attendant in the small building wave at him. "Just the day," he said.

"Gimme your credit number."

That done, Khadaji and Veate alighted from the flitter.

"Not cold at all," Veate said.

"The mesh and hats and gloves were in case the flitter had problems on the way," her father said.

Most of the buildings were standard everwear plastic, still dark green, almost in mint condition. Here and there some of the structures had been painted, to change their appearance. The builders had been generous in the sizes allotted to housing and recreation. The streets were straight and wide. Those running east and west were numbered, while those going north and south were lettered. It would be difficult to get lost, and the entire town was only three klicks by three at its longest. Someone who lived in the northwest corner would be found near the intersection of Avenue A and 1st Street; a shop in the southeastern corner would be near Avenue J and 10th Street. Simple.

The address her father had was between 3rd and 4th on Avenue E. It would not be a long walk from where the flitter was parked. There were few people and fewer vehicles evident, and those people who were about stared at Veate when she passed close enough for them to see her clearly. She was used to that. Albinos grew up with constant stares.

As they walked, Veate said, "So, are you going to tell me anything about this ex-soldier or not?"

Khadaji said, "I'd rather get your reaction without a bias, if that's all right."

Veate shrugged. It irritated her, but she said, "Fine." Whatever game he was playing here, she wasn't going to let him think he was getting the best of it with her.

The address was of a small shop, and what it apparently sold was hand-knitted garments. There were shawls, caps, and mufflers artfully hung in a display behind the plastic window. The door slid open as they approached it.

Seated in a wooden rocking chair in front of a display case inside was a woman wearing a green wool caftan. She was perhaps eighty-five, white-haired and wrinkled, and was busy with her needles, knitting a sweater. She looked up at Khadaji and Veate and smiled, showing a fan of deep lines at the corners of her eyes. Veate found herself returning the older woman's smile.

"Good day," she said. "You're new, aren't you?"

"Yes, fem," Khadaji replied.

"Come looking for a nice gift, perhaps?"

"Come looking for Sub-Chief Heresh Vasquez of the *Soldatutmarkt*."

The woman's smile froze, then faltered. She sighed and put her needles down, nodding as if to herself. "Ah. I wondered if you'd ever get around to me."

Veate blinked, but held her face as calm as she could. This kindly-looking granny was one of the fearsome *Soldatutmarkt*? Come on.

"We aren't here to disturb your life, Fem Vasquez. We only want to ask you some questions. That done, we'll leave."

"Do I know you? You look familiar."

"I don't think we've ever met. My name is Khadaji. This is my daughter, Veate."

Recognition lit the woman's face. "Ah. I knew I'd seen you. You're *that* Khadaji, aren't you?"

"Yes."

"I'm honored. What is it you want from me?"

Something in the woman's attitude bothered Veate, though she couldn't quite figure out what. She seemed less disturbed maybe than she should. In her place, a war criminal, Veate thought she'd be a little more nervous about being discovered. Especially by somebody like her father.

"I need to know everything you know about a man named Massey. And about Marcus Jefferson Wall."

"Why? They both died during the revolution."

"So they did. I still need the information."

Vasquez stood. "Would you like some tea? There are chairs in the kitchen. We can talk there."

"That would be fine," Khadaji said.

They followed Vasquez into the kitchen.

On the ship bound for Earth from Fox, Dirisha, Geneva, Sleel and Bork sat in the pub talking. There were only a few other patrons there, and they mostly seemed intent on some sporting event being presented on the far wall's holoproj.

Sleel said, "So how is this sticky-fingered character supposed to help us find whoever is out to get us?"

"He is a wizard with any kind of complex electronics. He's improved or invented half a dozen major devices in use throughout the galaxy, including the best lock suppressor made. No patent on that one. He can backwalk computer input better than anybody, so it's said."

"And you figure he'll help us try to find out who is doing all this biz by computer?" Geneva said.

"Yes."

"How come?" Sleel asked. "Guy like this is probably pretty well off; he wouldn't have to do us any favors."

"He had a son who got into some trouble once. I happened to be in the right place to help him out of it."

"Oh, good," Geneva said. "A new story. You constantly amaze me at all you've done."

"That's us old folks, brat. Full of history."

Sleel said, "Yeah, but you're still missing one of the wonders of your life, Dirisha." He grinned and waggled his eyebrows.

She shook her head. "Never give up, do you, Sleel?"

"Just trying to help your sexual education," he said. "We came close once, remember?"

"You were in a Healy with an arm blown off; you don't think that would have put a crimp in your style?"

"Nah, it'd have just given us more room in the medicator. We'd have needed it."

Bork and Geneva laughed, and Dirisha shook her head again. The man had a one-track mind, sure enough.

Vasquez talked for more than an hour, responding to Khadaji's questions. He had a recorder going; she answered candidly as far as he could tell and he had no reason to believe she was lying. Even so, nothing immediately useful leaped out at him. He had known Massey when the spy had been his student, and later when the Confed had arrested him. He and Wall had met only once, but nothing Vasquez said added much to his research on the Factor before that. Wall had been fond of little girls in one way, and apparently of animals in another—less perverted—way. Khadaji had known about the former, not about the latter, but it did little to illuminate the relationship between the Factor and his *Soldatutmarkt* lap dog.

Whoever it was who had used the image of Massey on the holoproj, it wasn't Wall, anyhow.

Well. There were other people in hiding who might offer more.

"Thank you for your time and trouble," Khadaji said. "We won't bother you any longer. And you won't be getting any visits from the Republic."

"Thank you," Vasquez said.

As they walked back toward their flitter, Khadaji said, "What did you think of Vasquez?"

"She seemed nice enough, though I wouldn't have pictured her as a soldier."

"Everybody gets older. Anything else?"

"Well, it's just a feeling, but it seemed as if maybe she was hiding something."

"Any ideas as to what?"

"I didn't think she was lying about her answers. But she didn't really seem all that surprised to see us."

"I thought so, too."

"Does it mean anything?"

"Probably not," he said. "But you can never tell."

Deep in another of his fantasies, Wall received a com that demanded a portion of his attention suffcient to terminate the carefully crafted dream. He stored the scenario intact so that he could resume it later, and conjured the appropriate face to receive his caller.

The old woman's image sparkled to life.

"Reverend Father?"

"I am here, daughter," said the kindly-looking fat man.

"Someone has come to speak with me as you predicted."

"Of course. The Lord of All does not lie."

"You didn't say it would be Emile Khadaji himself."

Wall was only faintly surprised but of course he did not allow it to show. "You did not need to know."

"I told him everything he asked for, as you ordered."

"Good. You have done well, Vasquez. God will smile upon you for it."

"Thank you, Reverend. Bless you for your intervention."

"It is only my duty, daughter."

Mirth played itself upon Wall's biomolecular electronic pathways. Things were going along nicely.

Very nicely indeed.

FOURTEEN _____

ELBU RA JAMBI stood in front of the com unit, speaking to one of Wall's holoproj constructs. It was not necessary, since Wall had eyes and ears all over the compound and knew more about what was going on there than did anyone actually on-site; still, the fiction must be maintained, at least for a while longer.

Behind the man was the clean room of an advanced bioelectronics lab, built to Jambi's specifications, furnished with all that he had requested to fill it. The air glowed with purity, courtesy of pulselamps that kept the interior perfectly sterile. Jambi and his assistants wore noshed osmotic suits equipped with coolers so that their indigenous microscopic flora and fauna did not escape into the environment. Advanced nanogen computers worked silently creating tiny machines, a billion of which combined would not weigh as much as a gram; biogen units burbled quietly, rearing their colonies of tailored viruses and bacteria; and other computers mated the pieces into something quite unlike any natural life that had ever existed. The lab was a marvel all by itself. What it did was a miracle.

"You have results to report?" Wall's image said.

Jambi, a pale-skinned man with kinky hair and blue eyes, looked petulant behind his clear facemask. "I have made the initial infection and it is functioning properly," he said. "But I must protest once again the choice of subject. The test-beast is old and infirm; a younger animal would be much better."

The construct said, "Your objection is noted, doctor."

Noted and disregarded. The hybrid electrovirus and its host bacteria and nanomachineries now circulated within the body of Hizta. True, the mastodon was somewhat past his prime, but Wall had a fondness for the old beast, who had been used extensively in breeding experiments with young females for a number of years. During his peak, Hizta had possessed an astounding virility and a matching eagerness to copulate with anything that would hold still long enough to allow him to penetrate it. Elephants, mastodons, curlnoses, Hizta was not particular once stimulated.

"How long before the circuitry is complete?"

Jambi looked at his chronograph. "With the new enzymes and cell linkers, another two days."

"Call me as soon as the tests show he's ready."

"Of course. But I wish you would reconsider the subject. It would be easy to infect a better specimen and it would only delay the project a week at most."

"Hizta will do."

Wall broke the connection by dissolving his ersatz image. Two days! In two days, he would have at his command an organic brain rewired to be much like the viral matrix of the computer that he had become. In two more days, he could wear the flesh once again, albeit that flesh would be an animal's.

No matter. He would be able to *feel* again, to touch and taste and smell. Two days.

He did not allow himself to dwell on the possibility that the experiment might fail.

Jersey Reason lived on an island in the Puget Sound, between Old Canada and what had once been the States United.

DeCamp Island was twenty-five klicks west of the Bellingham Metroplex, and was a tiny, squarish-shaped chunk of land barely large enough to show even on local maps. Due to the neighboring military installation in the plex, the airspace over the island was restricted. Due to a freakish combination of atmospheric and magnetic factors, DeCamp Island was in a dead zone, impenetrable by all but the most tightly focused of radio beams. The place could be reached by private watercraft, but there were no scheduled ferries coming and going. DeCamp Island was a small and insignificant spot in a cold, gray salt waterway, and a place one had to make an effort to find and reach.

Dirisha explained this to the others as they headed toward the island in a pearly mist kicked up by the fans of the ten-passenger hovercraft they had rented in Bellingham. Bork piloted the vehicle, which must surely qualify as an antique even here. The day was gray, and though the temperature was mild, the air felt chilly.

"Man likes his privacy, hey?" Sleel said.

Dirisha said, "So it would seem."

Ahead, the island loomed, and from the look of it, it was hardly impressive. Barely large enough to support the structures Dirisha could see through the thin fog. There was a large house, flanked by a smaller building that could be some kind of vehicle housing or workshop. The house was old, a three-story-high box with plastic textured-sheet

siding and a blue tile roof, built in a vaguely pre-space
Spanish style, complete with tall, arched windows. The
garage or workshop was in the same mold. A third
structure, a squat plastcrete oval, rose only a couple of
meters from the ground at its tallest. There was something
of a yard around the buildings, with grass and low, trimmed
bushes. There were no signs of a boat or any other vehicle.

"Doesn't look like he gets out much," Geneva offered.

"You think he knows we're coming?" Bork asked.

"I expect so," Dirisha said.

"I don't see how," Sleel said. "We didn't call; you
pointed out that the place is shit for radio or vis reception.
He got a crystal ball?"

"Well, he could just look out the window," Geneva said.
"He could see anything for ten klicks and if he's got any
kind of optics, he'd notice something this big to the
horizon, you think?"

"I'd love to have this place in a defense scenario," Bork
said.

Sleel chewed on that. "Yeah, maybe so. If you can't
come at the place by air without a couple of military
hoppers bracketing you, that narrows it down. Got to move
over the water or under it. And you'd have to come up when
you got to the island. You could line the perimeter with
proxy-mines or a trip-track gun and make things hot for
unwanted company."

"Unless the company was official," Geneva said. "Then
air would be okay."

"Still see it coming a long way off, though," Bork said.
"Couple of missiles on the roof . . ."

Dirisha grinned. It was good to see her friends thinking
tactically again. They'd all been away from it a long time.

"Yeah, that's all well and good," Sleel said, "but you got
no place to run if the heat comes down. Same rules apply to

you. You can see them, they can see you. You try to take off, you're just as visible."

"Maybe he's only worried about unofficial visitors," Dirisha said.

"Yeah? How good was this old geep?"

Dirisha chuckled at Sleel. "He was the best thief in the galaxy at one time. In the biz for forty-some odd years and never did a day of lock-time. The Confed never could pin anything on him and he mostly retired by the time the Republic came online."

Sleel nodded. "That's not bad."

Geneva laughed. "Damn, Sleel, that's almost a compliment. Better watch yourself."

"Yeah, well, if we can just come tooling up to this guy this easy, he's maybe not so sharp anymore. We could just as easily be out to splash him as not; how's he to know?"

That was a good question.

Veate had to admit that Khadaji had so far been operating at a level a lot higher than she had expected. Or had wanted to expect. As they left the frozen area around the bubble-town, she considered her thoughts about her father. True, they had not found Juete. Still, Khadaji's confidence did not seem dimmed. If he had any doubts, they were not apparent. And while their progress did not seem to have brought them any closer to her mother, Veate felt in a way she could not put into words that they were getting closer somehow. It was an eerie sensation, but no stranger than sitting next to a man she had grown up hating and finding that despite that, she was beginning to *like* being around him.

No. She was not ready to give that particular anger up yet. It was a wound that she did not want to heal.

Still, Khadaji did not behave as she had pictured him

behaving. There was none of the megalomania she had expected, no arrogance. He admitted to being afraid, he confessed that he felt doubts, he easily spoke of luck being a major factor in his triumph. No, he didn't pretend to a false modesty, he said he was good—but he never hinted at being great.

As the flitter zipped through the frigid air, Veate stole a quick glance at Khadaji. Despite all her years of anger, there had always been a tiny piece of her that took a certain pride in what he had done. She never voiced it to anyone, but he *was* her father and he *had* changed the galaxy in which people lived. And for the better, too. Maybe he had done it for more than just his own ego. He hadn't hesitated before agreeing to help her find her mother. Maybe he still did feel something for Juete as he had said.

Maybe he wasn't all bad.

In that moment, Veate realized she was going to have to work at it if she wanted to maintain her anger. It was a major thought. It made her want to shut her eyes and pretend that it hadn't come to her. Damn! Why couldn't he be as bad as she had wanted him to be?

"Where are we going?" she said.

"To the Bellingham Metroplex. To meet some old friends."

Wall maintained a calmness he certainly did not feel when he spoke to his hired medic. "The computer checks are all successful?"

"Of course. I did not expect it otherwise."

He was an arrogant bastard, but if he pulled this off, he had earned the right, Wall thought.

"Give me the relay codes."

"You are ready to begin the transfer?"

"Immediately."

"Very well. My monitors are in place," Jambi said. "There's an automatic abort and retrieve set at—"

"No," Wall said. "Don't pull the program unless you get a direct request from me."

"Unwise. The transfer is risky. The computer you intend to use is fragile in many ways. It could overload the organic brain. Such damage could rebound."

"The risk is minimal."

"Still, it is there. Another specimen can be infected and brought to term in ten days, should anything happen to the mastodon, but the rebound might damage your computer's circuits. Certainly it would scramble the program somewhat."

"Then I trust that you will make certain that there will be no problems."

"I can't guarantee that—"

"I thought you were supposed to be the best there is at this?"

"I am! But even the best cannot lay claim to omnipotence!"

I think perhaps you might be wrong, Wall thought. But he did not communicate this to the doctor.

"We will take the risk. Stand by for the transfer. I will upload my program into the comcircuit."

"It's your computer."

You don't know how right you are, Wall thought.

A hidden sensor must have seen Dirisha and Sleel as they approached the front entrance to Jersey Reason's house. While Bork and Geneva had also left the vehicle, they had separated and stayed well away from the others.

"Do I know you?" came a voice from the entrance. The voice was gruff, fairly deep, and age-roughened. Dirisha recognized it from her last meeting with Reason, even though that had been ten years earlier.

"Dirisha Zuri. We did some personal biz once."

"Ah. Dirisha. Hold on a second, I'll open the door."

"This is my friend, Sleel. And I've got a couple other people with me."

The door swung open on noiseless hinges, operated by remote control, since no one was there. "Sure. Bring 'em in."

Dirisha didn't need to relay that, since her dentcom was running. Bork and Geneva drifted into view.

"Down the hall and first door on the left," Reason's voice directed. "The library."

Nice place, Dirisha thought. Thick carpets made to look like some animal pelt, a dark, rich blue-black. Walls done in a complementary color, no pictures.

The library door opened, revealing an impressive room. Most of the walls were shelves, floor to ceiling, and stacked with antique tape cases, disk cartridges, and even bound hardcopy books. A wood fire or close approximation of one was burning cheerily in the gray stone fireplace to their left, and Reason himself sat in an overstuffed wingback chair— the thing had to be eight or nine hundred years old, if Dirisha was any judge of such things. He had a book on his lap, and he smiled at the four of them as they entered the room.

Jersey Reason was not so impressive as the room. He was a short, almost tiny man, with thick, white hair and a very short beard, also white. His face was wrinkled, especially with smile lines at the corners of his pale blue eyes, and his skin was sun-damaged and tanned. He wore a black-and-white patterned kimono belted at the waist, and slippers.

"Ah, my night-child Dirisha. How long has it been? A decade or more, eh?" He smiled, showing perfect teeth.

The size of the man belied the deep voice. Dirisha had thought that Reason talked a lot bigger than he was when she'd met him before, and the ten years had shrunk him even more, but the voice still boomed with power.

Sleel leaned over to whisper to Dirisha.

"Something's wrong here," he said. "If this geep is so good, why'd he let us just stroll in?"

"For all you know we're standing in a zap field or under a dozen gunsights."

"Maybe. But something's wrong with him, too."

"So, Dirisha, what brings you to Earth? You and your three friends?"

"Excuse my manners," Dirisha said. "This is Sleel, Bork and Geneva."

"I've heard of them," Reason said. "Nice to meet you."

"We need some help," Dirisha said. "We've run into something strange."

Reason raised one thick, white eyebrow. "Yeah?"

At that point, Sleel raised his left hand, slowly and casually—and fired his spetsdöd, aiming directly at Reason's forehead.

Dirisha snapped her gaze away from Reason. "Sleel!"

"Told you something was wrong," Sleel said. "Look."

Dirisha glanced back at the old man. He smiled at them. "What—?" she began.

"That dart should have hit him right between the eyes," Sleel said. "It didn't miss and it didn't bounce off; I was watching. Where is it?"

Reason stood, and while he did it slowly, all four of his visitors pointed at least one weapon each at him as he moved. The old man's grin increased. He turned and put one finger against the back of the overstuffed chair. "There's your dart, Sleel. Right where you aimed it."

There was a tiny hole in the fabric of the chair.

Dirisha understood almost immediately. Bork said it first: "He's a holoproj."

Reason walked toward them, until he was no more than two meters away.

"Incredible," Geneva said. "Even this close I can't see the scan lines."

Bork stepped forward and waved his hand back and forth. As his arm entered the image of Reason, it disappeared as if it had plunged into a solid.

"That's the best holographic projection I've ever seen," Dirisha said.

"It's the best *any*body has ever seen," said the image of Jersey Reason. "And the chair is rigged with a pheromone and scent pump. At five meters, it can fool a dog because it *smells* like me, too. How did you figure it out, Sleel?"

Sleel shrugged. "It didn't feel right."

"I'm in the blockhouse," Reason said. "Come on over and let's talk."

Dirisha looked at Sleel, who grinned and waggled his eyebrows. She shook her head. Gods. There'd be no living with him for at least a month.

FIFTEEN _____

IF WALL HAD tended toward believing in the metaphysical, he would have probably gone mad when first he had awakened to find himself reincarnated as a computer. Even though he had known the theory, the practice was another thing. The idea of transferring a portion of his self into the radically altered brain of a mastodon would have seemed equally crazed only a few short years past. And yet, here he was.

It began with a flow, an electronic flux that might be likened to white-water rapids, though it was altogether different. Some of him stayed on the shore, in the shelter of his computer trees, watching as another part of him floated away on the surging electron currents to a place no man had ever been before.

The rapids vanished. There came a sensation of falling, that flutter-in-the-gut tightness that happened in space vessels too small to bother installing in them ersatz-gravity generators.

A sense of coldness gripped him, but intermingled with streaks of heat, alternating patches of fire and ice.

Now there was a feeling of speed, and of high energies swarming like a hive of maddened insects, frantically searching for something indefinable.

Now Infinity yawned like a frozen canyon to the sides of a narrow trail, and one slip would hurl him into a fall that never ended.

It was a journey that seemed to take forever, winding through mental constructs that ran the gamut of travel, floating, walking, flying, crawling, until at last—

Until at last, without any sense of having arrived, he was *there*.

Alive. Blood coursed through his veins and arteries. Air came into his lungs. Muscles shifted under his thick, but somehow tender, skin. He felt strong, massive, he could hear, taste, he could see; he was flesh!

It had worked! He was a mastodon, but with the sensibilities of a man.

He was three meters tall at the shoulder; he had tusks of gleaming ivory that stretched outward almost two meters in a lazy curve. Intellectually he knew these things, but more importantly, he *felt* them.

"Program in place?" came a voice.

He heard the speaker with his ears, but also within the chamber of his thoughts, as if hearing two men speaking in two languages at once. It was the doctor, standing next to him—so small!—an insignificant being painted in shades of gray. He knew that he would see in black and white; he had expected it, but even without color, the picture was so vivid that it put to shame his most advanced computer sensing gear. Here was the essential difference in the kinds of life: the flesh was made to be sensual, the circuit could never be anything but electronically cold.

Using the great strength of the thing he had become, Wall nodded. He curled and uncurled his trunk—what a powerful coil of ridged muscles it was!—and reached to the communicator built especially for him. He tapped the fat, square plate marked "Yes."

A billion kilometers away and a billion years past, far back there in the forgotten distance behind him, the machine that he had been, that he still *was* somehow, also acknowledged the same query. He spoke with two voices and the division seemed almost complete.

"Very good," the tiny doctor said. He touched a control on a smaller panel that released the padded shackles holding Wall, a precaution against the possibility of transfer damage. A crazed mastodon could create a lot of grief in such a finely tuned place.

Wall stretched, glorying in the feel of his ability to do so. His tusks flashed in the sterilizing lights.

"Can you walk?"

Again Wall nodded, and proceeded to demonstrate his control. He took three steps forward, then three back. He felt an urge to trumpet his triumph. He restrained himself. No point in scaring the little man next to him.

"Excellent! Now, for the other tests—"

Wall reached out with his trunk and began to tap at the giant keyboard.

"A moment," the doctor said. "This is not scheduled."

Wall ignored him and continued to spell out his message. The flesh would not be denied.

BRING ME A FEMALE, he wrote.

"Not wise," the doctor said. But even with his reduced vision, Wall could see that the man was intrigued.

DO IT.

Jambi shrugged. "It's your money."

Anticipation filled Wall with a delicious ache.

The blockhouse on Jersey Reason's island was not so easy to enter as had been his house. The door that cycled open was more than a meter thick; the worm-gear hinges were of squashed steel and braced by plates of the same. The locking mechanism was of solid carbonex—it must have cost a fortune—and the center of the door showed at its edge another plate of carbonex sandwiched into the plastcrete.

"Nobody's gonna come in uninvited," Bork said.

Dirisha nodded. "Wonder if the whole place is carbonex shielded?"

"Take a long time to dig through, if it is," Sleel said.

The four of them walked through the open portal and down an arched hallway lined with what looked like stainless steel, floor and walls. "Straight ahead and right at the end," came Reason's voice.

Despite the look of the interior, it felt comfortably warm, Dirisha noted. The lighting was from sconces set into the walls at three-meter intervals, and the design of the fixtures was art deco, sort of like an inverted letter "A." There were no windows or obvious openings to the outside.

A steel door slid open to admit them at the turning, and the four found themselves in an elevator. There were no controls apparent.

"We sure this guy is our friend?" Geneva asked, as the door slid closed.

"I hope so," Dirisha answered.

"Very funny," Sleel said.

"Feel a little better about the old geep's security?" Dirisha said.

"Maybe."

After dropping for fifteen seconds at a slow speed, the elevator stopped and the door opened. Jersey Reason stood there, waiting.

He looked the same as he had in the holoproj, and the

room in which the four visitors found themselves was a match for the library in the house above the ground.

Bork said, "Man. The whole room was a projection. Furniture, books, everything."

"Except the chair," Sleel said. "Which didn't have to be there. Why was it?"

"I like to play fair," Reason said. "To see who is paying attention." He smiled. "Good to see you again, Dirisha. How can I help you?"

"We had somebody come back from the grave on us," she said. "We'd like to know who raised him from the dead."

"Solov manages a surfing resort on the Great Barrier Reef these days and is lucky to be alive to do it. I'll be happy to see what I can do."

Sleel, who had been looking at a leatherbound book he'd taken from a shelf, turn around. "Solov is your son?"

Reason inclined his head slightly.

"You named your son 'Solov Reason'? No wonder he got into trouble."

Reason laughed. "I'd like to talk to you, Sleel, about how you saw through my illusion. No one ever has before, you know."

Sleel shrugged. "I know real when I see it."

"We must discuss this at length. Meanwhile, let us see if we can solve your problem."

There was a rec room in the hotel at which Khadaji and Veate registered, and she told him she was going to work out the kinks in her muscles. Khadaji nodded absently.

"I'll join you there in a few minutes."

After she had gone, he lay on the bed in his room. Were they any closer to Juete? He felt as if he were somehow moving in the right direction, doing all the right things, but there was no way to be sure. Whatever all this represented, it was an intricate web. He had the feeling that if he could only catch a single strand, he could unravel it all.

He spent another five minutes trying to meditate, hoping to empty his mind of thoughts and allow the monkey brain to rest. The monkey was active, however. It didn't want to rest, it wanted to dance and caper and throw rotten fruit at him. Get up, fool! Your albino mistress is captured and your daughter by her hates you. Somebody out there wants you and all who know you dead. You don't have time to rest! The skies are going to fall and crush you!

Khadaji arose. So much for quiet meditation.

He took the lift to the recreation area, sixteen floors above their rooms. The lift doors opened to reveal a fair-sized gym, smallball court, and a long and narrow swimming pool. Six people, all naked, stood on the banks of the pool, watching a solitary swimmer.

Veate churned the water, her pale arms rising and falling evenly, her legs scissoring and creating foam in her wake. As he watched, she reached the far end of the pool, dug into the water and did a flip turn; her nude buttocks flashed under the lights. She twisted and pushed off powerfully, gliding under the water like an alabaster fish for a moment before surfacing to resume her mechanically perfect face-down crawl. She rolled every fourth stroke to breathe.

Normally his entrance into a small area would have drawn stares, dressed as he was in his orthoskins and spetsdöds, but the six people—four men and two women— were all held captive by Veate's magic. One of the men had an erection he was trying in vain to cover with his hands, and one of the women was flushed red and breathing heavily.

Khadaji found a plastic chair against the wall and sat, noting automatically the entrances and exits to the big

room. The echo of Veate's feet and legs as she slapped the
water during her turns bounced hollowly from the walls,
and the air held an acid tang of some bacteriostatic agent in
the clear water.

After about fifteen minutes of flashing whitely back and
forth, Veate came to a halt. She hung on the lip of the pool
for a moment, allowing her breathing to slow, then pulled
herself from the water in a single motion, to stand on the
rounded edge. She was naked, and she squeezed water from
her hair before padding toward a towel and robe draped over
one of the plastic chairs.

Khadaji sighed. She was lovely, every bit as beautiful as
her mother had been when first he had seen her naked.
Perfect in every way, not a gram of surplus fat, each muscle
in harmony with all the others. Her shoulders were a bit
wider than her hips, her torso sleek, her breasts small but
shaped well, her buttocks and legs without flaw, the wispy
white pubic hair downy, even while wet. Beautiful? Here
walked Beauty incarnate.

What he felt, however, was not lust, but a kind of pride.
True, she got her looks from her mother. But he was her
father. Some of her genes were his.

The naked watchers hung on her every motion, staring as
Veate toweled herself dry. One man turned his head and
pressed his hand over his mouth as Veate slipped into her
robe, white on white. Was it because he could not stand to
see such beauty covered? Or merely to keep himself from
drooling?

Veate wrapped the towel around her head, enshrouding
her hair, and turned and walked toward Khadaji. She wore
a half smile, and he knew that she was only too aware of the
effect she had on those fortunate enough to be allowed to
see her form in all its glory.

"I feel better," she said. "All that flying had me stiff."

"It must be catching." He nodded at the half dozen observers.

She laughed, a sound full of pleasure, and once again he knew her for her mother's daughter without any doubt. Her laugh could have been a recording of Juete's. "None of those will come within ten meters of me," she said. "Were I to approach the one whose penis longs for me, he would stammer and retreat. I can always tell."

"Of course," he said.

"So, do we have time to eat before these friends of yours arrive?"

"I think so."

"Well, Father, would you have me starve?"

There was a sting to the word "Father," but it seemed less venomous than before. Or maybe that was only his imagination.

The being that was Wall/Hizta felt a tremor in his rear legs as the female elephant was led into the room by the mahout. With them was the zoo's director, a thin woman with a worried look. She moved toward the doctor.

"This is Gretl, the only elephant we have in heat. What do you want with her?"

Jambi smiled. "What does one ordinarily want with an elephant in heat, madam?"

The director shook her head. "Hizta can't fertilize her; his strain is not close enough. And he's too old."

Wall's musth glands throbbed. The thick, oily secretion ran from his temples down and into the corners of his mouth, and the taste and smell of it was exquisite, adding to the urge to rush to the female and mount her. His heart thudded faster, until he could feel it throbbing all over his body, synchronized with the throbbing glands in his head. His penis grew hot within its sheath. Old?

Jambi said, "I don't think our client is interested in whether any offspring result from the mating. Just in the act itself."

"I protest—" she began.

"And I have carte blanche, madam, as you well know. If our client wishes to experience the fucking of an elephant, it is up to him."

Wall could stand it no longer. He was a man, but his body now sang to him a most basic song, older than language and more compelling than any words. He flung his trunk up into the sterile air and screamed his mating cry.

The young female elephant—Gretl—might have doubts about whether a mastodon was suitable for a mate, but there was within her some racial memory that recognized Hizta's desire and his call. She twisted her head around far enough to see him as he began to run toward her.

Gretl saw a male and that male knew *she* knew *exactly* what he wanted. She bolted.

The mahout dug his hook into the tender spot, but he was wasting his time. Gretl slapped the man aside with a sharp sweep of her trunk and fled. The mahout was slammed into a table, flipped over it, and landed in a broken sprawl.

She was, Wall knew, only being coy. The females did that sometimes, they ran from what they wanted. Hizta knew, if Wall did not. She was in heat. She would receive him.

Wall could not separate his desires from that of his host; he was pulled deeper into the mating urge every second. He did not think he could stop even if he wanted, and most certainly, he did not want to stop.

Even a large room such as this one had little space for an elephant and a mastodon to run before reaching a wall. While some small part of Wall's senses noticed Jambi tending to his instruments and the director moving to the

fallen mahout, it was the female who called to him. Her
smell overpowered all else, beckoning.

He caught her gaze as she turned to lurch away from the
wall, shook his head and let his ears, smaller than her own,
flap.

She understood the signal well enough, he could see that.
She cocked her head at an angle.

Wall danced with Hizta to her side. He touched her back
with his trunk, urging her to turn, to present to him. He was
prepared to be firm and insistent, as insistent as need be,
because he was not prepared to be denied.

Gretl spun and raised her tail, opening herself to him. So
much for being coy!

Hizta lunged forward, stretching his aged body. He raised
up, mounted her, and gripped at her with his forefeet,
resting much of his weight on her. He thrust with his penis,
now swollen and ready, and found the opening. He entered
her.

Wall's excitement was like a red madness. It burned in
him. Neither Hizta nor Gretl made any sounds, and it was
not like human thrusting; it was less a thing of friction than
of connection, as though they were joined together as one
creature, a little movement here, to dig himself deeper, and
within twenty seconds it began, he could feel it in his
quivering rear legs, in his spine, shuddering in his belly as
his penis became a nozzle, a hose pouring forth a hot, a
burning hot ejaculate, Oh, gods, the pleasure of it, the joy
of it—!

Wall's left eye went blank and a needle of ice jammed
into his skull. He roared in sudden pain, falling away from
the startled female, his semen splashing as he pulled himself
out of her.

What—!

His left foreleg went dead and he fell to his knee,

slamming his great head against the female's rump. She snorted and danced away. His chest hurt; it was as if a giant knife had pierced him there, skewering his heart. His other foreleg gave way. Then the back legs went. He fell to all four knees and started to topple to one side.

The instant knowledge erupted from the depths of Hizta's being:

He was dying!

Panicked, Wall screamed, his voice now only a croak from within the collapsing mastodon. Help! Get me out! Get me out!

And from billions of miles away, that small and distant memory of who else he was reacted and sent the message to Dr. Jambi at his controls: "The animal is having a stroke! Pull the program out! Pull it out now!"

Hizta's last sight was of the doctor frantically working his controls.

A moment later, the old mastodon was dead.

SIXTEEN

VEATE AND HER father finished their dinner and strolled through the hotel toward the lifts. There were maybe fifteen people doing various things in the lobby, checking in or out, sitting and chatting in the small alcoves around the edges of the larger room, walking about. Some of them were aware of and watching her, she was used to that. Of a moment, however, the attention changed. Her father saw it before she did, and a grin lit his face as he turned to look behind him.

His friends had arrived.

When she was twelve, her mother had taken her to visit the Darkworld, the place where Juete and Khadaji had met. For some reason they had gone to a zoo. It was one of those all-natural places, where the animals were kept in fairly good reproductions of where they had lived in the wild. The only thing keeping the people separate from the animals' enclosures were strategically placed sheets of one-way denscris. Behind one of those nearly invisible plates had been a family of vulps.

The vulps were some off-shoot variety of lupe, smaller than the gray wolves in the adjoining enclosure. At first glance, they looked much like medium-sized dogs. They were a dark gray, almost black, and there were half a dozen of them around something that looked to be the hindquarters of a deerlike animal. Only two of the six were feeding, and these were pups, half the size of the adults. The four grown vulps stood in a ragged circle, each facing outward, guarding the young ones as they ate. That alone impressed Veate, who knew that in most canine families, the hunters ate first and left the scraps to the young. The yellow eyes of the two vulps facing in her direction were even more impressive. The animals were alert, watching, ready. She could feel their gazes through the denscris, even though they couldn't possibly see her. Nothing was going to come through the reflective plate, any more than anything was going to leave, but the vulps didn't trust that, and they were prepared to fight to protect their young. Ready to fight and die, Veate knew. She had never seen such chilling looks of offhand determination on any face before, human or animal. It seemed an almost unnatural keenness, a tuning in to everything around them so that nothing could possibly come as a surprise.

As she watched the four people dressed in dark orthoskins move toward her and her father, Veate was very much reminded of the family of vulps in the cage on the Darkworld. The two men and two women seemed to be at total ease, moving easily, relaxed, smiling. But if something came through the invisible wall at them, it was going to be in deep shit. There was an undercurrent of competence radiating from them that Veate could feel across the room. Their shifting gazes told her that they were very much aware of what was going on. It would be more than a little dangerous to provoke these people. A person would be well advised not to make any sudden moves around them.

And the leader of the deadly pack was standing right next to her. Head of the family of watchbeasts.

So. Here were the most famous of the matadors.

One was big. His musculature looked to be so dense that he'd sink in a bath of mercury. The man exuded power, he had an aura that made him seem unstoppable. Probably could walk right through a wall if it got in his way, Veate thought. He had some gray in his hair, but she couldn't have guessed how old he was from the way he moved.

Then there was a smaller man, a little younger than the giant, who moved with an indolent grace that fairly screamed at any watcher: Hey, I'm the best there is, mess with me and find out.

Two women, vanilla and chocolate. Both with hair cut short and tight. The black woman was green-eyed and a little bigger than the blonde, and the orthoskins left no doubt that both were female, though they both walked with the athletic grace that Veate usually associated with men. Very nearly a swagger, especially by the dark one.

All four wore bilateral spetsdöds, as did her father. And all four were happy to see him.

Khadaji embraced each of them in turn, hugging them with real affection. The others watched, scanning her, the room, being aware, staying alert.

The big man hugged her father last, and lifted him clear of the floor as easily as a mother does a small child.

The black woman was in charge; Veate could see that even without her speaking, though speak she did. "Put him down, Bork. That any way to treat the hero of the revolution?"

Khadaji grinned, not offended in the least, and turned to his daughter. Veate found herself feeling like an outsider. This was a family of vulps, and—did she have a place in it? She suddenly found she wanted that. She recognized the black woman's voice. She had heard her father talking to her on-com.

"This is my daughter, Veate."

Veate smiled nervously.

Khadaji nodded toward each of the quad as he spoke. "This is Dirisha Zuri, Geneva Echt, Saval Bork, and Sleel."

Veate nodded, putting living faces to the names. She had heard about these four, of course. No history of the revolution would be complete without them.

"I have rooms uplevels," Khadaji said. "Let's go talk."

The six of them started for the lift.

When the lift opened, one of the hotel's staff was inside, a short and muscular man in a tight gray coverall who was angrily pushing the control buttons on a cart loaded with luggage. The cart was canted forward and the dozen or so large cases and bags on it were tilted precariously.

"Got trouble?" the one called Saval Bork said.

The man flashed a tight smile at them. "Yeah, sorry. The front repellors went out on the cart and the damn backup wheels collapsed. Looks like I overloaded it. I'll have to get a couple of guys to help me haul the damn thing out. Would you mind waiting for another lift?"

Veate started to turn away, but stopped as the big matador stepped into the lift. "No problem," he said. "I'll get it."

"I got maybe three, four hundred kilos loaded on this sucker," the man said.

Bork squatted, hooked one hand under the front of the cart, and came partway up. The cart leveled.

"Excuse me," Bork said to Veate, who stood behind him.

Veate stood there for a few seconds before she realized she needed to move. She hurried to get out of his way. He smiled at her patiently, and when his path was clear, he backed out slowly, towing the disabled cart. Once he was out of the lift, he gently lowered the weight so as not to disturb the luggage.

"Jesu Damn, mister," the man on the left said, "that ain't possible with one hand!"

Bork shrugged. "Sorry."

Veate looked at Bork and blinked. It was not a sarcastic comment. Sorry? Why was he sorry? Because maybe he embarrassed the man? Because he was stronger than a bull? Given what he looked like, that he was powerful was no surprise. But his response was. It didn't go with the wide shoulders and thick arms.

In that moment, for no reason she could name, Veate saw past Bork's size and strength. It was one of those too-seldom flashes of insight she sometimes got of what somebody was truly like. This great hulk of a man, she suddenly knew, whatever his training and abilities with those weapons and his big hands, had the soul of a poet. Bork was, in his heart, as gentle as a mother with a newborn baby. Wasn't *that* interesting?

As they moved onto the lift, Veate turned the revelation around in her mind. If this ape-strong giant was really what she thought, then maybe she was wrong about other people she had so often quickly relegated into an easy category. She already had been forced to change her opinion of her father. That she might be wrong again was unsettling. As an Albino Exotic, you had to learn how to size people up fast, or you might find yourself at a bad disadvantage. Missing easy shots, even from the hip, was dangerous.

Veate found herself standing next to Bork. She looked up at him and smiled slightly, knowing her pheromones were flowing and calling to him. All right. Let's see how all that testosterone bubbles when it's heated, big man.

He looked at her. Shifted a hair away from her. And

blushed as he suddenly found something fascinating about
the tops of his boots.

Blushed!

Veate was charmed. She smiled, a thing of pure joy, and
almost laughed. What an interesting man. Not her usual
type at all, of course, but obviously there were depths there
that Bork did not allow anyone to plumb. She had made the
mistake she was willing to bet others had made, taking him
at face value. Judging him by what he had carefully crafted
for people to see. He was, she knew, hiding behind all that
mass, and he didn't think anybody could get past it if he
didn't let them.

Well. We'll see about that, won't we?

Bork wished the lift was bigger. He wished he'd thought
to stand near the front and not next to Emile's daughter. He
didn't know what to make of her. The way she looked in
that moment, she reminded him of Mayli; there was
something hidden under that mysterious smile, some great
power, just like Mayli always used to have.

He was drawn to her. That was probably only because she
was an Exotic and all, though, right?

Wrong. It was something else. Something beyond the
beautiful face and come-hither hormones. Bork knew about
sex and he knew the difference between lust and love; Mayli
had taught him that. There was desire, sure, but there was
something else going on here. Surely not love, but something. He hadn't felt these kinds of stirrings for five years.
And she was looking at him funny, too. Did she feel it, too?

Yeah, and she is Emile's *daughter*, and young enough to
be *his* daughter. What was wrong with him?

Control, Bork. Control.

Wall was shaken. On one level, he knew that his escape
from the dying mastodon's brain had been relatively easy,

that the essence of himself back in the computer would not allow him to be trapped. But on another level, he felt the truth of what Jambi had said. His program—he—could have been damaged by the experience. How much damage would have been done had he died with Hizta?

He was glad he had not found out.

But the important part of the experiment, the most significant thing, was it had worked. He had been able to become Hizta, to function within the body he had taken, to wear the flesh. It was a major step—major!

Back in the persona he created for Jambi's benefit, Wall spoke through the construct shimmering from the holoproj to the doctor.

"How long before we can transfer into a man?"

"A year. Maybe eighteen months."

"What?! That's too long!"

"The test animal's brain was both larger and less complex than a man's," Jambi said. "The principle is the same but the technique must be much more refined. This is not some cheap, mass-grown education virus we are speaking of here, but a complete restructuring of a neural network, plus a new personality overlay. A healthy brain is required, and the anima of a healthy brain is not apt to stand by and allow itself to be extinguished as would that of a lower animal."

"If you had unlimited funds and staff at your disposal, how much time could you save?"

The doctor blinked at the image. "Unlimited funds and staff? Hmm. Well, if I could get Thromberg from Delta and Chan Li from Anaheim Research, plus another three biogens in the billion-kay range . . ."

"How long?"

"If everything went well, we might be able to cut that in half. Perhaps less."

"Could you do it in three months?"

"Unlikely. Not impossible, but unlikely. If we eliminated safety testing on primates, perhaps."

"If you can do it in three months, I will fund whatever research you choose to do for the rest of your life. At any amount up to a billion standards a year. And if you want, you will also be installed as Director of the Helsinki Institute."

"The Helsinki Institute! Impossible! And a billion standards? That—that's unheard of for pure research!"

"I can do both of these things. There is your carrot, doctor. If you can transfer my . . . program into a man successfully within three months, you win the prize."

The doctor was speechless. Wall could almost hear the man's mind whirring with the possibilities. And in truth, probably he could manage both promises, given his abilities in the computer-run worlds. Not that he intended to keep those promises, of course. If the doctor could do as he wished, he would no longer be necessary, and funding him for the rest of his life would be cheap, given how long the man was apt to live. The secret he would know would make him much too dangerous to leave alive.

Three months was not so long to wait for a miracle. And in the meantime, he could keep his enemies hopping, dancing to his tune. They wouldn't have a chance.

And as to the man who would become the new Wall?

That was easy. There had never been any doubt as to that, none at all.

SEVENTEEN _____

KHADAJI'S HOTEL ROOM was large enough so that even the four additional matadors did not overwhelm it. They had things to discuss. He let Dirisha take the lead.

"We talked to Jersey Reason," she said. "He says the recording we showed him is a computer construct. It wasn't Massey or an old recording of him, nor was it an actor."

"Interesting," Khadaji said.

"It gets more so," Dirisha said. "Whoever did it was the best at it Reason has ever seen. Given that he produced a holoproj that fooled us into thinking it was real, that is saying something."

"It didn't fool *all* of us," Sleel put in.

"I stand corrected," Dirisha said.

"So what does that tell us?" Khadaji said.

Geneva said, "Whoever is playing this game has big stads and big resources."

"We knew that," Sleel said.

"Can Reason give us any leads?"

"Yeah, we got some names," Dirisha said. "Half a dozen people who can program simulations close to what we saw.

181

He says none of them were that good a couple years back, but they might have had some kind of breakthrough."

"Well, it's another path to explore," Khadaji said.

"We've got Black Sun doing some checking for us," Bork said. "Courtesy of Dirisha."

"You do get around, don't you?"

Dirisha grinned and gave a little shrug. "How's things on your end?"

Khadaji said, "Slow. Veate and I interviewed one of the *Soldatutmarkt* high-ups. Didn't get much, but we'll poke around in that area some more, maybe.

"Rajeem has his people rolling on it, and we have whatever official help we need."

"None of which is getting my mother back," Veate put in.

"Somebody took her for a reason," Dirisha said. "If she's dead, she's dead and there's nothing we can do about it. If she's alive, it doesn't make any sense for them to torture her, so she's probably being held somewhere in relative comfort."

"This is bigger than just Juete," Khadaji said. "She's one of the cogs but not the whole machine. We'll find her sooner or later."

Khadaji saw his daughter's distress and impatience. She was an Exotic and used to getting what she wanted without having to wait for it. But she also knew she couldn't solve this problem on her own. She would have to learn that sometimes you had to wait and there was no help for it. That didn't make it any easier, knowing it, but there was nothing to be done.

"Okay, we have computer people to check out," Khadaji said. "We'll get started tomorrow."

"They got a gym in this place?" Bork asked.

"Uplevels," Veate said. "I'll show you."

Bork glanced at Khadaji, and it was all Khadaji could do to keep from smiling at the big man. Veate was interested in Bork; Bork felt it, and he was worried about what his old boss would think about that.

And how *did* he feel? She had probably slept with hundreds of lovers before he knew she existed, and she was an adult. It was maybe a little late to start getting feelings of fatherly concern, wasn't it? Besides, they didn't come any better than Saval. If anything, he ought to be concerned about what his daughter might do to Bork. The mue was still grieving over Mayli Wu, dead these five years past. He was more likely to get hurt in an affair of the heart—or other glands—than was an accomplished Albino Exotic, daughter or not.

"I'll go with you," Dirisha said. "I could use a workout myself."

"Me, too," Geneva said.

This time Khadaji did smile. Dirisha and Geneva had also seen Veate's interest in Bork. It seemed as if the giant mue had himself a couple of chaperones.

He saw a tiny frown pass over Veate's face.

There were other things to which Wall needed to attend, aside from his artificial fantasies and worry about the medical side of his plan. He sent forth splinters of himself to take care of these tasks.

A robot ship carrying several million tons of high-grade uranium ore through the outreaches of the Haradali System garbled a beam-reflect, despite the triple-rendundant navigation gear designed to prevent just that. The ship veered off course and slammed into a city-sized asteroid at speed. The ship was destroyed, the ore scattered, and the asteroid was knocked sufficiently out of its safe orbit so that it would make planetfall on Tatsu within three months. Such an intersection would destroy a fair chunk of real estate on the world, probably killing a few hundred thousand in the bargain. It took a military-engineering unit nearly four thousand work hours and three million standards to correct the course of the asteroid.

A computer error infected the Bank of Spandle's mainframe and backups so that every customer on the planet, as well as any in the four wheelworlds in the Mu System, suddenly had their account balances tripled. Most of the customers reported the mistake. Some of them withdrew their new wealth in negotiable precious and caught ships for other systems. Some of it would be recoverable, when the thieves were caught, but the upfront loss amounted to several hundred million stads.

The air-ground traffic control grid on Mason went into a snarl during rush hour on a busy Firstday, effectively shutting down three fourths of the planet's transportation for seven hours. It was worse than if the system had simply gone completely blank; it was as if some malevolent force had entered the grid. Landbuses were directed into dead ends; traffic signals on noncontrolled roadways all instructed manual controllers to go ahead; half the bumper magnetics switched polarity. Two hundred people died in accidents, another six hundred were injured, and the property damage was estimated in the ten million stad range, not counting lost work-time.

The leader of a reincarnation cult on Maro, the eldest son of the Martyr of Maro, received a divine visitation, after which he and fifty of his most faithful devotees took to the streets of Notzeerath, armed with ancient temple axes, striking down any who chanced to be in their path. Seventy-three people were ritually decapitated and seventeen more were badly injured before the local police managed to shoot or capture the surviving fanatics.

The galactic edcom channel aimed at Level 1 children (bright T.S. three-year-olds to average T.S. five-year-olds) interrupted its showing of holographic number and counting animations with a broadcast of a hardcore entcom feature depicting a highly graphic multiple-partnered sexual orgy. This was followed by what at first seemed a personal apology by the head of the Galactic Network, until, in the middle of it, the camera flashed a wide-angle view of the man, showing him naked and masturbating.

Tens of millions of parents suddenly found themselves answering billions of questions they had not expected to be asked for some years.

In his computer cocoon, Marcus Jefferson Wall smiled an electronic smile. The lack of flesh had some compensations. Power was one.

The gym in Emile's hotel did not have any free weights, but there were some magnetic piston machines, and full range-of-motion swivel gear. It was better than nothing. Dirisha and Geneva were practicing the Ninety-seven Steps in the area behind the pool, gliding along smoothly in the intricate sumito fighting dances.

Emile's daughter leaned against a wall next to the muscle-building machineries, watching Bork.

Bork was nervous. He'd stripped to a pair of shorts, a workout shirt and slippers, although he kept his spetsdöds on. Since the swivel machines had padded grips, he didn't need gloves.

The machine looked something like a big exoskeleton, mounted to thick uprights that ran from floor to ceiling, where they were anchored on structural I-beams. There were several braces, to simulate benches in front and back, and side supports for the more esoteric exercises. The device was simple enough to operate. You stepped into the shoe clamps, stuck your hands into the grips, and were ready to work out. This was one of the old voice-actuated models; the newer units had myosensors that read impulses and lactic acid build-up and adjusted automatically to take the worked fibers to a preprogrammed percentage of use, ranging from mild to failure, depending on the initial setting. Bork didn't much like the machines, preferring his own biofeedback, but you had to make do with what you had.

He stepped into the machine, adjusted the height and reach, and ran through a fast r-o-m warmup with a few kilos. There were a lot of ways to do a workout, but Bork preferred the old standard of going from the center of the body outward. He usually started with rowing and latpulls for his back, crunches for his abs, pecdeck and upright benches for his chest, then worked his low back, legs, shoulders and finally arms. Thirty or forty minutes a session, four or five times a week, was all it usually took to keep the tone up, three or four sets a body part were plenty, though you had to do more if you wanted to build new muscle or gain strength. He was already big enough and strong enough.

Once he got his joints warm, Bork forgot that Veate was watching him. There was no point in working out if you didn't concentrate on it, and he'd learned how to shut out distractions a long time ago. He'd see somebody come through the door with a gun if that happened, but anything less dangerous would have to wait until he was done.

Lats, first, he decided. Start light and pyramid the poundage. "Lat pulldowns," he said. "A hundred kilos."

He felt the muscles under his arms adjust to the strain as the r-o-m gear took up the slack and pulled his hands up over his head. "Wider," he said. The grips moved slowly apart. "Hold."

The motion was the same as if he were doing wide-grip chins when he pulled the handles down. Since it was less than body weight, it was easy enough. Once he kicked the resistance up, he'd have to use the braces and shoe clamps to hold him in place.

He brought the grips straight down until they were level with his shoulders.

Okay. That's one . . .

Because Bork was calling out the amounts of weight he was using in the exercises, Veate got an idea of just how strong he was as she watched him. She had known some powerful people, men, women, mues of both sexes, but none of them came close to Bork. With his back braced he was currently pushing straight in front of himself to arms' length, something close to four times her weight as if it were no effort at all.

And he had forgotten she was there. She moved several times, in ways she knew attracted sexual attention, but she was wasting her time. He was into this, and she could have been invisible.

Several other people in the gym had stopped what they were doing to watch Bork, and Veate heard one man gasp as Bork ordered the machine's computer to increase the resistance on the squat exercise. His muscles bulged under the thin skin; she could see the ridges and lines of them, the tortuous veins popping up across his thighs and in his calves as he moved. He was pumped up even larger than he had been before; it seemed as if he would burst if the swollen knots got any larger, but they increased and somehow, he did not explode.

His breathing was heavy, sweat runneled down his back and face, and his skin grew redder. When he worked his arms, first the backs, then the fronts, then the backs again, they grew so that they were easily as big around as her head.

The harder he worked, the more excited Veate became. She fought it, because she knew it was unreasoning. Here was one who could protect her from anything and the call was primitive and urgent, built somehow into her genes with her pale skin and sexual self. Seek the dominant male for a mate. It went against her sense of being, of mindful determination, of her unwillingness to depend on anyone but herself, but it was there nonetheless. She could resist it, but she could not deny it. Mine, she thought, as a two-year-old child will claim all she perceives. Mine, mine, mine!

After a time, Bork began to warm down, using smaller and smaller amounts of weight. Finally, he was done.

Veate tossed him a towel as he disengaged himself from the machine and stood there breathing heavily.

"Thanks," he said, wiping the sweat from his face and neck.

She wanted to leap on him right where he stood.

"Come to my room," she said. She allowed her pheromones to sing, she became the most potent of Sirens, she was totally ready for him. She would make him weak before she finished with him. She had never met her match, and he might be as close as ever she would get.

He took a deep breath and let it out. "I don't think that would be a good idea, Veate."

If he had slapped her she could not have been any more surprised. "What?"

"I'm as old as Emile."

"What has age got to do with anything? Don't you want me?"

If he said no, she would kill herself. She couldn't be that wrong, she could feel him yearning toward her.

"Yeah, I sure do. A whole lot. But it's not right."

"Listen, Bork, if I want you and you want me, what the hell is wrong with it?"

"You don't love me. I don't love you."

She stared at him, still unable to believe it. "Love? What are you talking about? You've never been with anybody as good as I am! You never will be!"

"Yes, I have. It isn't about technique. It's about love."

Her rage was too much to bear. She turned and stalked out of the gym, striding past Dirisha and Geneva and the other patrons of the gym. Even in her anger, she could feel the others watching her, was aware of how many of the men and women looking at her would give all they had to possess her in the way she had just offered to that apish lout who had turned her down.

Turned her down! Nobody had *ever* refused her! Not ever!

"What *did* you say to her, Bork?" Dirisha asked. "If eyes were lasers, you'd be a grilled slab on the floor."

Bork shook his head. "We, uh, had a disagreement."

"Wait until Sleel hears that one," Geneva said. "He thinks Dirisha is the master of understatement."

Bork twisted the towel uncomfortably in his big hands. Sweat dripped from it onto the floor.

Oh, man, he thought. She sure enough was mad, all right. Maybe he ought to try to explain it to her. It wasn't her fault.

Then again, given how upset she was, maybe he'd better wait awhile before he said anything.

EIGHTEEN

VEATE'S ANGER STILL bubbled in her, but it was more a simmer than a roil when she happened across Sleel in the hotel's bookstore. He was in the philosophy section looking at a holoprojic display when Veate found him. For just a heartbeat, he looked embarrassed to be discovered there.

"How's it going?" Sleel said. He edged slowly out of the philosophy display, past the racks of marble-sized stainless steel recording spheres in their soft rubber sockets, trying to seem as if he hadn't had any real interest being there.

"Tell me about Saval Bork," she said.

Sleel laughed. "What's to tell? He's a big mue, got muscle he'll never use and more testosterone than a ball transplant bank."

"Then why won't he have sex with me?"

The comment obviously caught Sleel off guard. "Huh? Uh, well, if you're looking for somebody to, uh, fill in, I, uh—"

"I'm not," she said, snapping out the words. "What about Bork?"

Sleel shook his head. "Let's go to the bar. This might take a few minutes."

She followed him from the bookstore. She was not fond of puzzles and she wanted to solve this one, now.

"Can I ask you something?" Bork said to Geneva.

The blonde was watching the metroplex's traffic from the balcony outside Khadaji's room, as Bork stepped out to stand next to her. Below on the surface streets, wheeled vehicles rolled past; in the air above the ground, computer-controlled carts stayed in their tightly defined lanes, carrying passengers to and fro. None of the lanes inside the city were stacked high enough to reach the level of their rooms.

"Sure," Geneva said. "About Veate, right?"

"How did you know?"

"Come on, Bork. How long have we known each other? Ten, eleven years?"

"Yeah, well, I can't figure out why she's so mad at me."

"Let me guess. She wanted you and you turned her down?"

"What, you taken up mind reading? How'd you know that?"

Geneva turned and flashed her smile at him. Even though most of her attention was focused on him, he could see her scanning the air and hotel facade, much as he continued to do. "I can't think of anything else that would piss off an albino so much. She'd be more than used to getting proposals; turning somebody down would be as easy as breathing for her. But *getting* turned down isn't something she'd have much experience at, if any. Especially by you."

"Why would I be anything special?"

"Because even a blind woman could tell you wanted to go somewhere and roll around and break furniture with Veate. Chang, anybody who tried to walk between you two would have bounced off the lust like it was a force field."

"Yeah. But it wouldn't be right," he said. "She's Emile's daughter. And besides—"

"You don't love each other," Geneva finished.

Bork shook his head. "You could get work in a carnival or something, you know?"

"Bork, Bork, Bork. I can see. Back at the Villa, you remember how I looked when I fell for Dirisha?"

He grinned. "Yeah. Dopey."

"No more dopey than you did whenever Mayli was around."

He turned and stared out at the city.

After what seemed like a long time, he said, "I really miss her, you know."

She laid a hand on his arm. "I know. We all miss her. And some of that is going on now with Veate."

He shook himself out of the memory. "Still doesn't explain why she got so mad."

"You took away her power," she said. "Look at it like this: suppose you went into a weightlifting contest against somebody, and he could somehow wave his hand and reduce your physical strength to, oh, say, my level. He's over there pressing half the planet overhead and the best you can do is maybe fifty kilos. How do you think that would make you feel?"

"Pretty bad," Bork admitted. "No offense, Geneva."

She laughed. "No offense taken. But you see my point? Your physical strength is something you take for granted. It's a part of you. If it suddenly disappeared, if somebody could *make* it disappear, you'd probably resent the hell out of them."

"Yeah, I expect you're right."

"That's what you did to Veate. Her attraction is something she's always had. She was born with it, it's her power, and when you turned her down, you raised a doubt in her she probably never had to deal with before. I imagine it scared her worse than anything else you could have done."

Bork sighed. "I wasn't looking to do that."

"I know. Eventually she'll figure it out, too. But her first reaction was from fear. Her very best, her most potent trick suddenly didn't work anymore. Her first thought probably was that something was wrong with you. But her second thought would have been that something was wrong with *her*. Had to be pretty scary."

"Yeah, I guess it must have been." He reached out and hugged Geneva, being careful not to hold her too tightly. "Thanks," he said.

She beamed at him. "Sure. What are friends for, if not to point out when you do stupid shit?"

The hotel bar was like a dozen Veate had been in before; the colors were too bright, the sounds too loud, the decorator's taste less than superb. She sipped at the small beer she'd ordered, then shook her head. "Mayli Wu was a whore?"

Sleel nodded. "Best I ever had. They called her Sister Clamp; we all met at Emile's pub on Greaves, back when he was doing his one-man war against the Confed. We didn't know it, what he was doing, but that's where Dirisha, Bork, Sister and I first got together.

"Mayli was a medic, full M.D., before she went into the pleasure business. Applied research, she called it.

"Later, she was at Matador Villa with us. Taught a course in love. She and Bork, they wound up partnered, and it was something to see them together."

Veate felt an irrational stab of jealously. "So, what happened to her? Why'd they sunder, if this was such a cosmic connection?"

"She got killed. We hit a power station on Earth, during the Revolution. We lost Geneva's father, Red, there too."

Sleel rubbed at his shoulder, as if it suddenly pained him. "I was wearing a prosthetic arm at the time. It ate a couple of explosive rounds and got blown away; I also lost a foot. Wound up having to regrow the stupid damned foot along with the arm. Anyway, I went down, looked like I was gonna be a war history footnote.

"Bork was right next to Mayli and Red when they got hit. He grabbed them both up, carried them to our transport, then came back and collected Dirisha and me like we were toys. I'd have been dead otherwise."

Sleel laughed. "Hell of a business, revolution. Maybe I'll skip the next one, run an ammo concession or something. Anyway, that's Bork. Always saving somebody's ass.

"So that you don't take things personally, you ought to know that I don't think Bork has been with anybody since Mayli died. He took it hard. Real hard."

Veate stared at Sleel. "He's been celibate for more than five years?" Such an action was beyond anything she could personally imagine. Oh, sure, she knew it was possible. Not for an Albino Exotic, but for tintskins; there were religious reasons and like that, it sometimes happened.

"That's what I'd bet on."

Buddha. How could she compete with a ghost? And this Saval Bork was getting more complex every time anybody said anything about him. Maybe it wasn't her. Maybe she had been right when she'd felt him want her. But now what was she going to do? Sure, there were billions of lovers out there; she could just walk away and do what she had always done, pick the lucky ones from the lines waiting. Somehow, though, that didn't seem as satisfying as once it had. She wanted Bork. He intrigued her as no one else ever had. She had never wanted a lover she couldn't have. It was a painful feeling. Was that what other people felt like when she refused them?

Damn, she wished she'd never gotten mixed up with her father and his crew of misfits.

No? came the truth seeker in her. When have you ever been more stimulated, had a more interesting time? Don't tell me, sister. That ship won't fly.

On Rift, after having escaped death when a boxcar from orbit unexpectedly lost power and plowed into the building next to his, Full Professor Steven Manning Thromberg received a job offer from Earth. The offer was accompanied by a certified credit cube worth an amount equal to three years' salary, for "incidental expenses." It took Thromberg all of five seconds to make his decision. If Elbu ra Jambi had this kind of money to throw around, he'd be unstoppable, and Thromberg wanted to be there. He started packing his travel case immediately.

Chan Li disliked Elbu ra Jambi as much as he did anyone, but he respected the man's abilities. The communication and the stads attached convinced Li fast enough. If Jambi said he was close to full implant, you could put that in the bank and draw interest on it. Li wanted very much to be on the winning team when that biological miracle happened. Better a part of the credit than none. You didn't have to be a meteorologist to ascertain wind direction. He left within hours.

"Salinas Biogentics," the bored salesman said. "What? What?! Hold it a second." The man on the com waved his hand and put the call on hold. He turned to the other order board salesman and said, "Heysoo Damn, Flint, I got somebody on the com who says he wants to buy three biogens in the billion-kay range! Yes, I think he's serious.

"Hello, still there? How, ah, soon would you need these units, mister—ah—?"

"*Doctor* Elbu ra Jambi," came the crisp reply. "I need them yesterday."

"And on what terms . . . ?"

"Full payment on delivery."

The salesman was already punching in a credit code request. J-a-m-b-i . . . Holy Mother Wesaw's Left Tit! Look at that stad balance! The guy was worth billions!

The Vice-President in Charge of Sales came running in, having noticed the conversation on his monitor. He waved his hands excitedly at the salesman. "Tell him they'll be in the air in an hour! Get an address for delivery! Get a jet; if he's out of the hemisphere, charter a suborbital boxcar!"

The size of his potential commission was making the salesman feel giddy. "If you're on Earth, you'll have them before dinner time, doctor. Is that fast enough?"

"It'll have to do, I suppose."

"Here's an idea," Sleel said to Dirisha, as they took an early evening stroll along the walkway next to the hotel. "Let's leave Bork and Emile's daughter alone in a room with the door locked."

"Anybody ever tell you what a nasty man you are?"

"All the time. Hell, Bork's got his spetsdöds. He can always shoot her."

"I'm glad I never slept with you, Sleel."

"Aw, come on. Don't talk to *me* about being nasty. You were just afraid I'd spoil you for any other lover."

"You got me. That was it, all right." She punched him lightly on the shoulder. They both laughed.

A bomb went off in the sub-basement of the Office of the Galactic Census Bureau, destroying a cross-index computer. This in itself would not have been so bad, except that the back-up data for that particular computer was destroyed in a mysterious fire inside a shielded vault only moments after the explosion. The information could be reconstructed, of course, since it had been gathered at the planetary level by field workers and subsequently logged into local computers, but it would take two things always in short supply in any bureaucracy: time and money. Certain political boundaries that would have shifted because of population changes therefore stayed the same, since system-level reappointment had to be approved by official Republic sanctions. On Mwanamamke, where a put-upon and heretofore patient minority of ethnic Mtuans had been held in check only by the promise of better representation in the Bibi Arusi System Council, riots killed a hundred and eighty-eight people when the Council vetoed Mtuan reparations for injuries offered the Mtuans during the last days of the Confed's reign.

The White Radio relay station orbiting Ago's Moon in the Faust System malfunctioned, tapped somehow into the local comnet, and scrambled a hundred million communications in ways beyond anyone's experience. The most interesting example of the misrouted calls came when a shop owner in the Bom Chu shopping complex in Boot City on Bocca called his wife from his business, a distance of some nine kilometers, to tell her he would be late for dinner. The local toll call was picked up by the Galactic Net, bounced from the Faust System out through the Mu, Nu, and Tau Systems, sent through nineteen substations, at a distance/station charge of some one hundred and six light years, before being sent back to the intended spouse. What should have been a call amounting to a cost of less than two demistads was billed to the shop owner's account at seven hundred and fifty-nine standards. The mistake was caught and apologies tendered later, of course, but not before the shop owner punished his teenaged daughter.

A weathersat weighing over a thousand kilos orbiting Aqua took leave of its ellipse and came down through the roof of the galaxy's largest indoor aquarium. Fortunately, the aquarium was closed for the evening. Nearly a quarter of the marine animals died when the largest of the exhibit tanks, a one-of-a-kind denscris display holding more than eighty million gallons of seawater, was ruptured. Several workers drowned in the resulting flood. Since the aquarium was the only building complex on Renfrew Island and the island itself the only land mass for two hundred kilometers in any direction, the satellite could not have picked a more precise location to which it could have done more damage.

Wall found that he was enjoying himself more and more. It was not so much what damage he could effect that interested him, but the style and manner in which he could manage it. He had only himself with whom to compete, after all, and his limits and imagination allowed him much leeway. They were such easy creatures to manipulate, he realized. Trapped by their own technologies and at his mercy.

And Marcus Jefferson Wall had little mercy left in him. Very little indeed.

Alone in the elevator, Veate pondered what she had learned. Her neat life was out of kilter. Her mother was gone, she had discovered that her long-held beliefs about her father were almost entirely wrong, and now there was this hard hulking man with an inner softness who bedeviled her more than any man ever had.

It was not fair to have to deal with all of these things at once.

She couldn't find her mother any faster, not with the best hunters in the galaxy on her side, so there was nothing to be done there.

As for her father, well, he just kept surprising her. She couldn't hold on to her old anger, it kept being blown away by the truth, and she was too smart not to see that.

Then there was Bork. She had waved her sexuality at him; it had never crossed her mind that he would be able to resist it, and yet, somehow, he had. Like it was nothing, no strain, no bother. Nobody had ever refused her before. It hurt.

What could she do? How could she convince Bork that she was worthwhile, that she had something to offer? She had offered him the ultimate treasure, hadn't she?

Well, that hadn't been enough. What would she have to do to get to him? What part of her hidden self would she have to risk?

Scary thoughts, those of change, and Veate would have preferred that they not come up, but—here they were. She couldn't just turn away and pretend they'd never happened.

Ah, Mother, why didn't you tell me this might happen? What am I going to do?

NINETEEN _____

FINDING HIMSELF ALONE in his room, Khadaji put in a call to Pen. The connection was made, and the local comnet quickly gave him the image of his old teacher. He was, after all, only halfway around the planet, not across the galaxy.

The holoproj of the shrouded figure tendered an invisible smile. "Ah, Emile. How is everyone?"

"Still alive, so far. We haven't located Juete yet. How are things there?"

"Pretty much back to normal. Diamond discovered the source of the oxidation explosive, but it's a dead end. The sale and delivery were done via com; nobody saw the buyer."

"That doesn't surprise me. We're dealing with somebody who is an expert at computer manipulation. The casino on Vishnu had its security breached when Juete was kidnapped and later when half a dozen hired assassins bypassed it, and the system showed absolutely no signs of tampering. The attack on Rajeem's ship, the phony evidence against Sleel, the fake Massey, every way we turn we have someone's fine hand performing more electronic wizardry."

The image of Pen nodded. "We live in an age where such things are inseparably entwined with our lives," he said. "There have been more than a few other unnatural disasters around the galaxy of late, most of which are connected to major computer systems."

Khadaji said, "Any of this causing problems with your comp set-up?"

"No. Our program security has held firm thus far. Even a genius would have trouble overcoming the dozens of geniuses who thickened the defenses over the last couple of hundred years."

"And what does integratics have to say about all this?"

"That it will come to a head in roughly eleven point three weeks," Pen said. "Give or take a few hours."

"Three months. Got a location, by any chance?"

"A stellar system. Here."

"Let me know when you narrow it down."

"Of course. You should know that there is great personal danger involved, Emile."

Khadaji chuckled. "So, what else is new? You skate the edge, sometimes you get cut."

"Nonetheless, you should take particular care."

"You are getting soft in your old age, Pen. You never warned me back when I was hacking away at the roots of the Confed."

"You were not in as much danger then as now."

That brought Khadaji up short.

He was tempted to stay online, to chat with his old teacher about inconsequential matters, but it would have been forced. They had never been much on small talk, not at the first when Pen had found him, not later, when the revolution had begun moving in earnest. Khadaji discommed.

That he was in some personal danger was no surprise, though the comment that it was worse now than when he'd opposed the Confed was news. Back then, there were armies that wanted him dead, literally billions of enemies. What kind of opposition today could compare to that?

It was a sobering question.

Dirisha and Geneva had found a little restaurant specializing in Tomadachi cuisine, not more than twenty minutes' walk from the hotel. Dusk was beginning to shade into night as they left the place. The stillwalk was thick with people going about their business, but most of them gave the two armed women plenty of room. The evening air was crisp, with a fresh breeze from the water bringing a faint tang of salt with it.

"The eel was pretty good," Geneva said.

"The loopfish was better. Maybe just a tad too much smoke, but it's a long way to Tomadachi to find better."

"Coming from a woman who can't cook failsafe soypro, that's quite a compliment."

"Yeah? Well, it's hard to master everything, brat. If I wasted my time learning how to cook, when would I practice my swaggering?"

"You've never going to let me forget I said that, are you?"

Dirisha grinned. "Are you kidding?"

"Ahead and to the left," Geneva said.

"I see him. You spot any company?"

"Not yet."

He was slim, moved like a young man at first glance, though that was sometimes hard to say in these days of surgical and hormonal reconstruction, and he was pretty good at shadowing. He was doing a front-tail, staying well ahead of the two matadoras, acting as if he had no interest in them at all. He would have fooled most people, Dirisha figured. He had been with them since they'd left the restaurant, at the least.

Geneva said, "I think he's alone. What do you want to do?"

"Let's see how he plays it. So far he's the only devil we know."

The local shops began to thin somewhat as Dirisha and Geneva approached the underpass for the eight-lane main highway through the plex, and the patrons grew fewer in number. The boy—Dirisha guessed his age at sixteen or seventeen from his moves and general appearance—stayed well ahead of them as he neared the underpass. More of the other pedestrians found shops or left the walk for other reasons, so that only a few continued on to the underpass, a well-lighted rectangle of smooth-walled stressed plast-crete. He'd be a lot more visible there, and Dirisha figured he realized it, because he stepped into a smokeshop to the right.

"He wants to get behind us," Geneva said.

"Yeah, probably wants to see my swagger from that angle."

"I'm going to hit you."

"You getting perverse in your old age, brat?"

"Bork is right. We've been married too long."

"You want a divorce?"

"I really *am* going to hit you."

Dirisha smiled at her lover. Geneva smiled back.

"The smokeshop is as good a place as any," Dirisha said.

When they reached the entrance to the shop, Dirisha went first, stepping immediately to the left as she entered the building. Geneva was immediately behind her, and she moved right.

The smokeshop smelled great, a combination of sharp and spicy scents made up of tobaccos, janes, *rok'eed,* and others she could not name. The boy stood at the counter, his back to her, pretending to look at a display of handcarved pipes and injector tubes. He was good, she had to give him that, good enough to know he'd burned the tail and was boxed. He turned, nodded once to let Dirisha and Geneva know, and made to leave the shop.

Geneva went outside first, ahead of the boy, Dirisha following him. The black matadora didn't think he meant them any direct harm, but if he did, he wouldn't be able to get them both without eating a spetsdöd dart, and he knew it.

Something about him seemed familiar. Dirisha searched her memory. She hadn't dealt with many children, and it took only a little while to scan those she had known.

He kept his hands away from his body, fingers spread wide, posture relaxed. Outside, he turned to face Dirisha. Geneva had him covered from behind.

"Long time," the boy said.

Dirisha remembered. "Resh," she said. "Long time and a long way from home."

He nodded, as if he'd expected her to recognize him. It had been more than six years since she'd seen him, and then only once. He'd been a street rat who delivered a message when she'd gone to her homeworld to collect Rajeem from where she'd stashed him. What was Resh doing here?

"The man said to give you this."

Even though his hands had seemed empty, Resh produced a thin circle of hard plastic the size of a demistad coin and held it up for Dirisha to see.

She nodded and took the message disc from him. Black

Sun had a long reach. That the boy had come from them she didn't doubt.

"Tell the man we owe him."

"He knows."

Dirisha glanced at Geneva and gestured with one hand. To Resh, she said, "See you later."

"It's a small galaxy," he said, grinning. He nodded once at Geneva, then strolled away.

"Do we know him?" Geneva asked, after the boy had gone.

"Picture him about this high"—Dirisha held her hand at chest height—"before we started moving on the Confed."

"The kid who brought Emile's message in Flat Town?"

"Good for you." She looked at the message disc. "Word from Maro. Something we can use, I hope."

The Fifty-Seven stood ready to attack, prepared to die for the glory of the One True God if need be, but convinced that they would not fail. The One True God had spoken to them through Three, the Holy Conduit, and the Word filled the Fifty-Seven with unmitigated joy beyond what any mere unenlightened mortal could understand. It was the work of a lifetime for any of the lesser faithful to become one of the Fifty-Seven, to be thus linked to the original members of the First Church. The original Fifty-Seven had been privy to the Words of the Prophet Himself, had been washed in the Light of His Being, and to achieve Fifty-Sevenness was to bask in that same glow. There was no sacrifice too great, no task too hard, no thing whatsoever that could be denied to the One True God. He had not spoken so directly or forcefully to any Fifty-Seven since the Beginning as He had recently to Three. Members One through Five had been witnesses to the Divine Communication, and Five had been so overcome by the visitation that she had fallen into a coma for several hours afterward. The word of the One True God was power beyond compare.

But all were alert and prepared for the assault now. Ancient holy weapons had been made ready, new ones procured, and preparations finalized. The Fifty-Seven had ingested the Holy Chemicals; they were thus impervious to pain, filled with the Spirit of the One True God, and subject to visual flashes of His Glory. They wore the ceremonial robes of green silk and laughed among themselves as the chartered bus took them to their rendezvous with destiny. They'd had to kill the driver, of course, and put Forty-Nine in his place, but that was only a small detail. The work of the One True God could not be denied. He had commanded and it was theirs to obey. They all knew the words by heart; the Holy Orders were seared into their souls:

The President of the Republic is an agent of Evil. He must die. Who accomplishes this will be at my right hand, yea, even until the end of Eternity.

To sit at the side of the One True God forever? There was not one among the Fifty-Seven who wouldn't kill a billion presidents for that!

The elevator doors opened and Bork started to enter the lift.

Inside, alone, stood Veate.

Bork hesitated.

"Are you going to just stand there?" she asked.

Bork took a deep breath and let it out, then moved.

The lift began to move upward. Veate said, "Hold." The elevator stopped.

Bork regarded the young woman. He felt a coldness in the pit of his stomach.

"When I was twelve," she said softly, "my mother introduced me to my first lover. There had been others who had tried to be before him, of course, but Juete was diligent in her watchfulness. She didn't want me to start too early."

Bork shifted his weight uncomfortably.

"His name was Arl, and he was maybe fifty T.S. He had been my mother's lover a couple of years past, and she had picked him for me then, against the day when I was old enough. He was from Spandle. Old enough to be my grandfather.

"Arl was a teacher. It was his job, his avocation, his reason for being. He lived to teach. He made me feel cherished, he spent weeks preparing me, weeks, so that when finally we breached my virginity, it was but one part of the total experience. As a lover, he was kind, gentle, and expert. It was a beautiful thing, my first time.

"On most worlds, sleeping with a twelve-year-old human or mue is a crime—and rightly so. But an Albino Exotic is not made the same way normal humans are, and twelve is old by our standards. Many of us start years earlier. We reach puberty, on average, at nine. I was sexually mature at eight. But I was protected by my mother, who wanted me to have an experience most of us Exotics do not have time to enjoy.

"Arl was patient, he was careful, and he showed me how good lovemaking could be, if one took the time and effort to make it so. I have been with scores of partners since— men, women, humans, mues—and some experiences have been better, though not many. I have learned more about myself; it is not bragging to say I've become skilled to the point of artistry. It is what my kind were created to do. It's something we *have* to have, to feel whole."

She looked up at him, locked her gaze to his, and he could feel her willing him to see and understand her.

"You said that it isn't about technique for you. That it is about love. It is beyond my understanding that a person could, for some abstract principle, give up something around which my life and the lives of my kind are based. That you would refuse my offer, something that many have fought for and at least one has killed to have, impresses me. Especially since I *know* how much you want me."

Her voice, when next she spoke, was quieter still, and he heard the quivering undercurrent in it.

"Arl taught me about sex and until now, sex has always been enough. I know what there is to know about technique, I know the ways of pleasure, and—I don't know why—it suddenly isn't enough anymore. That scares me. I never worried about love. I don't know about love. Before, it didn't matter, I didn't need it; but now, I *need* to know."

She took a deep breath. "Will you teach me about love, Saval Bork?"

And in that moment, she had no defenses; he could see her for what she was: a young woman who only pretended to be hard and invulnerable. And one who had just opened her heart to him. Just as Mayli had done, so long ago. You can't force it, she had told him. Love comes as it will and it may leave just as quickly. You must be in the moment or you will lose it. You can't define it, but you will know it when you see it.

Now, in this moment, Bork saw something he had never expected to see again. It was like a hammer to his solar plexus. He felt weak. He felt blessed. He felt cursed.

Damn.

He sighed. There was really only one choice. "Okay," he said.

He gathered her into his arms and hugged her, that was all. Not quite like a father holds a child, but not like one lover holds another. Not yet.

She started to cry. After a little bit, Bork did too.

Damn.

TWENTY _____

THE BUS FANNED to a stop in front of the Presidential Office Building in Brisbane, settling to the safety wheels in a blast of dusty air. The three side doors slid open and the passengers, all dressed in billowy green robes, began to pour from the bus like offworld tourists discovering a historical marker. Only instead of cameras, these tourists carried weapons. Some bore modern carbines, some had military wands, others brandished antique rifles or hand-guns. A few in the small mad sea of green even waved swords. There were fifty-seven of them, all human men or women. They screamed and chanted as they began to move, yelling "Death to the Evil One!" and "Carlos must die!" and "For the Glory of the One True God!"

They rushed the nearest entrance gate, which the security computer immediately closed and locked.

The attackers began firing at the control mechanism.

Three of the green-clad people were splattered by ricocheting bullet fragments seriously enough to be knocked down bleeding, while several others were wounded but not incapacitated.

Eight of the more impatient leaders leaped into the densethorn hedge, trying to bull or cut their way through to the grounds beyond. It was like trying to shove through a nest of fishhooks. All eight were impaled upon the brambles, held fast as bugs in amber.

As the gate continued to withstand the barrage of small arms fire, four more of the screaming fanatics set themselves as human catapults, using their interlaced hands to launch others of their fellows into tumbling flights over the living barrier. Two of these pseudoflights fell short, ending in falls into the hedge, trapping securely the would-be birds. Two fliers attained the grounds. Of these, one broke her left tibia upon landing, and the other sprained his ankle. The one with the sprained ankle continued to hobble toward his goal. The one with the broken leg crawled.

The gate, not designed to hold up under the concentrated hammering of more than a dozen weapons at once, finally sprang open. The remaining attackers boiled through the breach and charged the building.

The grounds' automatic zap fields triggered, and thirty-one of the running figures were immediately knocked sprawling, unconscious.

The remaining group, it would be learned later, were pumped so full of analgesic and psychedelic chems that the zap field only stunned them slightly, a thing known to be possible but seldom seen in practice.

With the partial failure of the zap field, the security computer automatically heated the antipersonnel lasers and brought them online, and the high-wattage beams of coherent orange light fanned across the grounds in three-quarter-second pulses, at a preset height of just under a meter.

Two of the running attackers, both of whom were later found to be wearing stolen class-three military armor under their robes, continued moving, as did the crawling woman

with the broken leg. The rest of those not already flattened
by the zap field were cut down by the lasers. Only two
would die from massive shock when major arteries and
organs were severed. All the others would be treated in
time.

Thus far, the security computer recorded, eighty-eight
seconds had elapsed since the arrival of the bus.

Of the three remaining attackers still moving toward the
building, the two in armor reached the door first. Each fired
the better part of a full magazine of AP slugs at the
carbonex, which ate the metal pellets as if they were so
much popcorn. When the pair stopped to reload their
weapons, the door snapped open and two of Rajeem
Carlos's personal matadors leaped out and shot the fanatics.
Tam Staver's spetsdöd dart caught his target on the forehead, slightly above the right between the eyes, knocking
the man unconscious almost instantly. Beryl li Rouge put
three shocktox darts into her target, one smack on the chin
and one into each of his bare hands, dropping him.

The crawling woman with the broken leg managed to get
one wild shot off from her handgun before both matadors
put darts into her. The woman's shot hit the building wall
two meters above the front door and did no damage. Even
so, Staver and Rouge were very unhappy that the fanatic
had managed that much.

Elapsed time, according to the security computer, was
one hundred and seventeen seconds.

In the largest of his rooms, Khadaji waved a hand and the
holoproj faded. The others looked at him with varying
degrees of disbelief and wonder.

"Pretty stupid attack," Sleel said. "They could have had
three or four times that many and still gotten chopped into
slaw."

"They could have all gotten into the building and never reached Carlos," Veate said.

"Why'd they do it?" Bork asked.

"Their god told them to, according to the survivors," Khadaji said.

"Who really told them?" Geneva asked.

"Well, the inner sanctum of their temple was wired into a mainframe computer. That give you any ideas?"

"Whoever is doing this could have taken a page from your book," Dirisha said. "You used to do the same kind of shit to the Confed."

"I wasn't the first," Khadaji said. "It was an old tactic, guerrilla hit-and-run. Stir up enough dust, your enemy won't see what you are really doing."

Sleel said, "Anybody notice that there's *always* a computer involved in these things somewhere?"

Veate, sitting next to Bork, pressed her leg against his, just to watch him blush. She said to Dirisha, "What about the information you got from Black Sun?"

Dirisha held the info disc up. "Right here." She walked to the computer and adjusted a control, then fed the disc into the reader.

A face shimmered into being above the comp, a close view of a man, the POV then pulling back for a full-figure shot.

Veate gasped. "That's the man in the recording from my mother's cube!"

Khadaji nodded.

A chunk of stats lit under the image, listing a name and personal physical information about the man.

"Cteel," Khadaji said. "Where do I know that name from?"

"It's pretty common," Dirisha said.

Geneva said, "Probably an alias."

"Nah," Dirisha said, "who would deliberately choose a name that sounded like some kind of sea creature?"

"Funny," Sleel said. "Very funny."

"He was spotted here, on Earth," Bork pointed out. "Look."

The others fell silent as they read the information.

"Do you think my mother is here? On the same world?"

"The guy who took her is," Bork said. "If she's still with him, that'd make sense, wouldn't it?"

Khadaji didn't say what he knew at least some of the others were thinking. Traveling from Vishnu to Earth with a kidnap victim wouldn't be the easiest thing anybody had ever done. The kidnapper might not have brought her, and if he left her, maybe she wasn't alive.

He didn't want to think about that. He'd walked away from Juete once; he didn't want to lose her again, not like this.

"He was seen in New Rio de Janeiro. Computer, give us a map of Rio de Janeiro, and five hundred kilometers around it."

The air lit with the map.

"Oh, yeah, the country that looks like somebody's nose. Southern Hemisphere, right?" Sleel said.

"That's the place," Khadaji said.

"So, what do we do? Go down and cruise the streets looking for this guy?"

Khadaji looked at Sleel. "I'm open to other suggestions. If Black Sun spotted him there once, they must have people who can spot him again. I can get Rajeem Carlos to send some of his people."

"Maybe not," Dirisha said. "We don't want to muck up the water too much. Might scare our fish off. If a few of us went down and were discreet, we might do better."

"You have a point."

Veate said, "He could have left."

"True," Khadaji said, "but a cold trail is better than none at all. If we can find this guy, we might convince him to tell us about Juete."

"Oh, no doubt about that at all," Sleel said.

Bork and Veate went to rent a long-distance vehicle. What they found was a ten-passenger hopper with a cruising range of eight thousand kilometers. Bork piloted the craft from the rental agency back to the hotel, handling the chore with an offhand expertise. They could take commercial transportation and rent flitters locally, he explained, but the closer you got to a quarry, the more careful you had to be, so better that they had sure transport sooner than later. There was no way to tell if the guy they were hunting had connections where he was, and maybe somebody might tip him. Better safe than sorry.

Veate had mixed feelings. She very much wanted to find her mother. She also wanted to stay next to Bork and continue learning what he was teaching her.

She watched the muscles play quietly under his orthoskins as he adjusted the hopper's controls, still somewhat amazed at herself. They had not become lovers. They talked a lot, they sometimes touched, but the connection lacked the carnal heat to which she was accustomed. The fires were there, but banked and in control. He wanted her, but he would not do it. Not yet. They didn't know each other well enough, he'd said. And maybe that would happen and maybe it wouldn't. It was rattling Veate no end.

Bork told her about himself, things he kept private, and she still wasn't quite sure why he was doing it.

During one session, he spoke of his father.

"Yeah, we didn't get along too well, my da and me. He was big, bigger than I am now, and strong. He was a lug-hauler, he did physical work all day, and he liked it. Our kind of mue, we were originally designed for heavy-gravity work, our bones are denser than yours, our ligaments levered better, our blood richer. Course by the time I was born, my parents had lived on four worlds. I started out to be a lug-hauler, so'd my sister, but neither of us turned out quite like Da wanted."

"You have a sister?"

"Yeah. Four years younger. She's a local cool on Tembo."

"Street police?"

"Detective."

Veate tried to imagine what a female version of Saval Bork might look like. And how she might appear to some wrongdoer as she collected him. Impressive, no doubt.

"Anyway, my da kept order the old way, the back of his hand. One day I blocked the slap. I was about seventeen T.S. He beat the crap out of me; he was still twenty-five kilos heavier and a lot stronger. So I started working out harder. When I hit nineteen, I was almost as big as he was and I was pretty sure I was stronger."

"So you clobbered him the next time he tried to hit you?"

Bork shook his head. "No. We used to arm wrestle, when he was in a good mood. Course, he'd always beaten me. When I was nineteen, one night after dinner, we arm wrestled again. That was when I knew I was stronger. I could feel the power of his grip and his arm, but I knew I could win. No doubt at ll."

"Ah, a symbolic victory. So what happened when you won?"

"I didn't. I let him win."

She blinked. "But—why? You could have defeated him and made your point. He'd have known you were capable of defeating him in a real fight, or at least of giving him real competition."

Bork shrugged. "I knew I could, so I didn't need to. My da was fairly limited in what he could do. His strength was all he really had. I didn't want to take that away from him. I left pretty soon after that anyhow."

Veate shook her head. She'd been right about one thing. Bork wasn't stupid. He did have the soul of a poet. How many people were content to know a thing about themselves without having to prove it to others? How many men had she known who would have let their enemy escape when they had the advantage? Few. If any—

"Landing in a minute," Bork said, breaking into Veate's memory scan. She smiled at him. He was going to look for her mother and she was not. Her father had told her that having another Albino Exotic running around down there, one who was the image of the kidnapped woman, might throw grit into the machine. Better she should pursue other avenues. But she was sure going to miss Saval. Every time she found out something about him, she learned something about herself. It was, in its strange way, quite amazing.

Impulsively, she said, "I'm going to miss you."

He grinned. "Yeah. I'll miss you, too."

That simple statement gave her more pleasure than the best lover she'd ever had. Which made no sense at all.

"Progress, Jambi?"

The doctor nodded at the holoproj of his employer. "Yes. My assistants, men of not inconsiderable talent, have begun to come up to speed. Our new biogens are nearly ready to go online. The computations and nanomachinery programming are in synch. At this rate, we can hope to test in four months."

"And if you skip, as you said, the primate studies?"

"Perhaps nine weeks."

"Very impressive, doctor. Have you written your acceptance speech for the Kothar Prize yet?"

This drew a small smile from Jambi. "One must not count embryos before the ova are fertilized. Still, it is not an impossibility to consider the Kothar within reach."

"Succeed in this and that will be the least of your glories, doctor."

Jambi tried to keep his face neutral, but Wall had no trouble at all watching the dreams play across his features. It would indeed be a biological miracle and one of which any scientist could be rightly proud. Perhaps the visions would keep the good doctor blind to the dangers until it was too late. Wall hoped so.

Part Three
Point Death

TWENTY-ONE _____

THE HOPPER HAD more than enough room for the four of them. Bork piloted the vehicle, as he usually did whenever he was on a mission. The big man had a way with aircraft. Must have been a bird in some past incarnation, Dirisha sometimes said.

Sleel was asleep in the back row of seats, sprawled and obviously comfortable, since he hadn't moved much in the last couple of hours.

Geneva peered through the thin sheets of denscris that made up the double window next to her seat, watching the ground far below. They were over the giant farming complex of central NorAm, east of the Rockies and west of the Mississippi River. Vast overlapping circles of greenery dotted the land, robot-tended fields of various crops too far below to be distinguished as to a particular kind. Some of the circles had to be several kilometers across and there were hundreds of them. The world's breadbasket, they called it. Ten decades past, the entire area had been replanned, and many of the cities had been deserted and eventually plowed under for more cropland.

Dirisha herself sat staring into nowhere, remembering the adventures of years before, and realizing how much she had missed the action. After the fall of the Confed, an enemy she'd never really thought they'd defeat, life had shrunk somewhat. Sure, she and Geneva had good times together; love was always a major factor. They'd toyed with the idea of having a child, maybe a couple, but it hadn't ever gotten beyond the wouldn't-it-be-interesting? stage. Geneva would make a good mother, but Dirisha had her doubts about her own abilities in that direction.

No, they had started to get fat and lazy, if only in the mental sense, and both of them had to admit they felt a lot more alive since all this latest crap had begun. Maybe some people just weren't built for peace. After all her years of martial training, despite the philosophical aspects of being taught to avoid fights, to sit idle seemed a waste, somehow. Sure, she'd quit the Flex, but that was more because she'd been winning consistently than anything else. The game isn't so much fun when you don't think you can lose.

So, this problem would be resolved eventually. What then? If they lost, well, that settled that. Dead was dead. If they won, then what would be the next direction? Dirisha was pretty sure Geneva would agree with her, that teaching classes or freelance bodyguarding was going to be too dull to go back to again. There would always be some kind of big trouble somewhere, even in the tamest of civilizations. If they survived this round, Dirisha was pretty certain of what she would have to do: go looking for a piece of that trouble to make into her own.

Hell of a thought, turning into some kind of galactic do-gooder. Well. Everybody had to be somewhere.

After a few minutes, she dropped into a light sleep, thinking about her future.

• • •

Bork said, "On approach to Rio, folks. Anybody want to freshen up before we put down, this is your chance."

Sleel came out of his sleep all of a moment, noticing that Dirisha and Geneva were half a second behind him.

"How long?" Sleel said.

"We're in de Janeiro airspace on autolanding beacon to Aeroporto do Guanabara, the new space and international port set on the renowned and beautiful artificial island of Santos Pedro in the sparkling baia to the northeast of the city. ETA, now fifteen minutes."

"What, are you a tour guide?"

"Just furthering your education, Sleel. Maybe you'd like to hear the rest of the canned feed coming in with the beacon?"

"Thank you, no. I'll settle for your digested version."

Sleel went to the fresher, splashed some water on his face, relieved his bladder, then returned to the passenger section of the little ship.

"Wow. Look at that," Geneva said.

Sleel moved to a window to see what had interested Geneva.

The city, full of high-rise buildings and the usual attendant civilization, sprawled for kilometers in all directions away from the edge of the water. There was a small loop of land, a mountainous finger jutting into the east side of the bay.

Upon this projection of land was a giant head.

Sleel looked, as the autopilot banked the hopper and took it around the huge carving. Other ships looped around the stone at various heights and distances.

It was big, all right. Somebody had spent a lot of time working it. Hard to tell exactly how tall it was, given the scale, but a couple hundred meters, easy.

The face was that of a woman, quite beautiful, with a

straight nose, full, sensual lips, and large eyes. The hair was cut short. It was as impressive a sculpture as Sleel had ever seen, and easily ten times as large as the faces of the four political leaders carved on that mountain back in the Northern Hemisphere.

"The Pao de Acucar Monument," Bork said, repeating what he was hearing from the landing com. "Here, listen." He punched the volume up. A deep female voice filled the hopper.

"Originally called Sugar Loaf, named for its shape, the tallest spire now bears the likeness of Maria Passos Guerra Viera, First President of the United States of South America. It was created after the Revolucion Grande in the last days of the Twenty-First Century. Formerly Chancellor of the Universidade do Estado da Guanabara, winner of the Solar System's Pushkin Prize in Literature for her novel, *The Snake With Warm Blood*, and mother of five children, Presidente Viera was assassinated during her third term in office by a crazed divisionist zealot.

"As one, the decent peoples of South America mourned Viera's loss, and the greatest sculptor in the galaxy, Chin lu Reilly, was entrusted with the honor of creating her monument. The work took seventeen years, cost six billion and twelve million standards, and reduced the size of the spire by nearly one third. Even so, the monument is the largest single sculpture in the Solar System, and second in size in all the galaxy only to the Canuto Nude on Koji. Over five million tourists come to see the sculpture each year, making it the most visited attraction in the Southern Hemisphere of Earth."

"They treat their heroes well down this way," Sleel observed. "I wouldn't mind having a monument like that after I'm gone."

"Yeah, but who'd want to work on a giant phallus?" Dirisha said.

"You're right," Steel said, shaking his head in mock grief. "They'd never find a rock big enough."

Dirisha laughed. She tried to speak, but kept breaking into more laughter every time she got started.

"Sleel's point," Geneva said. "You didn't get your next shot off quick enough, Rissy."

"Caught me flatfooted," Dirisha said. "I concede."

The hopper pulled away from the sculpture, leaving the swarm of other small aircraft buzzing around the monument in their preset patterns like so many flies.

"Should be on the ground in about five minutes," Bork said.

Sleel gave the statue one last look. Nice, but they hadn't come for a vacation. There was work to be done.

Veate followed her father into the governmental computer complex in SoCal, where they were to meet one of the leads given to Dirisha by Jersey Reason.

They had to pass through a series of airwalls, each of which circulated bacteriostatics, just to get to the visitor center. The viral-molecular computers deeper in the complex had to be protected from contamination, and to get there required elimination of *all* possible fauna and flora, including that which lived inside normal people. Even with the hurryup *E. coli* inoculations and designer chem that workers got each day when leaving, computer experts lived on the edge of diarrhea all the time. So said her father, as they reached the heavily protected visitor's center.

The expert was already there, a short, rather rotund woman of maybe forty T.S., dressed in spraywhites and hood. She reminded Veate of a great predatory bird she'd seen in a nature exhibit once, something called an owl.

"So you're Khadaji, eh? I thought you'd be taller."

Her father grinned. "Dr. Pemberton," he said.

"Between that old fart Jersey's rec and your clout with the Prez, I am at your service," she said. "What can I do for you that you couldn't ask for over the com?"

"I need a complete list of computers that are capable of a certain level of complexity. Some of the requirements are fairly technical."

"I'm recording. Shoot."

He began to rattle off statistics that meant little to Veate. He spoke of galactic interactions and holoprojic parameters, of gigabytes and googlums, and it surprised Veate that he could repeat the things from memory.

Pemberton nodded as she listened, her wide eyes blinking now and then. She asked a couple of questions, noted the answers, and then pulled at her lower lip with a thumb and forefinger. "Hmm. I'll have to run the lines, but offhand, I'd say you are looking at thirty, maybe thirty-three possibilities. Twenty-five of those are Republic brains, stellar system Apex-class units. The rest are in private hands."

"How many in Sol?"

"Nine. Six belong to us, three to corporate factions. Ours are the four governmental mains, plus one military and one scientific research. I don't know all the uses on the corporate machines, but I can probably get a pretty good run-down. It sounds like the system you want has a lot of dedicated space, I dunno who could swipe that much from any of the guv's machines without it being noticed."

"You would guess a private system?"

"Yeah, I'd bet stads against toenail clippings. You really think the comnet is compromised?"

"See what you can find out, Dr. Pemberton. Here's my code, I'll be on Earth for a while."

"You got it."

As they left, Veate said, "Did that help?"

"Yes. If we can find the particular computer the bad guys are using for their games, we can get into it and maybe figure out who and where they are. If Pemberton is right, there are only three computers big enough to play by the rules they're using. It could be outsystem, of course, but I think maybe not. And I know who owns one of those comps—it belongs to the Siblings—so that narrows it down."

"We're getting close, aren't we?" she asked.

"Yes. We're getting close."

While scanning the continuous flow of billions of bits of incoming information, a warning flag lit in Wall's security net. He routed more than a routine share of his attention to the flag.

Well, well. A small rental vehicle had just landed at one of the nine airports in New Rio, the pilot's name being Saval Bork. The passenger manifest listed three others with him, also matadors of some repute.

Wall allowed a small measure of electronic amusement to dance within his being. Ah. They were getting closer. He did not know precisely what had led them to Rio, but that city state was only a mere fifteen hundred klicks from the Old Brazil zoo, nothing compared to the galactic distances they had already covered to get this far. Very interesting. He had thought he would have to provide more obvious clues eventually, but it seemed that would not be necessary.

Care must be taken to slow them somewhat, of course, for there still remained a number of weeks before he was ready. And Khadaji wasn't with them.

They were better opponents than he had thought, and that gave him a nanosecond's pause. Underestimating his competition had been very costly to him before; best he not fall prey to the same trap twice.

A hundred scanned scenarios later, Wall decided that the most likely reason the hunters had arrived at their present location had to do with Cteel. Certainly he was the most obvious bait, and the best thing to dangle before them at this juncture. They were tricky, these matadors. It would serve him to give them something to occupy their time.

Wall put in a call to Cteel. Once again, his old friend's current-generation namesake would serve his master. That would likely mean he'd have to create a new one pretty soon, but that was of no importance. One Cteel was as good as another. One could not use one's cannons without the proper fodder.

"Cteel."

"Here."

"I have a job for you."

"Moon, here," said the holoproj.

Khadaji smiled at her. "I would ask your assistance."

"Ask."

He explained to her about his visit to the government computer complex.

"And you would have us cross-check their results."

"Yes."

"It could be a slow process."

Khadaji nodded. "Better a slow process than none at all."

"We'll let you know what we find."

The Black Sun contact was to meet the matadors in the Nova Praca, the New Square in the Offworld District near the ruins of the Old Stadium. He or she would find them, the scrambled voice said in the communication.

Dirisha was the focus, with Sleel as close back-up, Bork

and Geneva circulating through the crowds of tourists shuffling across the square. The district was flush with hotels, on a direct transportation line to the offworld port, and festooned with colorful attractions. A replica of an old-style market occupied one corner of the square, small booths selling wares ranging from personal electronics like translators, music players and vid gear to stalls hawking local fruit suitable for offworld export. The locals dressed in bright reds and blues, and shouted at the passersby in the native language, as well as standard galacticspeak. It was hot as the sun headed for its zenith.

"Some party," Sleel said, as he looped past Dirisha and continued walking his circuit.

"Yeah, takes you back to the good old days."

An offworld tourist carrying a holocam around her neck on a strap and a bag loaded with souvenirs glanced at Dirisha, away from her haggling with an erotic toy merchant. The woman was heavy, sweaty in the heat, and she wore badly tailored shorts and a loose-fitting silk shirt. The look was quick, one that anybody might give to an armed black woman in matadora orthoskins, but Dirisha was scanning for contact. The woman was all too obviously a tourist, not worth a second look, except that she had a small hand wand tucked into her waistband. The weapon was pretty much hidden by her shirt, but it helped Dirisha decided that she'd made her connection.

"Don't you have one with a bigger *thing*?" the woman said to the merchant. She waved a small doll with a vibrating and erect penis in front of his face.

"Ah, sí, my lady, you want the hero model. A moment."

Dirisha made a small hand signal, alerting her three companions, and sidled up next to the woman.

"Hello," she said.

To the fat woman's credit, she knew she'd been spotted.

"Never mind," she said. "I'll take this one."

She paid the toy seller, shoved the anatomically explicit doll into her bag, and nodded at Dirisha. "There's a small restaurant over there in the shade," she said.

Dirisha followed the woman to the restaurant, where they managed to find a table in the courtyard. The table was under an umbrella-field that wafted cool air over it.

"How did you spot me?" the woman asked as they sat. "Professional curiosity."

"If you are going to carry a weapon, don't wear a clingy shirt."

"It hardly shows, and it could be a pager or a medkit," the woman said.

"People who are armed carry themselves differently. It's a thing of feel."

The woman nodded. "There was a black woman who used to walk the Flex a few years back," the contact said. "She was in the top five players when she vanished. Green eyes, real good with her hands and feet."

"You were a player?"

"Yeah, ten years and thirty-five kilos past."

"We all move on."

"Ain't that the truth. Um. Well, you're good, sister, and I see your back-ups are buzzing around pretty good, too. You wouldn't think you could lose three like them, even in a crowd this big, but they're hard to keep track of."

Dirisha said, "We've practiced a lot."

"Um. Anyway, the man you are looking for was last seen by our people in the Escola Naval, used to be the navy station on the Ilha de Villegaignon. That's just east of the old Santos airport. Whole place has been turned into a red light district, pubs, trullhouses, casinos. They call it Meantown here; it's not a place to take the family, if you understand what I am saying."

"I think we can probably take care of ourselves."

"I expect that is so, but you need to understand that our organization has little power there, the Republic even less. Meantown has been there for a hundred years. They managed to resist outside control even during the Confed's heyday. The local law is completely in charge, and it is run by the Nine Families, who pass it all operating money. If you get into trouble in Meantown, you are on your own."

"Thanks for the warning."

"Your quarry, when he comes to town, likes to spend some time in the MAN house, a small casino and whoring operation in the worst section of Meantown. The initials stand for Manina Apretida Novata, it's run by one of the Families, originally a Mexican group. They, ah, specialize in exotic tastes. The name means 'the tight little green pussy.' They aren't talking about color."

"I see."

"I appreciate the tip about the wand. Go with your gods."

The woman stood and shuffled away.

If he thought the Dogtown docks were bad, Sleel was gonna love this.

TWENTY-TWO _____

JAMBI WAS AT a critical stage in the organization-level mitochondria nanomachinery replications when his employer called. "Yes, what is it?" he snapped.

Wall didn't mind that the man was on edge; he actually worked better that way. There was a fine line between help and hindrance, and it was his intent to keep Jambi teetering on that edge.

"You had promised a progress report. A breakthrough, you said."

"Yes, yes, I recall. One of my assistants has had a thought about programming. On the face of it, it seems a relatively sound idea. However, if we follow it and it fails, it will delay the project by approximately four weeks."

"And if the thought is successful?"

"It will eliminate the need for hormone bioformates, or nearly so, and allow a faster growth curve for the third-level nanocyclics."

"Saving how much time?"

"Six weeks."

"Do it."

"The risk factor is about evenly balanced for success or failure, you must understand."

"I said to go ahead. I'll take the risk."

Back in his own thoughts, Wall felt a kind of elation. If this new idea worked—and he already knew what it was, being privy to the computer storage—it would cut the time to under a month. He could hardly stand it.

Perhaps he should grow himself a new flower to share this delicious joy with?

Yes. He would. And no sooner thought than done. . . .

On the face of it, in daylight, Meantown didn't look any worse than several other such places Bork had seen. When you work as a bouncer in public houses, you can find yourself in some tough situations, dealing with hard people. Bork had done a job in a pub on #313-C, a world commonly referred to as "Ohshit"—the nickname coming from what most people said the first time they saw the place. There had been a lot of miners on the planet, since that was what they mostly did there, and the men, women and assorted mues were more than passing strong from working in the gee-and-a-half. When things start falling in that kind of gravity, they hit the floor real hard. He used his experiences there as a kind of comparison whenever he went into a new situation, and the MAN casino did not seem to measure up. Then again, as he'd also learned, looks could be deceiving. Geneva here could pound most men into the ground without raising a sweat, and she looked like your kid sister, or maybe how you wished your girlfriend would look.

It was a midmorning, maybe why the casino section of the place was fairly calm. There were the usual things found in gambling houses: roulette wheels, sturz-booths, various card game tables, number matching machines. A small

restaurant bounded one end of the main room, a long
blue-plastic bar with matching stools ran the length of the
opposite end. There were mirrors on the walls and ceilings,
pop-lights set to go off when a machine paid, and soothing
subsonic generators that gave the required auditory ping
every thirty seconds. Opposite the entrance was a reception
area that led to the brothel rooms uplevels.

When the four matadors arrived, a pair of uniformed
local cools playing five-stad-limit halycon with a bored
dealer looked up from their game. One of them, a tall,
wide-shouldered, narrow-hipped man with a shaved head,
stood, adjusted the pair of hand wands on his hips, and
walked over toward Bork. This one had moved some
flexsteel, Bork saw; he had the dense musculature of a
powerlifter, and his arms were thick where they strained
against the short sleeves of his shirt. Strong, armed, and
backed by the law, he'd be pretty sure of himself. Bork
guessed he'd go a hundred twelve, hundred fourteen kilos,
maybe ten less than Bork's own weight. Bork recognized
the look the man gave him: Which of us is stronger?

"Help you with something?" the cool said.

Dirisha produced the holoprint of Cteel and held it up.
"We're looking for this man."

The cool kept his gaze on Bork, weighing, measuring,
calculating. "Never seen 'im," the cool said, not even
bothering to glance at the picture. To Bork he said, "You're
not basic stock?"

"HG mue," Bork said.

The cool nodded. "Thought so. What's your PR in the
bench?"

"Three-forty-five. A triple. Three-sixty single."

The cool nodded. Maybe he believed it, maybe not. He
wasn't going to seem impressed. "I did three for two once."

He glanced away from Bork at the others. "You all licensed to carry?"

"Yes," Dirisha said, putting the holoprint away. "Republic permits."

"Republic docks don't shine much light in Meantown. Don't cause trouble, we'll get along fine." He turned and went back to his card game.

"What were all those numbers about, Bork?" Geneva asked.

"Guy's a weightlifter. We were exchanging personal bests in the bench press."

"He thinks with his triceps," Sleel said. "You two ought to get along fine."

"How do you want to play it?" Bork said to Dirisha, ignoring Sleel's barb.

"Well, we can't hide if the house wants to let our boy know we're here. No point in playing subtle. If he shows, we grab him."

"And if the cools object?" Sleel said.

"We didn't come all the way here to sit this dance out, deuce."

Sleel grinned. "Good. That bald baboon irritates me. Too bad Spasm is illegal; I'd like to see what kind of knot he'd make. Probably disappear up his own asshole."

Dirisha shook her head in mock disgust. "Sleel, Sleel. What am I going to do with you?"

"I could make some suggestions."

"I didn't doubt it for a second, Sleel. Okay, let's spread out."

"I'll be happy to check uplevels," Sleel said.

"Somehow I thought you might say that," Dirisha said. "But no. We'll see him here if he comes or goes. And don't even bother with the cheap shot about seeing him come better uplevels."

"You wound me," Sleel said.

"Nah, she just gives you too much credit for brains," Bork put in. "You'd never have thought of that one on your own."

"Let's go to work, folks."

Veate and her father waited in SoCal, spending most of their time in or around the little hotel cabin they'd rented near the beachplex. He spent hours every day in front of the com unit, sometimes even using the *betydelse* space. Veate had once had a lover who had the ability to comlink using that rather esoteric device, and as always, it was eerie to watch somebody work it. The machine transmitted by three different codes, signals from each hand and by voice. The latter didn't even have to be spoken aloud, merely subvocalized, so that watching somebody in a *betydelse*, one saw the fingers of the operator's left hand twirling this way and that, the right hand making noticeably different gestures, and what looked to be silent mumbling. Veate had never tried it, but her lover, a rich Mtuan businessman, had told her it was like writing a novel with one hand, doing your taxes with the other, and giving a speech about something else altogether. She hadn't known her father could work it.

There was a lot about her father she had yet to learn.

More, she was interested in knowing it. Whatever happened with her mother, Veate realized that learning about her father no longer filled her with anger. It might take some adjusting to get used to that one. Being with Bork had helped. The big man knew things about people that Veate had never suspected existed.

After about ten minutes, Khadaji came out of the trance. He shook his head, blinked several times, and looked at her.

"Is it that difficult?"

"For me it is. I can last about fifteen minutes before I lose my concentration. I know a man who can go for an hour and come out looking as if he has just had a refreshing nap."

"Learn much?"

"A number of things, many of which are interesting. And useful. This path grows more convoluted all the time. We've located the right computer, and the registration and operators are being traced. It is not what it seems."

"Is anything ever what it seems?"

He smiled at her. "Probably not. Some of the information is very disturbing."

"In what way?"

He sighed. "Can you stand a bit of history?"

"Of course."

"I'll try not to bore you with old war stories, but there are some things you probably ought to know."

"I am listening."

The matadors had spent three days in the MAN house, doing little but watching and waiting. Dirisha hadn't liked the place when it had been described to her; she liked it less after having been inside it. It reminded her all too much of her own upbringing, such that it had been. She had been born to a whore, raised sister to a whore, and had even begun the trade herself when she'd had the realization that changed her life. But for an accident of place, she could have been one of the too-young girls or women uplevels in this pit, waiting to lose her virginity for the first or the hundredth time. Such things as hymens were easily built by a competent surgeon, and if you looked twelve, then the customer was apt to believe he was your first. Some of the girls would probably be here by choice, others would not. Dirisha didn't much like the idea of children as prostitutes either way. For a bent demistad, she would pull this place down and laugh while it burned.

The cools changed, the customers ebbed and flowed, and the management and owners seemed content to let the four matadors alone as long as they didn't bother anybody. So far, they hadn't had any reason to disturb the paying customers. They drank little, not enough to dull their perceptions, rotated positions, and kept each other alert. They took turns eating and sleeping, overlapping at the busiest times. Such as now.

Even so, when Cteel showed up, they almost missed him.

Dirisha was sitting in a juice booth, feeding the thing coins but keeping the coils turned off. She happened to glance at the front entrance just as the quarry walked in, saw Bork or Sleel or maybe both, then turned and darted back outside.

Dirisha stood, started for the door, and bit down on her dentcom twice, clicking her teeth. "Heads up, everybody; our boy just stuck his nose in the door, then turned and ran. Let's go."

The rest of them dropped whatever they were doing and moved.

The bald cool caught it. And decided to play games.

He filled the doorway, flexing his muscles and grinning.

Moving in next to her, Sleel said, "You want me to shoot him?"

Bork was closest to the cool. "No. Bork will move him."

"He's pretty big."

"Yeah, and we've all got moves we'll never use. Bork can dazzle him so he doesn't know which way is up."

"It won't happen that way," Geneva said, behind her. "This region was big on man-to-man stuff back before space flight. Some kind of stupid male honor thing. Called it machismo. Bork figured it out. Watch."

She was right. Bork could have kicked or punched or danced around the man and flattened him with one of the many sumito moves they had all mastered. He didn't, though. He raised his arms, hands wide, and the grinning cool matched him.

"Not leaving in such a hurry, eh, compadre?"

"Afraid so," Bork said. "You'll have to move."

"Not gonna happen, amigo."

Bork and the cool slid into a wresting hold, arms locked, and their hands on each other's shoulders. The cool strained to his left, Bork in the opposite direction. The cool's bald head flared red with the effort, and the men shook as though afflicted with some nerve disease. A long second passed, then Bork said, "Sorry," and tossed the cool into a lazy sideways flip that sent him sailing into a card table three meters away. The table shattered under the man's weight and the players scattered, yelling.

"The other one is to the right," Geneva said.

"I got him," Sleel said. He snapped his arm out in a backfist and pointed his index finger at the second cool, who was dropping into a gunner's crouch, his hand wand clear of its holster and coming up. Sleel's spetsdöd coughed once.

"Right between the eyes," Sleel said.

Bork had the door open and was halfway through.

The cool with the muscles rolled free of the destroyed table and, still on his back, went for his hand wand.

Geneva shot him.

Two seconds later, all four of them were out in the street.

"There hc goes," Bork said. "He's got a flitter."

Dirisha looked. Sure enough, the one called Cteel was piling into a brand-new shiny machine half a block away. Their own hopper was fifty meters in the opposite direction. Dirisha didn't need to say anything. All of them ran for the hopper.

Bork got there first. Despite his size, he was faster for

short stretches than any of them. He had the repellors lit and cycling up by the time Dirisha brought up the rear. They strapped into their seats as Bork lifted.

Cteel's flitter flashed by, climbing sharply, breaking speed and level laws.

The hopper was slower off the ground, but would be able to keep up with the other craft once it reached cruising speed. Automatic alarms blared over the com as the local traffic control simadams screamed at them.

"Come on," Sleel said. "He's getting away."

"He can run but he can't hide," Bork said. "I got his signature locked in. We can doppler him from now until doomsday."

"Unless he's got a confounder."

"Don't matter," Bork said. "I got him. I can follow the blank spot just as easy. Watch."

Bork touched a series of controls, and waved his hand over other light-sensitive switches. The hopper shook.

"What are you doing, Bork?"

"I just launched our copydrone. We'll pull back far enough so he can't make us on visual, like so . . ."

The hopper's speed decreased. Thirty seconds later the flitter ahead disappeared in the distance.

"Then I light the drone, like this . . ."

Bork waved his hands over his board. "He thinks he's lost us," he said. "The drone kicked in and took his radar lock with it, so his scopes'll show that we turned. And our confounder will keep him from picking us up again. As long as we stay back a few klicks so he can't eyeball us, he'll never know we're here."

Sleel shook his head. "That's not bad."

"Watch it, Sleel," Geneva said. "You're being nice again."

"Oh, fuck you," Sleel said.

"That's a clever one. Can I write it down?" Dirisha said.

Sleel smiled. "Better I should show you."

"You wish."

"Faint heart ne'er a fair lady won," Sleel said.

"Chang, Sleel, is that *poetry*? Are you reading poetry these days?"

Sleel looked uncomfortable. "Uh, no. I—uh, I heard it in an entcom vid."

"Sure you did."

Dirisha and Geneva gave each other looks of mock amazement. "By all the gods, Sleel is a poet," Dirisha said. "Who'd have even thought it?"

"Fuck both of you."

"You wish," they said together.

Bork's laugh was the loudest, but barely more than Dirisha's and Geneva's. Sleel didn't even crack a smile. But they all knew he wanted to.

TWENTY-THREE _____

VEATE CAME OUT of a light sleep to the sound of her father calling her.

"What?"

"That was Dirisha on the com. They've found the man who kidnapped Juete. They're following him."

Veate sat up on the bed. "Do you think he'll lead them to my mother?"

"No way to be certain, but, yes, I think so."

Veate felt her pulse quicken. "Still think this fits in with what you told me?"

"Yes."

"What now?"

"We'll have to be sure about where Cteel is going, though I have an idea about where that might be. I've got to go see Jersey Reason for some rather esoteric supplies."

"May I come along?"

"Sure."

Wall sent an order to Cteel, still in flight.

"Land at Uberlandia and spend the night," he said.

242

Cteel flashed puzzlement at him. "Why? I told you I lost them in Rio. My screens are clear, nobody is behind me, there's nothing else in the air but farmwagons."

"I'm sure you are right, but humor me."

"Well, okay."

"And tomorrow, I want you to put down at Golania and spend the night. The day after that, Jetai, and the next day, Poxereu. After that, you can return to the zoo."

"You're the boss."

"Indeed."

Wall broke the connection. It was time to finish this. True, his tame genius was not yet ready, but Wall had assimilated all of the research, even that which Jambi had taken such pains to conceal, and he realized that the man was stalling. The doctor was afraid of failure where even the smallest chance of it existed, so he was duplicating and triplicating every facet of his work. Wall had the information and he knew it was so; he also knew that it was unnecessary. And by eliminating the scientific rigors and the cover-one's-ass mentality, the experiment could be completed in a mere three days. The miniature implant could be, no it *would* be, finished in less than seventy-two hours.

Not by Jambi, of course. The man would not allow himself to be rushed that much. But certainly one of his able assistants could be persuaded. One with more greed than principle, or one with more survival characteristics.

Jambi would have to go. Wall had something in mind.

Between the combine ag stations, small patches of thick, tropical woods remained or had been reforested, a testament to a somewhat late period of land use planning. There were rumors, according to infocom, that certain native peoples had thrown away most of civilization's implements and returned to some of these new forests, to live as had their long-ago ancestors. There were reports of nearly naked tribes who lived off the land, drove small internal combustion engine scooters run on petroleum analogs or alcohol, and who would kill any outsider who came looking for them. The matador's hopper had just passed over another of these mini-jungles, a mere thousand meters below.

"Hope they can't throw their spears this high," Sleel said.

"Surface-to-air doppler spikes," Bork said. "According to some reports."

"That's back to nature, huh? Great."

"So our boy is landing. What'd we have here?" Dirisha asked.

"According to the net, a little farming town called Uberlandia. The main crop is a hardy offworld grain that grows well here, *rizvete*, a kind of cross between rice and wheat."

"Good place to hide, you think?" Geneva said.

"Good as any," Sleel said. "What's the plan?"

"We put down under cover, hike in, and see what's what. If Juete's there, we get her out."

"Just like that," Sleel said.

"Whatever it takes. Unless you have a more pressing appointment?"

"Not me. I came to dance."

"That's nice."

Since a stranger in such a small town would surely stand out, the matadors stayed hidden until after dark. The old stealth skills might be a bit tarnished, but it was not as if the farmers here were particularly expert in spotting intruders, and the four matadors had no trouble sneaking in and through the village. Apparently nobody here liked dogs or *mbwa*, for none barked or howled at the four as they slipped through the night. Made it even easier.

"There's his flitter," Bork said.

"Looks like he's got a house. Not much of a place. We should be able to spot her if she's in there," Sleel said.

"I'll go," Dirisha said. "I blend into the dark better."

She worked her way through the warm night toward the house, a cheap blue-plastic prefab box, faded from its time in the tropical sunshine. Insects buzzed around her; they'd still need those for pollination of things in such a backrocket operation, she guessed.

Through an uncovered window, she spotted Cteel sitting on a beat-up couch, fondling a naked woman. The woman had black hair and swarthy skin, was maybe twenty-five T.S., and she laughed too loud at whatever Sleel was saying. It didn't take a particularly bright observer to recognize a local whore.

Dirisha circled around the house and peered in through the windows, but there was no sign of anyone else. Since Cteel seemed occupied and since there were no signs of a security system, either, the matadora slipped the latch on a back bedroom window and entered the place. She moved quickly and quietly, checking each room. The laughter had stopped, but it was replaced now by the sounds of a woman pretending coital passion. Dirisha left before the counterfeit orgasm noises began.

"Nope," she said when she got back to the others. "Our boy is in there with a woman, they're playing dork-and-bush, but no sign of anybody else around. No stray white hairs in the fresher, no clothes. I don't think she's been there."

"So he stopped just to get laid?" That from Sleel.

"Funny, coming from you," Dirisha said.

"I guess we hide and wait to see what he does, right?" Bork said.

"You called it."

As they left Jersey Reason's house, Veate asked, "What did you get?"

"An old memory," Khadaji said. "In this." He held up a tube the size of his little finger's tip. He explained.

"Will it work?"

"Reason says so. I hope I'm wrong and don't have to find out."

"Now what?"

"A few more pieces of the puzzle, then we need to go see Pen."

There was a small stone building not far from the main complex of the zoo; inside was a room upon which Cteel and his assistant had spent much time and effort. Aside from a chair in front of a comp terminal set into the wall farthest from the door, the room appeared empty. It had no windows or doors save the one.

Into this room came Elbu ra Jambi, a brilliant man who had made, however, one bad mistake.

"Have a seat, doctor," Wall said. He allowed a holoproj image to appear over the com.

"I know your voice, but the face is different," Jambi said as he moved to the chair.

"The real me," Wall said. "I resorted to a subterfuge before; I hope you'll forgive my little deception."

Jambi shrugged. "It is of no importance. I do find it somewhat interesting that you are an albino."

"In my first incarnation. Later, I looked like this."

The holoproj swirled once, like a stirred drink, and cleared to show the face and body Wall had last worn, when he had been Marcus Jefferson Wall, Factor, adviser and puppetmaster controlling the Confederation President.

Unlike some men in his profession, Jambi was not politically illiterate. He recognized the face.

"Really? I had heard that you died during the revolution."

"Alas, it is so."

"Then how—?"

"Surely you are not unaware of the theory of encoded information transferral from organics to viral matrices?"

"Stevenson's Practicum," Jambi said.

"Precisely. And the simpler side of the coin upon which you have lavished so much admirable work."

"Ah. So that's why you hired me. You want the process reversed for *personal* reasons."

"You speak that word as though it were blasphemy, doctor."

Jambi shrugged again. "Your reasons don't matter, I suppose, only the end result."

"True. And I have it on the best authority that you are dragging your feet on your experiment."

"I beg your pardon? Who has lied to you about this?"

"It's true enough. You could finish the implant within a few days; is this not true?"

"It is not. I could complete the *device*, but this is not the same as finishing the *experiment*. There are protocols that must be adhered to, tests that need to be run. To proceed without them would be scientifically absurd. I'd never be able to publish; I'd be laughed off the planet."

"I'm afraid I'm in a hurry and must insist, though."

"I won't do it."

"Not under any circumstances?"

"That is correct. And you must be aware that I hold the trump card here, sir."

"You would think so. Still, it's a pity. Ah, well."

The image of Wall raised its hand and pointed its forefinger at Jambi.

"What are you doing?"

"Adieu, doctor."

Wall's finger seemed to explode.

The frangible ceramic pellet hit Jambi square on the left eye; on impact, the thumb-sized bullet shattered into thousands of corkscrew-shaped fragments that sliced and carved the man's brain into mush. He was hurled clear of the chair by a final muscular spasm. He wiggled on the floor for a few seconds, then died.

The holoproj vanished, and the tracking gun retracted into the wall, hidden by a permanent projection that looked like the rest of the stone.

There came a hydraulic whine, and the floor of the room split down the middle. Jambi's body and the chair slid toward the center of the room as the trapdoor mechanism widened. Beneath the building, some five meters below, a large vat of contact-activated acid received the mortal remains of Jambi and the chair upon which he had last sat. The acid hissed and roiled. In ten minutes there would be no identifiable part of Jambi or the chair remaining, only a slight organic thickening of the soup in the special denscris vat. The organics would eventually be boiled off and then vented through special pipes into the swamp some kilometers away, the pipes then being flushed and cleansed with a different kind of acid brought to a hard stream and sprayed through them several times.

Elbu ra Jambi's transition in the way of nearly all flesh was thus greatly accelerated. Somebody looking for him would really have to work at it to find any identifiable trace.

It was, Wall thought, a great toy.

• • •

"There he goes," Bork said.

Sure enough, Cteel emerged from the small house and started toward his flitter.

"Let's get back to the hopper," Dirisha said.

"He's poking along awfully slow," Geneva said. "You think he's spotted us?"

Bork said, "I don't see how he could."

"Yesterday he was heading almost due northwest," Dirisha said. "Now he's altered his course farther to the north. What's out there?"

Bork called up a map.

"There's another farming town about two hundred klicks ahead of us," he said.

"Past that?"

"Nothing but swamp and mountains for a couple thousand kilometers, not until the Monte Alegre Metroplex on the Amazon."

"Can he get that far in his flitter?"

"Not unless he's swimming to the eyeballs in fuel. Thing's got a range of maybe eight, nine hundred klicks, tops."

"He didn't refuel last night."

"So, if he stays on this heading, he'll land in this farming town."

"Unless he knows something we don't," Sleel put in.

Dirisha shook her head. "Something doesn't feel right here."

"So, what do we do?" Geneva asked.

"I don't see what we can do, except follow him."

"Maybe we could grab him and convince him to tell us where Juete is," Geneva said.

"Yeah, and maybe he's got a suicide zap charge built into a tooth or something," Dirisha said. "Better not chance it.

He's going somewhere. We'll stay with him until he gets there or we figure it out."

Veate was with her father as he crisscrossed back and forth over the western half of the country, stopping no less than six times for certain errands before they refueled and headed for the Siblings Compound on Manus Island.

As the sun began to settle into dusk, the computer control piloted the little ship at a cruising height of nearly eight thousand five hundred meters across the glittering Pacific Ocean, racing at twice the speed of sound.

Inside, the wind noise was muted by the insulation, so the ship was almost quiet.

There passed what seemed a long time of silence.

"My mother said you were a mystic," Veate finally said.

Khadaji, looking through the sea far below, nodded.

"I used to be. I had a vision during a battle, when I was soldiering for the Confed. It's what drove me to do what I did."

"It must have been powerful."

"It was. The single most powerful event in my life. It reshaped me totally."

The sunlight reflected in a vast sheet on the water so far below, growing dimmer. They were too high to see waves, if there were any.

Veate said, "You said 'used to be.' Not a mystic any more?"

"No. I burned too many bridges, I saw too much grief to believe in a benevolent cosmos any longer. I caused much of that grief myself." He paused.

"Pen and his priests have a computer program that can almost predict the future. I mentioned it earlier, remember?"

"Yes."

"Integratics, they call it. They study the butterfly-and-tornado effect."

"I've heard of the theory," she said.

"Mmm. If you can gather enough information, can put it together correctly, it takes on a life of its own. Very large patterns have to be interpreted, but it is possible to make some sense of some of them, some of the time. It's still a fledgling science, much like chaos-theory was a couple hundred years ago, but eventually, there won't be anything that can't be predicted."

"That hardly seems likely."

"Oh, it might take a couple million years to evolve computers and beings capable of managing it, but I expect it to be possible. Certainly the Siblings of the Shroud believe it."

"I don't think I want to see that," she said. "It seems awfully dull, somehow."

"I agree. But knowing that it will happen, along with all the experience I've had in my short span, has helped turn me into a cynic."

She laughed.

"Something funny?"

"Yeah. You. You're the least cynical person I've ever met."

"You think so?"

"I didn't want to like you before I met you, you know. I had some grievances, most of which weren't valid, but they were treasured wounds I didn't want to heal. Bork has made me let go of a lot of those. He thinks that love can pretty much redeem just about anything, and I'm beginning to believe maybe he's right."

"What's that got to do with me?"

She smiled. "You're a man who kicked over the supports of a repressive government and literally made a change that affected the entire galaxy, just because it was the right thing to do."

"That was then—" he began.

She cut him off. "Yeah, and half a decade later, you're the same man who came out of retirement to mobilize the best bodyguards in the known universe to scour the galaxy to find a woman you once loved—because a daughter you didn't know you had *asked* you to do it. You can space the cynic pose, Father. There's probably not a bigger idealist and romantic alive."

He tried to keep a straight face, she could see that, and it amused her no end that he couldn't manage it. He grinned.

That was what she needed. It was the final push. She had seen how he acted, seen what kind of loyalty and love he inspired, and there wasn't any way he could have faked that. People were willing to put themselves on the line for Khadaji, to risk death, because somehow, he called up that kind of belief. Almost a devotion. Bork had said it simply: "Your father is a great man." And damned if she didn't believe it.

Her grin mirrored his. "Hi, I'm Veate, your daughter. And I'm glad to meet you," she said.

And damned if it wasn't true.

TWENTY-FOUR

PEN, WRAPPED IN his enigmatic shroud as always, came to meet them. Veate marveled at how well he moved, given that he was, according to her father, easily in his eighties.

In Pen's office, the information came quickly. The priest handed her father a small recorder.

"The computer is a top-of-the-line viral matrix maxi-frame with multiple attendants, constructed during the final days of the Confederation. The start-up order came directly from Limba Kokl'u."

Veate watched her father. Kokl'u had been the President of the Confed, killed at the hands of a mob in Brisbane during the revolution. Khadaji did not give away anything with his reaction. Not even a blink.

Pen continued. "The computer is ostensibly owned by a private company, Tenton Electronics, but the corporation is a dummy, as are the holding companies that formed it. We have backwalked the trail through nine false fronts and have yet to discover the real owner."

Khadaji shrugged. "Doesn't matter."

"Not to you, maybe, but we like to have things tidy around here."

"Go on."

"The ship is in geosynch just inside the perimeter of the Duralum Wall. Coordinates are in the recorder."

Veate said, "Duralum Wall?"

Her father said, "Since the first satellites were orbited hundreds of years ago, a lot of trash has accumulated in orbit. Most of the bigger stuff gets swept, but anything under a few grams is hard to track. Since it moves at different relative speeds, it can pack quite a punch. A paint flake or a shard of metal sheared from a nut barreling along at fifteen klicks a second relative will make quite a dent in an unprotected ship's hull. A chunk the size of your thumb will punch a crater in denscris armor. The Duralum Wall is a series of overlapping plates that protects a large satellite complex hung in geosynch orbit. Cheaper than sheathing each sat or ship."

"Ah."

"Your theory is just barely possible, according to what Diamond has learned," Pen said. "It's a reach."

"Makes sense, though," Khadaji said.

"We've figured the other orbit you asked for. If you're wrong, it could be an expensive mistake."

Khadaji grinned. "Yeah, well, that never stopped me before, did it? And I never noticed the Shroud falling all over itself to slow me down, either."

Pen laughed. "What will you do now?"

"A little more checking. Dirisha says their quarry is playing games, hopping back and forth between backrocket towns in the middle of nowhere. Maybe I can figure out where he's going."

"And after you find Juete?"

"Well, we'll have to see."

"Our projections have changed. Things are going to happen sooner than we figured. Days now, maybe even hours. The system is in flux; there are too many variables. We can't pin it down."

Khadaji shrugged. "I figured."

"We can't be sure of your fate, Emile."

Her father smiled. "If you find out, don't tell me."

"Do you understand what it is I am asking of you?" Wall said.

The man in the chair said, "Yes."

"Is there any problem with compliance?"

"No. I cannot guarantee success, but no problem with doing it as you have outlined."

"Good."

"I had thought that Jambi was the galaxy's expert on this," the man said. "But you seem to be as knowledgeable as he is in every aspect."

"I am," Wall said.

"I am surprised that I haven't heard of you. I keep up with this subject."

"I value my privacy, doctor. Highly."

"Point taken. Too bad Jambi fell ill, though. He is going to be sorry he missed this."

"I'll try to keep him informed as we go."

"Well, then. Tomorrow. You'll have the subject for us?"

"No. The implantation will take place elsewhere. I have my own medical team."

"That is most risky. We have consulted the four best electroneurosurgeons in the galaxy and they are not of a like mind on exactly how the procedure should best be performed."

"I have access to a Ninth Generation Healy Surgidrome, doctor, fully programmed with *every* recorded operation your four cutters have done, along with over a thousand other most carefully documented procedures."

The man shook his head. "Really? I didn't think any of the multiunit dins were in private hands. I'd heard the Healy people've managed to get only three or four of them fully operational and online."

"You are correct. One of them belongs to me."

"Your resources are nothing short of amazing."

"I know."

"He has to know we're back here," Sleel said.

"I don't see how, but, yeah, I think you're right," Bork said.

Dirisha stared at the tracking screen. The blip that represented Cteel hung in empty space, moving slowly toward its next destination. "What's the town he's heading for now?"

"Poxoreu," Bork said.

"Another great outbrush metropolis," Sleel said. "Wonderful. We're being led around like a *chombu* on a leash here, folks."

Pemberton's call came as Khadaji and Veate were about to leave Manus Island. The transmission was voice-only, so they couldn't see the woman's face, but she sounded quite pleased with herself.

"I did some checking," she said. "I think maybe I got something for you."

"Appreciate any input," Khadaji said.

"You know anything about elephants?"

"Elephants?" Dirisha said.

"Yeah. There's a zoo full of them a couple hundred klicks from where you are now," Khadaji said. The comcircuit was a little out of tune; it made his voice deeper than it should have been. "That's where I think Cteel is heading."

The matadors looked at each other.

"Those big armored things with the nose horns?" Geneva said.

"No, those are something else," Bork said. "These are the ones with flexible snouts. They're bigger than the horned animals; some of them have these long white tusks."

"Oh, yeah, curlnoses."

"What makes you think that's where Cteel is going?" Dirisha asked.

"I've got a source that tracked the ownership of the place. Used to belong to Marcus Jefferson Wall."

"What's he got to do with this?" Sleel asked. "He's fertilizer, right?"

"He died, yes," Khadaji said. "But maybe he's got a brother. A twin."

Dirisha said, "There's a pleasant thought. You think Juete is on this elephant farm?"

"It's possible."

"Then maybe we should just skip the tour of the countryside."

"Give me your coordinates," Khadaji said. "I'll meet you there. We'll all go pay them a visit."

They were parked in a grassy area when Khadaji and Veate arrived and landed their flitter. It had been almost eight hours since they'd last talked.

The late afternoon's heat had hardly abated and the shade of the nearby trees offered a little respite. The group moved that way.

"So, what's the drill?" Dirisha asked.

"I expect they know we're going to show up," Khadaji said. "Our advantage is that they probably *don't* know exactly when or how. The place sits on the edge of a swamp, in the middle of a big grassland. Some of the vegetation is nearly twice a man's height. I think they can spot anybody coming in by air, but we should be able to get pretty close on the ground. They'll have some basic sensing gear to track the livestock, but nothing a flatpack confounder can't rascal."

Bork, who was standing next to Veate with one big hand resting lightly on her shoulder, glanced at Khadaji, then back at the albino woman.

Khadaji said, "Veate will stay with the vehicles. If things get out of control, she can come in blasting. I've had some modifications made to our flitter."

Bork relaxed a little.

Veate wasn't particularly happy about being used as a back-up, but she also knew she didn't have the skills her father and the others had.

"I've got the loan of five class-one shiftsuits, with coolers," Khadaji continued. "Yours might be a little tight, Bork."

That brought smiles.

"I've got some supplemental weaponry. Plus a construction plan of the zoo. We'll do a study, talk it out, and go in after dark, everything being equal."

Veate said, "Can you be sure she's there?"

"No guarantees," Khadaji said, "but everything points to it. Pen's projections say this is all about to peak. Wouldn't make sense for Juete to be elsewhere when it happens."

"I don't suppose negotiation with the kidnappers is an option?"

"No."

The matadors nodded but did not speak. They had all done similar scenarios many times, both in training and in reality. This kind of operation had to be fast and precise. Were it to succeed, there was little room for error. Their reflexes might not be as sharp as once they had been, but the old skills were still there. They'd see how well things worked soon enough.

"All right," Khadaji said. "Here's the aerial holoproj of the main complex. My information says there might be as many as thirty security people on the premises . . ."

"The implant is ready," the doctor said. "Packaged for transport."

"You have taken all the precautions I ordered?" Wall asked.

"You could drop the package from a flitter at ten thousand meters and it would survive the impact. Life-support systems all are triple-backed, vacuum-proofed, directional locators rigged for emergency. You have thirty-six hours and twenty-three minutes before the nanomachineries start automatic replication. Best you have the implant in place before then."

"I am aware of that, doctor. Load the package."

"You'll let us know how it goes?"

"Of course."

If it goes as it should, I'll let you know in person, Wall thought. If not, I'll need you for another try. You aren't expendable just yet, doctor.

They had flown in a ground-hugging circle to within ten klicks of the target, arriving just before sunset in a tangle of wooded swampland to the northwest. Both the flitter and hopper were rigged with confounding gear; they had traveled low enough to avoid normal radar, and had taken a route that they hoped had kept them out of sight of any curious locals.

Veate sat alone in the flitter, monitoring the emergency channel her father had designated. They would stay off the air unless there was something they couldn't deal with, he had told her. No news is good news.

Was her mother out there past the jungle that hid the vehicles? Veate couldn't tell; she didn't have any gut feelings that said yea or nay. Her father seemed to think his ex-lover was hidden there among the elephants, and Veate had begun to think his greatest talent was in being right before he took action.

She would know soon enough, one way or the other.

Despite the cooler, the shiftsuit was not the most comfortable thing Khadaji had ever worn. The viral-matrix computer was hardly bulky, given its single, simple task of matching the background closest to it, but the material itself was fairly heavy and stiff. It didn't make you altogether invisible, but as camouflage went, a shiftsuit came pretty close. In the jungle, in the dark, it would take somebody with almost superhuman vision to spot them. Between the suits and the confounders, nobody was apt to pinpoint them even if they suspected where they were.

It had been a long time since Khadaji had done this kind of work, and the old fluttery feelings came back, stirring his adrenaline and putting razor edges on his senses. If they'd had time, he would have gotten bacteria-aug circulating, to speed up their reflexes. The spookeyes they all wore gathered enough starlight to make the jungle a pale phosphorescent green imitation of day; they had flare-shields in case somebody started throwing photonbombs. Crowed to their belts were several varieties of their own explosives. The five of them were as well equipped as they could be under the circumstances. It would have to do.

It took nearly an hour to reach the edge of the plain. The nearest patch of gently waving grass was more than two meters tall. They moved into the new cover.

"Fuck!" Sleel said in a deep whisper.

Khadaji crouched, hands coming up reflexively, spetsdöds angled to cover almost a semicircle, seeking possible targets.

"Sleel?"

"Heysoo Damn, I just stepped in a pile of shit halfway to my fucking knee!"

Geneva laughed. "Careful you don't trip over one of the curlnoses, Sleel."

Khadaji chuckled. He hadn't realized how tense he'd been until Sleel's misstep had broken the mood.

"Let's keep it down," Khadaji said. "The night has ears."

"No, the night has turds," Sleel said.

The transport ship arrived, and Wall's mobile dins unloaded it with preprogrammed care, moving the container to the surgidrome. The package didn't look like much, a rounded aluminum block the size of a microwave oven, the operative part of it smaller than the last joint of a man's middle finger. Priced per gram, it was probably one of the most expensive items in man's galaxy. More than a hundred million stads had gone into the implant, not to mention the efforts of more than two dozen of the best man and mue brains ever collected for a project this size.

The Healy surgical environment was programmed to perform only this one task, and there would be no mistakes. The machineries were as precise as could currently be made, and the brainpatterns and vital statistics of the subject had been part of the programming from the start.

Now. All that was left was to make certain of his arrival.

Wall activated his com.

"Cteel?"

"Right here."

"You are in the air?"

"Almost to Poxoreu."

"Get back to the zoo, now. Put the security forces on alert. You are going to have visitors."

"Damn!"

Veate's computer gave her the ID on the small ship that approached the zoo: Cteel had finally come home. Did her father and the others know that?

Outside, local insects chirped and buzzed, filling the swamp with their noises. Should she call the matadors?"

No, better not. Her father must have seen or heard the ship coming in.

Hidden in the deep grass, the five matadors watched the small airship circle in and set down on the zoo's landing pad. They had their spookeyes shoved back; the bright landing lights showed the pad well enough so that they recognized the flitter.

Sleel said, "Well, well. Looks as if our boy got tired of his vacation."

Khadaji said, "Doesn't matter. Dirisha?"

"Geneva and I do the main power caster in thirty-two minutes from . . . now."

"Bork?"

The big man had his sleeve shoved back, He touched his chronograph. "Check. I got the aux in thirty-one minutes, fifty-five seconds."

"Sleel?"

"The front door'll be open, boss."

"All right. You all know the rest of it. We've got to hit this the first time. The Republic won't have a sat footprinting this spot for another hour and a half. Nobody is going to be calling shots from the air. On either side."

"Piece of cake, boss," Sleel said.

Khadaji took a deep breath. The smell of the night was musty, full of pollen and other organic richness. It was always like this when your life was on the line. Everything was so much more intense.

"Let's do it. Be careful, all of you."

Wall watched with amusement as Cteel and Tone moved about in mild panic, dispatching their security forces to cover the compound. The troops were mercs, ex-military most of them, veterans of life-and-death battles. They were well armed, well paid, and ready for action. Most of them bore military surplus weaponry, full-auto carbines or sleet launchers, and they had been supplied with enough ammunition to last a long time. Two dozen men and women against how many? Five, six? No more than that, surely. Were those coming not the spawn of Khadaji's training, Wall would have bet that his people would control the situation quickly. But he knew better. These matadors were the people who had toppled the Confed, and five-to-one odds was nothing compared to what they had gone up against before. That didn't scan well for Cteel's forces.

"You see something there, Mati?"

The second guard squinted into the darkness. The big floods didn't reach this far, and it was like the inside of a cave out past the perimeter.

Both men wore spidersilk body armor, including helmets and clear blast shields. Both men held Parker .177s slung in hip points. A wave with one of those carbines on full auto would spew a line of explosive pellets that could easily slice an unarmored man in half.

Both men were looking right at Khadaji, no more than ten meters away.

"Nah, there ain't nothin' there. You're getting jumpy in your old age, Sonk."

Khadaji raised both hands slowly. The blast shields the men wore left a thin strip of bare skin between the chin and base of the neck. And neither man wore gloves. Probably too uncomfortable in the muggy tropical night.

Too bad for them.

Khadaji fired, one shot from each spetsdöd. Both men crumpled without a sound.

He moved to his left, staying outside of the light's reach.

"We're way early," Geneva whispered.

"That's why they make timers, brat. Take the two on the right." Her voice was also too soft to be heard more than a meter or two away.

There were three guards posted at the only door to the main powercast generator. They could destroy the entire building if they wanted, by simply tossing one of the thermite bombs each carried, but the idea was to keep things quiet until they had to go noisy.

"I got the one on the left. On three. One . . . two . . . *three*—"

Both women fired their spetsdöds.

The trio of guards collapsed.

Thirty seconds later, Dirisha and Geneva reached the door.

"Not even locked," Geneva said, pushing the door open.

"Go set the popper," Dirisha said. "I'll keep watch." They dragged the three unconscious guards into the building. Dirisha closed the side-hinged door, save for a crack. Wouldn't be real bright to stand out there in the light, shiftsuit or no. Be trouble enough if somebody came round and saw that the guards were gone.

Geneva was back in less than a minute. "All set," she said.

"Good. Let's get moving."

"Sleel was right. This is a piece of cake."

"I know. That bothers me. It's too easy. Emile is right, it smells like a set-up. Stay sharp."

"If you promise not to swagger."

"Oh, you're gonna pay for that."

The two women squeezed each other's hands, and slid into the night.

Bork had to shoot two guards on his way to the emergency generator, but there wasn't anybody watching the power source itself. That wasn't too clever. Somebody didn't know squat about tactics here.

He set his popper, triggered the timer, and moved away from the shack. In ten minutes, it was going to get real dark around here.

Sleel was in position, watching the four circulating guards. He figured the quad for as good as the opposition was gonna get here; they were cautious, edgy, and paying attention. He sat with his back to a thick-boled tree to the right of the building, at the edge of the floodlights. Without the 'suit, he would have been visible; there was enough light to cast shadows here, but anybody looking his way shouldn't see anything but tree bark. He had his knees drawn up, his wrists propped on them, so he could see the timer crowed to the left sleeve of the shiftsuit. Moving slowly and with great care, he reached up and pulled his spookeyes down, leaving the power off and the lenses clear as he set them in place. With this much light, powered spookeyes would keep the shields up and he'd be effectively blind, but if things went like they were supposed to, there wasn't gonna be any light pretty soon.

Sleel grinned, but kept it tight. Wouldn't do to have one of those trigger-happy balloos see his teeth shining in the bark of the tree, now would it?

Gods, he loved this.

Khadaji glanced at his timer. There came two faint pops, not a second apart. The floods went from white to bright orange, then faded to a dull red. He powered up his spookeyes, stepped into the clearing, and shot the startled guard who had stupidly turned to stare at the dying lights.

The show was in the air. There would be no turning back now.

He took a deep breath and moved.

TWENTY-FIVE _____

"Now," DIRISHA SAID. With that, she pulled one of the pocketbombs from her belt and thumbed the six-second timer into life. She heaved the fist-sized chunk of heavy plastic in the general direction of the unguarded garage thirty meters away.

The bomb clattered on the roof, bounced once, and exploded. The deep *whump* of it resounded solidly in Dirisha's chest. Made more noise than it did damage, but the roof of the garage wasn't going to be stopping the afternoon rains any time soon.

"Good throw," Geneva said. "I felt that in my bones."

Geneva tossed one of her own bombs. It arced away in the eerie green nightscape, and both matadoras turned from the explosion. Somebody started yelling close by, somebody with quite a command of esoteric curses, too.

"Come on. We need to keep this pot stirred," Dirisha said.

Most of Wall's cameras went down when the back-up power did. He wasn't really surprised, and he had a few

safeties that ran on batteries scattered around, though not
nearly as many as he would have liked.

The hidden camera in the security office, for instance,
had a transmitter and basic sensors that could generate just
enough signal to reach one of his ground substations. It
would be good for maybe an hour, small as the batteries
were, but that should be more than enough time. The
available light wasn't much, but Wall had starlight boosters
on his pickups. Good thing the filters worked, otherwise the
camera would have burned out when Tone switched on an
emergency biolamp.

Cteel said, "Dammit, there goes the power!"

"Looks like they got the back-up, too," Tone said.

"Tell me something I don't know, moron."

Tone was standing next to a closed window. He manually
cranked the casement open. The transmitter's sensors were
good enough to feed Wall the stench of damp, burning grass
and the scorched-insulation smell of D-2 plastique that
came into the room. He couldn't smell it, but he could
catalog-match the molecules the sensor noted.

"The garage is on fire," Tone said. "I hope you parked
your flitter somewhere else."

"On the landing pad."

"Yeah, well, that's on fire, too."

"Shit!" Cteel looked nervous. Well he should be. He
knew what would happen to him and to Tone if they should
be captured. The same thing that would happen if he
responded to the Exotic sexually.

"I'm going for the woman," Cteel said.

"What do you want me to—?"

"Meet me behind the biolab. Five minutes."

"That cargo flyplate won't carry us a hundred klicks
before it runs down."

"Would you rather be here or a hundred klicks away from here come daylight?"

Another explosion rocked the night.

Both men ran from the room, temporarily out of Wall's ken.

The four guarding the door never had a chance, though one of them did manage to spew a hundred rounds from her carbine before she lost her grip on it when she hit the ground. It dug a three-meter-long trench in the earth next to where Sleel stood, but it wasn't even close; half a meter away, easy. He ran to the door, tried it and found it locked, and slapped a popper onto the control plate inset into the wall. He twisted away, and the popper went off, blowing the circuit. Sleel slid the door open, using it for cover, but nobody inside started shooting. He darted into the building. There was enough ambient light seeping in through the door and windows to see by using the spookeyes, and Sleel moved in an easy crouch across the entryway. This was the building most likely to be sleeping quarters, according to what they figured.

A guard carrying a sleetpistol came around the corner. "Who's there?" he called, waving the gun.

Sleel shot him in the throat, and the shocktox dart threw the man into a hard spasm against a table, knocking it over.

Sleel would've gone on looking, but he was supposed to wait for back-up.

All right. He'd wait. He'd give 'em thirty seconds.

Even six kilometers way, the sounds and light seemed loud and bright to Veate. It was happening. And she had to sit here and wait.

People might be getting hurt, they might be dying, and

she couldn't do anything about it. Her father, her mother, and Bork, they were all out there, in danger.

But she had to wait—

Fuck waiting!

Veate punched the flitter's repellors up to full power and lifted.

Khadaji came through the open door, rolled to his left, and ducked behind a free-standing shelf full of hand-held umbrella-field generators.

When he peered around the corner of the shelf, he saw what appeared to be several white dots floating in the air five meters away. It took him a second to recognize them as teeth against a shiftsuit hood background.

"Sleel," he said.

"Yeah, boss. Call it."

"Cover the door. I'll go look."

Khadaji moved down the hallway, spetsdöds questing as if they had a life of their own, seeking targets. He passed a small kitchen, turned into a long hallway, and saw a glow-in-the-dark exit sign mounted over a back door. The normally dim sign was made bright enough by the spook-eyes so that it seemed he was looking at the sun. Not quite bright enough to trigger the shields, however.

He tried the first door. It opened on an empty room.

Same with the second door.

The third door slid open and a blast of gunfire erupted from within the room. Craters appeared in the wall across the hall.

Khadaji was not so stupid as to have been standing in the doorway. Off to the side, he dropped prone and wiggled around the jamb.

The man inside had his carbine aimed at where a standing man's chest would be. The shiftsuit tried, but even it couldn't match a background instantaneously, and the man saw the motion. His aim was too high, his reflexes too slow.

Khadaji fanned four shots at the man. The last one missed, but it didn't matter. Three were enough.

Getting old, Emile, to miss at that range.

The last door on the right was locked from without by a portable bolt and screamer.

"Juete?" he said.

"Who is it?"

Khadaji felt a flush of joy as he recognized the voice. It was her! She was alive!

"Stand away from the door."

The popper blew the lock and he shoved the still-smoking door back into its frame. It stuck halfway, but that didn't matter.

There was no mistaking her, even in the foggy green of the spookeyes. After all the years. As beautiful as ever. Funny, she didn't look as much like Veate as he had thought.

"E-Emile?"

"It's been a while."

"How did you—?" She stopped and grinned. "Veate?"

"Yeah. She's really something. You did good."

"We did it."

"I hate to interrupt," came the voice from behind Khadaji, "but I'm holding a WD shotpistol and if either of you even bats an eyelid, you're both dead."

Biolum light flared and Khadaji's spookeyes shields popped on.

Veate brought the flitter down in the nearest clear spot close to the main complex. Her father had left her a small handgun, a 4mm needler, and she held this as she left the little ship.

Maybe this wasn't such a hot idea, she thought, but she had to do something. There was enough light from burning structures so she could see. Now, which way to go looking?

She almost fainted when she heard her father's voice over the com tacked to her belt. " 'Vring the flitter in 'vlasting!" he said. His voice was tight, and she realized it was a subvocalization, all quiet throat sounds. *Bring the flitter in blasting*, he'd said.

He was in trouble.

There was a small garbage can-sized and -shaped din rigged with camera and sensors that Wall had saved for the direst of emergencies. He powered the robot up, put it online, and sent it to where Cteel was to meet Tone for their escape. It wouldn't do to miss the grand finale.

Along the way, the din sent back an image of Tone, heading away from the rendezvous. Wall sent the din after the man, at a discreet distance. No need to get close when the gel-eyes of the camera could zoom to a close-up from a hundred meters away.

"Turn around and let me see you peel those dartguns off, very carefully," Cteel said.

Khadaji turned slowly, spetsdöd barrels pointed at the ceiling. He shifted the spookeyes back on his hood. "I can put a dart into you before you shoot me," Khadaji said calmly.

"Yeah, probably. But you're loading shocktox and if this building is still here in fifteen minutes, I'll wake up. You and the woman will bleed to death before anybody can get a vouch to you or get you into a Healy."

"Somebody will find us before you wake up."

"I'd say that's iffy, pal. Even so, I got this sucker pointed right at her head, and a brain shot or three won't leave much to work with. Best neuromedic who ever lived can't fix it if it's splattered all over the wall."

Khadaji thought about it. Sleel was watching the door; he'd come eventually, but it wouldn't do them much good. Of course, they were dead if he shucked his weapons, too. The only thing that was keeping Cteel from shooting was knowing he couldn't do it unscathed.

"I don't plan to stand here all night," Cteel said.

He had to play it for as long as he could. "All right." Slowly, Khadaji reached over and unsealed his right spetsdöd, peeling up the edge of the plastic flesh. He lifted the weapon and dropped it.

"Now the other one."

He had bombs on his belt, but he'd never be able to get to them fast enough.

Bork saw the flitter come down, but he was on the other side of the compound and by the time he got there, Veate wasn't around. Had Emile called her? Or was she here on her own?

Bork couldn't stand the idea of losing her. They hadn't become lovers yet, not in the physical sense of the word, but he knew he loved her. She called to him as Mayli had done, and he couldn't go through that kind of pain again.

He pushed the hood of the shiftsuit back, and the humid night air felt good on his bare skin where it touched him.

Veate. Where are you?

Khadaji peeled the second of his spetdöds free and allowed it to fall to the floor.

Cteel grinned. "Her I still need," he said. "You I don't. I never killed a hero before." He shifted his weapon so that it pointed at Khadaji's face.

"If he dies, so do you," Veate said from behind Cteel.

• • •

"Hey, isn't that our flitter?" Geneva said.

"So it is. Wonder what it's doing here? I thought we had things iced."

"She wasn't supposed to come unless Emile called."

"Yeah. Maybe we'd better go see what's up. That building, over there."

Bork saw a smallish man, one who would be forgettable in a crowd of three, moving toward the back door on the target building. Only Bork knew this face; it belonged to the man who'd been with Cteel when he'd taken Juete. Well, well. Wonder where he thinks he's going?

Wall's remote eyes saw the big matador following Tone. Not good for Tone, to be sure. Nor Cteel, if he was around, as certainly he must be. He was Tone's exit pass, he and the albino woman, and why would he be going there if they weren't still inside? He didn't have a battery-operated camera in the woman's room; too bad.

It looked, however, as if Tone and Cteel were about to reach the end of their usefulness.

Cteel spun, firing the shotpistol—

Too quickly. The first round punched a dozen fingertip-sized holes in the hall wall, angled in a widening fan pattern along the wall's length. The boom was deafening in the enclosed space—

Instinctively, Veate ducked and crouched away from the shot, raising the needler. She was not very good with guns. The little needler *twanged* twice, but both spikes went high and wide to Cteel's right—

Khadaji was already moving, leaping at Cteel's back—

The door behind Veate opened and a man stepped in, raising a weapon—

Khadaji slammed into Cteel with all his weight, arms circling around his neck in a simple tackle that knocked the man to the floor. Cteel's biolum flew, casting pale moving shadows, and landed on the floor. The shotpistol went off again—

The man in the doorway pointed his weapon at Veate—

Bork stepped in behind the man and brought his fist down on top of the man's head. Hard. "No, you don't," Bork said. The man fell as if his legs had vanished—

There came two muffled *whumps*. Khadaji felt Cteel vibrate under his grip, and blood oozed from the man's ears. What—?

He moved back and turned Cteel over. Blood also came from the man's nostrils and eyes. His expression was one of intense pain, of terror. After a few seconds, he went limp.

"This one's dead," Bork said. "Sorry, I didn't mean to hit him so hard."

Khadaji stood, glanced at the other corpse, and shook his head. "It wasn't you. Some kind of minibomb in his skull. Same thing happened to Cteel here." He nodded at the body.

"Mother!"

Veate ran to her mother and they embraced.

Behind Bork, Dirisha and Geneva arrived. "This a private party or can anybody play?"

"Mother, this is Bork," Veate said.

"Hi," Bork said. "Nice to meet you. I, uh, love your daughter." He glanced over at Khadaji. "If that's okay?"

Khadaji laughed. He and Juete exchanged looks.

Sleel sauntered down the hall. "I got better things to do than sit around out there waiting for you guys to finish taking care of business," he said. "Are we done here?"

"Yes," Khadaji said. "We're done. Except I've got to go see a computer about a man."

"Huh?" Sleel said.

"Veate will explain it," he said.

TWENTY-SIX _____

THE FLITTER DIDN'T have the capability to reach orbit, but Khadaji had access to a ship that did, courtesy of Rajeem. He flew to the spaceport at Fortaleza on the coast and found the little vessel, a six-passenger lighter formerly owned by the captain of a deep space liner, now owned by the Republic. The captain's tastes had apparently run to the plush side—most of the inside surfaces were carpeted in dahlteen, and to step onto it was to sink to the ankles in the soft green furlike material.

Khadaji checked the launch window he needed, found he had less than ten minutes, and so didn't have much time to worry about what he was going to do. He plugged in his orbit request and he rechecked for the fifth time the small pack he'd brought with him from the flitter. This would be a tricky operation, no doubt of that, and a mistake would probably be fatal. So many things he had done over the years would have been fatal, had his luck not been strongly good. He had cheated death dozens of times, but that did not mean he could take it as a given. A man needed only one fatal mistake to end the game.

The traffic computer gave him a three-minute launch warning, and Khadaji turned his attention to making certain the lighter's systems were all functioning properly. The previous owner's logo still graced all the computer reads, and apparently the Republic hadn't gotten around to repro-gramming the system. *Jacob's Ladder*, it was named. Khadaji didn't know what the significance of the lighter's name was.

"Launch in one minute," the computer said.

Khadaji vocally affirmed the notice. What a convoluted trip this had been. About to be over, one way or another. At least Juete was safe. And he had come to know a daughter, no small accomplishment.

"Launch in ten seconds. Counting to one. Nine. Eight. Seven."

Khadaji took a deep breath. Five seconds later, *Jacob's Ladder* took him into the heavens.

He was coming, Wall knew, just as he had known all along. He didn't have the vessel located yet, but he surely would soon. Most of his not inconsiderable attention was turned to tracking everything he could see leaving the Earth. There were hundred of ships, but most of those could be ignored. Within a matter of seconds, Wall had narrowed down the possibilities to a handful. Of course, other ships were leaving all the time, and those were also observed and plotted. The handful waxed and waned as destinations were logged or arrived at. No ship claimed a matching orbit with Wall's own, but he hardly expected Khadaji to announce it that blatantly.

If I were him, I would move into a higher or lower orbit and work my way down or up, Wall thought. With that idea, he expanded possibilities.

He was coming; he *had* to be coming. The bait had been

taken, the game had run its course when the albino had been
retrieved, and all the tactics Wall had used were narrowed
down to the final moves of the game. Khadaji had to come
because of who and what he was. He had been given
sufficient clues to solve the puzzle, albeit the clues had been
oblique enough to make it difficult. Wall knew what made
the man work; he had studied every scrap of information
available on him, including his own brief meeting before it
all fell apart. Khadaji was a hero; he wore the psychologi-
cally flawed psyche like a cape, he was a slave to fair play
and the belief that the universe was an innately *good* place.
Khadaji made it a point not to kill during his revolution, not
with his own hands. He could have snuffed Wall like a
flickstick when first they'd met, but he had not; he had
given Wall a chance to consider the error of his ways. What
a fool. True, he had engineered the assassination later, but
even so, he had chosen as his tool someone who would have
gladly killed Wall on her own, had she possessed the
means.

Of course, the Republic had enough weaponry to blow
Wall out of the skies, yawning all the while, but it would
not happen that way—at least not until it was too late. No,
Khadaji would feel the need to confront him, thinking that
he somehow would prevail. He would walk into the den to
beard the lion, certain of his own invulnerability, positive
he would triumph. That would be his last error. The lion
would take his soul.

Come to me, hero. Come and meet your match at last. I
will not make the same mistake I made before.

Wall stole a few seconds from his concentration to
construct a brief affair with another of his delicate flowers.
Soon, he would be able to hunt for them in the flesh again.
It was his most pleasant thought. What a garden he would
sow!

• • •

The first orbit Khadaji hung was tricky. It had to be exact, the speed and angle could not be off, and he could hold it for only seventy seconds at the most. If he could not manage what he needed to do by then, he would have to break it and try again.

It took sixty-nine seconds to accomplish his task.

Still shaving things right to the edge, eh?

Well, said his little interior voice, a second is as good as an eon, if you succeed.

Yeah, and as good as forever if you fail.

Jacob's Ladder scooted from the first orbit and spiraled outward.

Wall checked his input, crosschecked, and crosschecked again. He ran all the numbers, crunched all the data, and became satisfied with his conclusion:

There he was!

The ship was matching his orbit and moving closer, past the Duralum Wall, and there was nothing else within a dozen klicks with which to rendezvous.

Wall had an armory built into his vessel, of course. He couldn't wear battleship plate on the outside without arousing suspicion, but nobody could see what hid behind the standard ship-sandwich skin. Tracking lasers and railguns could come into action in less time than it took a man to blink. He could knock Khadaji's little ship to pieces with less effort than solving a nine-level spakulus equation, had that been his desire. Of course, that wasn't part of the plan, but in the remote chance that Khadaji brought help, Wall had the means to protect himself, at least for a while. He could go out in a blaze of glory.

He had no intention of so doing, however; he was certain he was right, and so it seemed. Khadaji's ship was alone, and there were no other vessels within close range. He continued to track anybody who might venture near, of course, but he was certain he was right.

The ship drew nearer. It rolled to match its docking plate with Wall's. Wall allowed it to come.

This was the one variable about which he could not be positive. Out here against the black of space with the needle points of the stars and planets unblinking, there was a slight chance—very slight—that Khadaji might be willing to sacrifice himself to take Wall with him. Get within range, trigger a backpack nuke, and die in the fireball that would shatter both ships.

But, no. Not until he had a chance to talk, to see if Wall had a way out. It wouldn't do him any good to destroy the ship if there might be another computer hidden somewhere, ready to take over. There was not, but Khadaji couldn't know that for sure. And once he thought he knew, it would be too late.

The smaller ship, tiny against the bulk of Wall's, neared the dock. Wall extruded the link.

Come into my web, foolish fly.

When Khadaji stepped into Wall's domain, Wall stood there waiting for him. A holoproj, of course, as good as any he'd ever seen. Just as he remembered Wall from years before: dark skin, blue eyes, black hair. He looked a fit forty T.S., and the image wore red silk and platinum fittings. He was braced by a pair of vaguely anthropomorphic dins, man-high, with heads and arms, each pyramiding to a wheeled base.

"Well, well," Wall said. "The hero arrives."

Khadaji still had his spetsdöds, but they wouldn't do him any good against the holographic Wall or the dins. He could have loaded explosive pellets but he was sure that he wouldn't have been allowed on the ship if he had been carrying any weaponry that might cause major damage. He'd recognized HO scanners, bomb and poison sniffers, and fluoproj gear in the lock. His one hidden ace was partially scan shielded, but wasn't a weapon in the real sense—it occupied the slot normally taken by his left spetsdöd's magazine.

"Marcus Jefferson Wall," Khadaji said.

"Not exactly in the flesh, but, yes."

"You are very resourceful."

"Especially considering that I am dead, eh?" Wall waved his hand and the ship rocked slightly.

"If you were planning on using anything in your ship in this encounter, think again," Wall said. "I've just kicked it loose and already it is on its way into deep space."

"You've gone to a lot of trouble just to get me here."

"No trouble at all. I've had a lot of free time on my hands of late. Care for something to eat or drink? I don't have much use for it myself these days, it's not very fresh, but I can have one of the dins thaw something."

"A last meal?"

"I am civilized."

"I'll pass."

"This way, then." He turned, flanked by the dins, and walked away.

Khadaji followed him. He glanced at his chronograph.

Wall led him to a wide door that slid back to reveal an operating theater. The centerpiece was a sealed unit the size of a small room.

"A Healy?"

"Of course. Only the best. You'll have questions now."

"And you will give me answers?"

"Why not? It won't matter, and as I said, I am civilized. Even to my enemies."

"I think I've got most of it," Khadaji said. "Stop me if I go wrong."

Wall smile.

"After you were assassinated, this ship became fully operational."

"Yes. The recordings run right up to the moment of my death. My old friend Cteel, a later incarnation of whom you met, was my security computer at the time. He kept the attacking forces out of my sanctum long enough to finish the final transfer."

"What took you so long to begin this operation? It has been five years."

"Well, I had some learning to do. Plus there was the question of reversing the technology that put me here. Rome wasn't built in a day, you know."

"And I was always the goal?"

"From the first. It is only fitting, don't you think?"

"I could have been dead or injured."

"The Man Who Never Missed? Hardly. I needed to draw you out; you were hidden rather well, I must confess I could not find you."

"And all the rest of it was just to keep us off balance."

"Yes. With the Republic running around putting out a lot of little fires, it kept them out of my hair, so to speak. I merely had to make sure my timing was right for the main show."

"You could have done it all so much easier."

"Of course. But when one has a muscle, one uses it. It hardly seems fair to waste such brainpower as I have in a straightforward manner. Much like playing fugue, the fun comes in the indirectness. Occam's Razor is such a bore when you control millions of blades."

Khadaji nodded. "And you think I'm stupid enough to walk into your trap unprepared, knowing what you intend?"

"Dear boy, no. I *knew* you would come, but I also figured you would have some kind of inept and inane plan to save yourself. My scanning gear is second to none, much better than what I had on Earth. You have nothing with you that can hurt me. A poison spew won't slow my dins a microsecond, they are sealed against corrosives, and I already know that you don't have any inert components that can combine to make either, anyhow. I, on the other hand, could flood this ship with sleepgases should I so choose. You'll have to breathe sometime. Your hipshooting reflexes won't help you now."

"But you don't want to kill me."

"To be sure. Nor do I want you to kill yourself. You won't, you know."

"Why is that? I could deny you your goal."

"Temporarily. My second choice would be your ex-lover or your daughter, or, failing them, one of your matadors. You would rather it be you than them."

"You think so?"

"Oh, I *know* so. I know just about everything there is to know about you. You probably had something on your ship—there was a shielded package next to the pilot's seat—upon which you pinned your hopes of defeating me. You aren't transmitting on any frequency I can monitor, and if you were, it wouldn't get past my jammers. Nothing on your person can be made into a weapon fierce enough to stop my dins from putting you into the Healy, and five minutes after that happens, you won't be *you* anymore, you'll be *me*."

"But if somehow I were to succeed, where would that leave you?" Khadaji said.

"Well, I could say I've got another me waiting to take over, but the truth is, I don't. It won't be necessary."

"You seem so sure."

"Oh, I *am* sure. You weren't sure of what you would find, so you had to come and see. And in your arrogant, simple-minded way, you thought somehow to find out and then escape, probably destroying me in the process. It isn't going to happen, Emile Antoon Khadaji. Your quickness and dead aim won't help you now, because I have out-thought you. In the end, it is the brain that is the more powerful weapon, no matter how large a gun you can mount. This is my victory."

"You think so?"

"I *know* so. And it is sweet beyond anything you can imagine. You took my life, and now you will replace it."

Wall waved one hand, and the two dins moved toward Khadaji.

Khadaji raised his right hand and fired his spetsdöd, forefinger held rigid in full auto. The darts pinged harm-lessly off the dins. He backed away from the slow-moving robots.

Wall laughed.

The spetsdöd ran dry. He lifted his left hand, pointed it, but nothing happened. Quickly, he reached to his right weapon and ejected the empty magazine. But when he repeated the action for his left side, he touched the minia-ture projector he'd gotten from Jersey Reason. It ejected and fell onto the floor as had the magazine.

Behind the image of Wall, a young woman appeared.

"Marcus?"

It was hardly necessary, but the image of Wall spun.

"Michelle?!"

The dins stopped.

The girl appeared to be no more than twelve or thirteen, right on the budding edge of womanhood, and she wore tight white thinskins that revealed every prepubescent line of her body. She looked to be a beautiful child, though the recording of her was based on a woman who had actually been closer to thirty T.S. years than to thirteen.

Khadaji stole a glance at his chronograph.

The girl held out her arms to Wall. "I've missed you so much, Marcus."

After what seemed a long time, Wall turned away and looked back at Khadaji. "Oh, no, you don't. You think I'm so stupid as to be fooled by this fake image? You had her kill me once; it won't happen again!"

There came a noise like a fist hitting a solid object.

The ship shuddered.

The image of Wall wavered. "What have you done?"

"I got your attention," Khadaji said. He turned and started to run.

"You can't escape!"

Another fist hit. Then a third and then a fourth.

Behind him, the holoproj of Wall vanished. He would have other things on his mind, Khadaji knew.

The ship rocked under more impacts, ten, a dozen, a score.

Khadaji ran for where he thought Wall would have his escape pod. There would be one, so that the new Wall wearing Khadaji's body could have a way out, in case something happened. He might well be able to whistle up a troop transport, but he wouldn't take any chances with his new body; there would be some insurance. Khadaji had spotted the unmarked hatch while approaching, and if his sense of direction could be trusted, he was heading the right way.

The artificial gravity wobbled, making Khadaji suddenly lighter on his feet. He was prepared for that; the soles of his boots were stiktights he could trigger if need be.

He started hyperventilating as best he could while sprinting. He could hold his breath for two and a half minutes while doing moderate exercise, and that had been augmented by a tailored aerobic bacteria circulating in his system that would stretch the time to perhaps four minutes.

The noseplugs he wore expanded and shut his nostrils, triggered by the invisible gas which must be pouring in around him. The special contact lenses sealed and protected his eyes. Khadaji held his breath and kept going.

"DAMN YOU!" came an amplified voice from the changing air.

More impacts against the ship's hull. Wall's self-repair machineries would be running at full speed, and losing the battle. The sandwich-hull, layers of metal and carbon fibers separated by dead spaces, would absorb the impact of a paint flake or metal shard that might somehow slip past the orbiting Duralum Wall, but it had not been designed to withstand the assault of sixty steel marbles moving at more than twenty-five kilometers a second.

The window in the Duralum Wall was open only once every ten orbits, for under three seconds, and then it was less than half a meter wide, giving odds that the chance of some stray orbiting particle getting through would be tiny in the extreme. But to somebody with the resources of the Siblings' computer and a conscious design, shooting through the small gap was not all that difficult. It was, as Wall had said, the timing that was important. Khadaji had gotten there ahead of the steel missiles, and had only needed to distract Wall in the final seconds before they arrived. Wall could not have seen them earlier, and after a brief instant when he might have been able to move, it would be too late.

He should be getting close to the escape pod, Khadaji figured. He hoped so.

How could this have happened? He was under attack; missiles slammed into him, shattering and tearing holes in his hull, some of them punching through into the ship itself!

Wall sent all his repair dins into the fray, patching head-sized holes that allowed the air inside to escape, where it turned to frozen crystals in the hard vacuum.

He didn't have enough units. Air continued to whistle forth.

One of the missiles found a hole made by a previous strike and slammed into a heater, splashing plastic and circulating fluid about as if it had been bombed.

Another missile tore through the ship's main engine, wrecking the Number One mix chamber.

He was being crippled.

He was going to die if he didn't do something!

Khadaji. He had to collect the man and make the transfer!

As the gravity lessened by maybe half, one of the ship's dins lurched out into his path. Khadaji didn't hesitate. Stable as the din was in normal gravity, it wouldn't be anchored by as much weight with the ship's systems cutting in and out. Khadaji ran straight at the din, then at the last second jumped and twisted, feet leading in a flying kick. His left bootheel hit the din high, and the momentum and his mass were enough to topple the robot. By the time the din could use its arms to right itself, Khadaji was well past. It would never catch him from behind.

If he was right, the escape pod was just ahead.

Analysis of the shattered missiles revealed spheres composed of iron, carbon, nickel, vanadium, chromium—

Steel, Wall realized. He was being beaten to death by steel marbles. He also realized what Khadaji must have done. Very clever. No weapon involved; they were only thrown rocks! He could have foreseen the possibility. He had made a mistake in trusting the Duralum Wall.

Where was Khadaji? Ah, there—

Wall went blind. He could not feel pain, but he knew he was damaged. More of the steel balls continued to thud into him, tearing into his entrails, destroying precious circuitry and hardware. But the Healy was self-contained. He could get Khadaji there and he would be saved. The implant was ready; even if his main mind was damaged, most of him would make the crossing, the memories were logged—

What? Did someone call him?

"Marcus? It's me, it's Michelle. Where are you?"

No, it was a trick! Michelle was dead, he'd had her aged, and the poison she had spewed at him had killed her, too—

"Marcus?"

Khadaji! He had to get Khadaji!

Khadaji found the pod. It was a two-person sled with enough rocket power to hold an orbit, and had rudimentary aerodynamic surfaces to fly in atmosphere, though it wouldn't be a comfortable time of it to ski down to land. He was almost out of air, his lungs burned, he wanted to breathe, it was all he could do not to breathe. He banked on the pod being unguarded and unlocked, because on a ship controlled by Wall, there would be no need to worry about somebody stealing it.

Another din, programmed to capture him, rolled out from behind a bank of transducers. He saw he could beat it to the pod's hatch; once inside, he'd be safe.

The gravity failed completely. Unprepared, Khadaji lost his footing and tumbled. He tucked, and managed a half turn before he slammed into the wall above the escape pod. He triggered the stiktight boot soles as he bounced off into the air. All he needed was a surface, wall, ceiling, floor, and he could regain control.

The din floated past and it clicked a three-fingered hand

shut on Khadaji's shoulder. He twisted and the claw dug into his orthoskins and shoulder, drawing blood, but missing a secure grip on his flesh. The tough fabric tore, and the din twirled away clutching a bloody scrap of his clothes, but nothing more.

Khadaji reached the ceiling and shoved his feet at it. The boots stuck. He looked at the pod. The din would reach a wall in a second and it too would be able to propel itself back in his direction.

He shoved away from the ceiling toward the pod, using his toes to flip himself in a layout half somersault so that he was once again moving toward a flat surface feet first. If he had guessed right, he would land in front of the pod's hatch. From there, it would only be a step to hit the control and enter the tiny ship.

The din reached the far wall and pushed away with inhuman strength toward the pod. Khadaji realized immediately that the din was now moving much faster than he, and that it would arrive at the pod before he did, blocking the hatch. He had no weapons with which to fight it, but maybe he could hit or kick it hard enough to move or damage it. There was nothing to lose by trying. . . .

The gravity came back on.

Khadaji was in landing position and he hit feet first and tumbled.

The din was still rotating toward its landing position. Unfortunately for it when the gravity started up, the din was head down. It fell from two meters up, smashing its sensor and control cap. The din managed to shove itself onto its treads, but only one side worked, and the robot began to spin in tight circles, beeping and waving its arms.

Khadaji rolled up, hit the hatch control, and dived into the pod. He scrambled to the control panel, blew the emergency wall bolts, and was kicked out of the belly of

Marcus Jefferson Wall into space. The little engines coughed to life and shoved the pod away from the larger ship.

Khadaji remembered to breathe. Canned air had never tasted so sweet before. He wasn't safe yet; Wall could still shoot at him. He had to get as far away as fast as he could.

He was, he reflected, getting too old for this.

Wall felt systems breaking down in himself. He managed to get a back-up camera input going by rerouting and crossing busses designed for communications, and what he saw was ruin.

One of the steel marbles had found its way into the Healy. The implant package was destroyed, an oozing ruin.

No!

A short in the main nuclear batteries was approaching critical. The control rods for the fusion furnace were only half operative. The solar collectors were smashed to useless bits. His main drives were out.

The escape pod had been deployed.

He was going to die, finally, in a form far different than he had planned. And the man who had killed him was escaping.

No. There was the self-destruct circuit, independent of the others, and if he must die, he would take his killer with him! The pod was close enough to be enveloped in the explosion. He would trigger it—

"Marcus?"

The camera showed her standing amidst the clutter next to the destroyed operating theater, curiously undisturbed by the destruction. A girl. A flower. Didn't he know her?

His thoughts were muddled, and for a second, he didn't understand why. Ah. He had been injured somehow. An accident?

"Marcus?"

But wait. Here was Michelle, his favorite flower of all time, such a darling child she was. Something uncomfortable swept through him as he regarded her, some darkness, but he could not quite get his mind around it. He felt . . . slowed, somehow . . .

"Marcus?"

"In here, dear one," he said. "This way."

The girl smiled at him. "Marcus?"

Wait. There was something he was supposed to do. What was it? Oh. He remembered. The self-destruct command. Yes. He had to—had to—had to—

The nuclear battery short reached critical. Energy flared, reaching out with hot fingers to score all that it touched. The claws of it found the core of Wall's mind and gouged deeply.

"Marcus?"

Wall had one instant left to him. "Michelle?"

Then he winked out, like a light bulb smashed by a hammer. All the systems linked to Wall's mind went down at once. The whine of turbines faded, but until the last of the air left to carry sound had escaped from the holed ship, a small recorded voice kept plaintively repeating its final question:

"Marcus? Marcus?"

But Marcus was gone.

TWENTY-SEVEN

THEY WERE WAITING for him when he managed to put the escape pod down at the cleared field in Brisbane. It had been a rough ride, but all things considered, Khadaji felt just fine. He stepped from the scorched pod onto the plastcrete.

The six of them hugged him, a tangle of arms and kisses and congratulations.

"You okay?" Bork asked.

"Yes. Veate filled you in?"

"Yeah," Sleel said. "You took a pretty big risk."

"Not really. I figured I knew Wall better than he knew me. His weaknesses were worse than mine. Made it easier."

Juete had her arm around his waist. "What will you do now, Emile?"

"I have a little pub," he said. "Maybe you'd like to come and stay with me there? There are some things to catch up on. Some things to think about in the future."

Juete smiled. "I'd like that."

Bork said, "Uh, Veate and I, we, uh, we want to, uh, to contract. To get married."

"Tomorrow," Veate said. "Tonight we have other business to consummate." She looked at Bork and he reddened. She put one hand on his back and patted him.

Dirisha and Geneva held hands, smiling at Bork and Veate. "Look how cute. Kinda gets your juices stirred up, don't it?" Geneva said to Dirisha.

"Yeah, ain't love wonderful," Sleel said, disgust in his voice. "The boss goes off with his beautiful lover, Bork the ape-man gets the beautiful daughter, you and blondie make tracks for the nearest bed, and here's old Sleel all by himself again. There ain't no justice."

Everybody but Sleel laughed.

Dirisha and Geneva exchanged glances. "What do you think, brat?"

"Well, it's been a long time, but I recall that he wasn't too bad. I'm willing if you are."

Sleel frowned. "What?"

Dirisha smiled broadly. "Come make tracks with us, Sleel. To the hotel bed. It's the least we can do."

"Huh?" Sleel's mouth gaped and the look on his face was worth a million stads. Khadaji wished in that moment he had a camera, but he didn't need anything else.

Not a thing in the universe.